T0375778

A good name is rather to be chosen than great riches,
and loving favour rather than silver and gold.

—Proverbs 22:1 (KJV)

MYSTERIES OF COBBLE HILL FARM

Digging Up Secrets
Hide and Seek
Into Thin Air
Three Dog Knight
Show Stopper
A Little Bird Told Me
The Christmas Camel Caper
On the Right Track
Wolves in Sheep's Clothing
Snake in the Grass
A Will and a Way
Caught in a Trap
Of Bats and Belfries
Stray from the Fold
Borrowed Trouble
Lost at Sea
Pride, Prejudice, and Pitfalls
The Elephant in the Room

MYSTERIES OF COBBLE HILL FARM

The Elephant in the Room

SANDRA ORCHARD

Published by Guideposts
100 Reserve Road, Suite E200
Danbury, CT 06810
Guideposts.org

Cover and interior design by Müllerhaus
Cover illustration by Bob Kayganich at Illustration Online LLC.
Typeset by Aptara, Inc.

ISBN 978-1-961442-93-1 (hardcover)
ISBN 978-1-961442-94-8 (softcover)
ISBN 978-1-961442-95-5 (epub)

Printed and bound in the United States of America
$PrintCode

MYSTERIES OF COBBLE HILL FARM

The Elephant in the Room

GLOSSARY OF UK TERMS

cheeky • insolent or irreverent, but in an amusing/ charming way

chuffed • pleased

cooker • oven

crisp • potato chip

dodgy • fishy; shady

fit up • incriminate someone with false evidence

fortnight • a period of fourteen days

holdall • a large rectangular bag with handles and a shoulder strap used to hold clothes and accessories; often used for a weekend holiday

jumble sale • garage sale; yard sale

mate • friend

ramble • a walk

scarper • run off

serviette • a table napkin

nick • steal something

uni • common abbreviation for university used in casual conversation

CHAPTER ONE

Basking in the unusually warm November morning, Harriet Bailey-Knight reclined in her patio chair in the garden and tilted her face toward the sun. "To be honest, I don't understand the appeal. A member of the nobility is the last thing I'd want to be."

"You'll always be a lady to me." Harriet's husband, Will, handed her a cup of tea, his tone affectionate.

Her hand wobbled, spilling her tea into the saucer beneath, as if to prove how non-noble she was. "You know what I mean." Living up to her grandfather's reputation as an excellent veterinarian when she first moved to Yorkshire had been hard enough. "I'd hate the social pressure members of the peerage face. Everyone would always expect every hair to be in place and that I'd wear the latest fashions. All the ladies wear those fancy hats. I don't look good in hats."

"You look beautiful whatever you're wearing."

She laughed. "You're just saying that because I made breakfast." And realizing how perfectly he'd made her point, she straightened in her chair. "See, that's the other thing that would bother me—never knowing if someone was pandering to me because of what I could do for them."

Will's eyes twinkled in that way they always did when he had her cornered. "Trust me. You making breakfast is just a bonus."

Chuckling, Harriet leaned across the table and kissed him.

Harriet's assistant, Polly Worthington, appeared in the garden. "All right if I interrupt?"

Will gave Harriet a peck on the cheek then pushed to his feet. "She's all yours. I need to go if I want to make this conference before the opening assembly."

Harriet stood and gave Will a proper hug, inhaling the comforting, woodsy scent of his aftershave. "I'll miss you. Drive carefully."

"I'll miss you too, but I'll be back before you know it." After a last kiss, he strolled away.

Polly helped herself to a cup of tea from the pot on the patio table and sat across from Harriet's chair. "You two are still like newlyweds," she teased when Harriet rejoined her. "So cute."

"This from the woman who's been married—what? A month and a half longer than I have?"

"That's right. Your voice of experience."

Grinning, Harriet picked up the toy Maxwell dropped at her feet. The little dachshund had to maneuver about the yard with a wheeled prothesis her grandfather had fitted for him to compensate for his paralyzed back legs, so Harriet tossed the toy only a couple of yards.

"Forgive me for being nosy." Polly swept her hair into a loose knot at the nape of her neck. "But who are you worried is pandering to you?"

"Oh, that. Ever since Will's dad befriended Sir Bruce and then discovered he was a long-lost relative, nobility seems to be a topic that comes up every time Gordon and Will talk. I was telling Will I don't understand why his dad is so psyched about being related to a baronet."

"Seriously?" Disbelief pitched Polly's voice higher.

Harriet rolled her eyes. "Not you too."

"Don't tell me you've never dreamed of having a handsome prince sweep you off your feet." Polly took Ash Wednesday, the gray kitten Will had adopted, into her arms and cuddled him.

"I tended to dream more about horses, dogs, and cats."

As if taking the pronouncement as an invitation, Charlie, the clinic's resident cat, jumped into Harriet's lap, purring loudly as she nestled in.

Polly gave an unladylike snort. "Not me. I loved to play dress-up. Mum would let me wear her wedding veil, and I'd pretend I was a princess." Polly brought her teacup to her lips with an exaggerated lift of her pinky finger.

Harriet burst out laughing.

Polly laid a hand on her chest as if affronted. "I'll have you know my mum worked in a manor house before she married Dad. And she took great pains to teach me proper etiquette in case I should ever be invited to dine with royalty."

"And your brothers?" Harriet deadpanned, recalling their rough-around-the-edges demeanor at her wedding reception.

Polly swept their behavior aside with a flick of her hand. "Lost cause. But I'd be happy to give you a few tips before your speech at Lady Miltshire's brunch next Saturday."

Harriet groaned. "You'll make me a nervous wreck—more than I already am." When Lady Miltshire had first asked her to speak at the fundraiser for rehoming retired racehorses, she'd felt honored. But the more time she'd had to think about it, the more anxious she'd grown.

Polly obliged Maxwell with a ball toss when he brought it to her. "So, your father-in-law is still into his ancestry research, is he?"

"Oh yes. He called again last night with his latest findings."

"I imagine the research is fun for him. Don't we all harbor a secret dream that if we give the old family tree a good shake, a long-lost estate or title of a wealthy ancestor will fall into our laps?"

Harriet's cheeks heated at the realization she'd been blessed with such a gift in the generous bequest of her grandfather, who'd left her Cobble Hill Farm, complete with his veterinary practice, home, and art gallery.

The sound of a car rumbling up the drive drew Harriet's attention to the time. She sprang to her feet, unceremoniously dropping Charlie to the ground, and called Maxwell. "We'd better get to the clinic. Sounds as if our first client is here."

Despite his handicap, Maxwell quickly led the way inside.

Polly collected the teapot and milk jug and fell into step behind them. "Your first client is Roger and his rottweiler. Her pups are due in two weeks, and he's become a nervous Nellie."

By the time Harriet had seen to Roger's dog—whose pregnancy was progressing smoothly—two other dogs, and the Yateses' budgie, Griffen, Polly had a short list of farm calls waiting.

"I rescheduled your one o'clock appointment for four, so you should have plenty of time to attend all three emergencies."

"Since it's Friday, why don't I pay Nancy and Rover a house call after the farm visits instead of them coming here? That way you can have the afternoon off."

"That's okay. I've been overhauling the files and want to get them finished."

"Are you sure?"

"You know me once I set my mind to organizing something."

"Yes, I do." Polly was the most organized person Harriet knew. Harriet read through the list Polly gave her and noted that *Castlegate Manor* was written at the top. "Are these listed in order of urgency?"

"Probably not. But the Castlegates aren't a family that likes to be kept waiting."

Harriet grimaced. Thankfully, no one at the estate had ever complained about her services. "This will be my first visit since Lord Castlegate passed."

"Oh, there's a new lord of the manor now." Polly donned a comically posh accent. "His Lordship's son, Clifford. He's the same age as me. I saw him at our secondary school reunion last weekend."

"He moved away after school?" Harriet asked.

"He attended the local school before his father shipped him off to boarding school for his last year. His sister, Edwina, stayed here. She was a year behind us."

"Why would their father send one off to boarding school and not the other?"

"Clifford was a bit of a prankster. But I'm pretty sure his father sent him away to thwart his romance with Maisie Coop. You know her as Maisie Aubert."

"Really?" Harriet widened her eyes in surprise that a chicken farmer would have turned the head of a lord's son. But maybe she wasn't a farmer at the time.

"They were inseparable. Until his dad intervened, that is. Although, judging by the way Clifford spoke to her at the reunion, he clearly thought their love should have survived."

"He said that to her? In front of everyone?"

"I doubt Clifford was paying any attention to the rest of us listening in." Polly's eyes twinkled with mischief. "He said he'd written to her faithfully for months, and it was obvious he was peeved that Maisie hadn't bothered to send a single reply. Although she claimed she had."

"That must have been uncomfortable for her and Pierre." Maisie's husband was fairly new to their community, having moved from France only a few years before to open a leather goods shop.

"Thankfully, Pierre wasn't there. It would've been very embarrassing for him, especially after Clifford came back to Maisie and apologized. He said he'd lashed out because it had hurt not hearing from her all those years ago. Then he kissed her hand and held it to his heart and declared that he'd never stopped caring about her."

Harriet winced. She didn't know Pierre well, having only chatted briefly with him now and again at church, but Clifford's behavior would have been upsetting for any husband.

"Maisie must have wondered how her life could have played out if she'd waited for Clifford," Polly went on. "But after his confession, she looked even more uncomfortable and made a quick exit."

"Didn't Clifford know she was married?"

"Someone told him after she left. You should've seen his face." Polly whistled.

"Yes, I can imagine. Anyway, I'd better get moving on the farm calls."

Fifteen minutes later, Harriet parked her grandfather's old Land Rover, which she'd affectionately dubbed "the Beast," next to her client's shiny new BMW.

Edwina Castlegate trotted from the field on a lively bay and met Harriet outside the stables. She alighted from the horse in one graceful movement and handed her reins to a groom then removed her riding helmet and shook out her long blond waves. Even in riding chaps and a light jacket, she looked as if she'd stepped off the pages of a fashion magazine, without so much as a hint of helmet head.

Harriet shook away the whimsical thought. "Is Thunder in here?"

"Yes." Edwina's voice quivered. She had a reputation for being passionate about her horses and clearly hated seeing them suffer. "I'd planned to exercise him this morning, but the groom noticed he was favoring his left hind leg."

"Let's have a look then."

The groom had the gelding in the barn's brightly lit center aisle. Thunder shifted his weight, and Harriet could see he was favoring his leg, just as Edwina had said.

Speaking to the horse in a gentle tone, Harriet skimmed her hand along his flank and down his leg before coaxing him to lift his foot for her. He did so willingly. She extended her free hand to the groomsman. "Could you hand me a hoof pick, please?"

He handed her the most beautiful horse pick she'd ever seen. The pick's end was polished to a high gleam, and the handle, made of wood inlaid with mother-of-pearl, fit perfectly in her grip. The Castlegates clearly didn't skimp on quality or aesthetics.

Harriet cleaned out what little dirt still clung to the hoof and gingerly poked around in search of tender spots. In the same way a person could bruise a foot if they stepped wrong on something hard, horses could too. And if that was the case, Thunder might favor the sore spot for weeks. But that didn't appear to be his problem. "Would you please walk him for me?"

While moving, Thunder's lameness was noticeable but mild. Harriet turned to Edwina. "When you last exercised him, did you detect a change in his gait? Or difficulty with transitions or with stopping?"

"Yes. He's been a bit off for the last couple of days." Edwina's gloved hands rested lightly on her hips as she scrunched her nose. "It's why I wanted to work with him more."

"Has he fallen recently?" Harriet motioned to the groom to turn the horse and bring him toward her.

"We took a tumble a fortnight ago, but we both got right back up and carried on."

Harriet palpated the horse's pelvis. "Please secure him, and I'll bring in my portable X-ray machine to take a few pictures. He could have a fracture."

Edwina's cheeks paled. Then she buried her face against the horse's neck and whispered apologies. His glossy coat shone like burnished copper, testimony to how well cared for he was.

As Harriet joined them in the barn with her diagnostic equipment, a young woman scurried across the drive toward them. "Is His Lordship in the stables?"

"No, he's speaking to that man who's redesigning the gazebo," Edwina said. "Why?"

"There's a foreign gentleman waiting in his office to speak to him."

"Did you get his name?" Edwina snapped.

"Yes, milady. Mr. Aubert, the man from the leather shop. I served him tea and had him wait in His Lordship's office."

Edwina's eyes flashed. "You left a tradesman unattended in the house?" She turned to Harriet. "Excuse me. I need to see to this." To the young woman, she added, "No need to bother my brother."

The pair strode off, and Harriet shook her head over the stark contrast between the woman's treatment of her beloved horse and how she treated her staff. Where Edwina's obvious bond with her horse had warmed Harriet's heart, Harriet doubted one would ever catch Her Ladyship apologizing to a servant.

With the groom's capable assistance, Harriet x-rayed the leg. "How bad does it look, miss?" he asked as she studied the images.

"It's not broken or dislocated. I suspect he's strained a ligament." She went over the area again. "There are definite signs of inflammation." She unpacked the ultrasound machine she'd also retrieved from the Beast. "This will give us a better picture of the ligaments."

Someone approached and stopped behind her, casting a shadow across Harriet's screen. "What's all this?" a man's voice asked.

She squinted up to find a handsome, blond-haired man about ten years her junior studying her. "You must be the new lord of the manor." The family resemblance was undeniable.

He extended his hand and shook hers in a firm grip. "Clifford Castlegate. And you're Old Doc Bailey's granddaughter, I presume."

"That's right. Dr. Harriet Bailey-Knight."

"Ah yes, Harriet. I remember you coming here a time or two when I was a kid."

"Yes, when I was a teenager. I'm surprised you remember."

He tapped his head. "I have a mind like an elephant's. Never forget. I heard you took over your grandfather's practice."

"About a year and a half ago."

Clifford nodded and motioned to Thunder. "And what's the matter with my sister's horse?" Before Harriet could explain, he added, "Where is she, by the way? It's unlike her not to be on hand when her horses are being seen to." This last part he directed to the groom.

"She had to deal with a tradesman, sir."

Clifford chuckled. "Leave it to Edwina to put unsolicited tradesmen in their place." He shifted his attention to the image on the ultrasound screen. "What are we looking at here?"

"I'm assessing the ligaments." Satisfied that the ultrasound images corroborated her theory, Harriet excused herself to retrieve the appropriate medication from her vehicle, hoping Edwina would return soon. With two more farmers waiting for her services, she didn't have time to go over her findings and care instructions twice.

Once outside, she spotted an irate Pierre Aubert tromping out of the manor house carrying a leather duffel bag. When he reached his car, he cast a furtive glance over his shoulder, shoved the bag into his trunk, and sped off.

Harriet wondered about his behavior as she carried the injection back to where Clifford and the groom waited with Thunder in the barn.

"What's the needle for?" Clifford asked.

"Inflammation. It should also help with pain. In fact, if you'll give me a hand by holding the ultrasound paddle right here"—Harriet moved the instrument into position—"I'll be able to see where the needle is going and inject the medicine precisely where it will be most effective."

Clifford's gaze was fixed on the screen. "Amazing."

With the injection finished, Harriet retrieved the paddle from Clifford and told the groom he could return Thunder to his box.

Edwina joined them at the stable door, muttering about the impertinence of tradesmen.

"Who was it? What did he want?" her brother asked.

"The owner of that new custom leather goods and repair shop." Irritation laced Edwina's tone. "Presumably to drum up more business. I don't know. I didn't give him a chance to make his pitch."

Clifford squinted down the drive in the direction the tradesman had disappeared. "Maisie's husband came to see us?"

Stiffening, Edwina crossed her arms. "Yes."

Clifford scratched his chin. "I wish you hadn't sent him away. I would have liked to meet him." Without waiting for Edwina's response, he strode toward the house.

Edwina huffed. "You'd think he'd be grateful I got rid of the man before he could make a scene. I still can't believe he canceled his weekend trip to Paris last week in favor of the school reunion."

Harriet wasn't sure if Edwina expected a response, and glanced at the groom for help, but he merely smirked and carried on with his work. Harriet needed to do the same, but her curiosity got the better of her. "Why would Pierre make a scene?"

Edwina rolled her eyes. "Because my brother is still in love with the man's wife, of course. I suppose since you're new to town, you wouldn't know they used to be sweethearts."

"Lady Edwina, Lady Edwina!" The same maid as before dashed across the lawn, her cheeks flushed. "His Lordship wants you to come straightaway."

"What is it now, Louise?" Edwina practically growled the words.

"The silver elephant statue, milady." Louise wrung her hands in the folds of her apron. "It's gone!"

CHAPTER TWO

Gone, as in stolen? Harriet reflected on Pierre's furtive glance over his shoulder when he'd stashed his leather bag in his trunk. Had he been trying to hide the bag? But surely Edwina would have questioned his leaving with it if anything had seemed untoward.

"That tradesman must've scarpered with the statue," Louise rushed on, her voice quivering, as if perhaps she was worried about being blamed for the theft herself.

Harriet shook her head. "I know Pierre from church. I can't believe—"

The flash in Edwina's eyes cut off Harriet's protest. "Wait here. Don't leave until I get back. I want to hear Thunder's diagnosis firsthand."

"But other farms are expecting me."

Already hurrying to the house, Edwina waved away Harriet's protest with an air of superiority that irked Harriet.

"You'd best wait for her," the groom advised. "You don't want to get into milady's bad books."

Groaning, Harriet looked at her watch. Which was worse—ignoring the direct order of a lady, or keeping other clients waiting unnecessarily? She was strongly leaning toward the latter. Of course, as an American, she hadn't been raised to defer to someone of noble birth.

Harriet packed her equipment in the Beast then prepared a prescription to leave for Thunder and wrote out his treatment plan. She was about to go over the instructions with the groom alone when Edwina returned.

"Thank you for waiting," she said, although her tone suggested there'd been no question of Harriet doing otherwise. When Harriet noticed that Edwina had taken the time to change her clothes, her temper frayed a little more.

Edwina lovingly stroked her horse's neck. "The police are on their way. And they've asked that no one else leave until they can be questioned."

Terrific. "I don't see what help I can be when I've been out here the entire time," Harriet said.

"I'm sorry to keep you," Edwina said. "But they *were* insistent."

"Fine. I'll wait a few minutes longer." She wasn't exactly eager to speak to the police, because as much as she couldn't believe Pierre was a thief, she also couldn't deny that his behavior had seemed suspicious. Harriet checked her phone to make sure she hadn't missed any messages. "If a client calls to say one of my patients has taken a turn for the worse, I won't be able to stay," she warned.

"Fair enough. Now tell me about Thunder's injury."

Harriet explained the horse's condition and treatment plan then answered Edwina's thorough questions. She was about to call the next farm on the list for an update on their cow's condition when Detective Constable Van Worthington, Polly's husband, drove up the driveway.

Harriet sighed in relief. At least Van wouldn't detain her unnecessarily. He knew he could speak to her anytime at the clinic.

Van parked next to the Land Rover. Since marrying Polly, he seemed less awkward and gawky than when she'd first met him. But with his light blond hair and easily flushed cheeks, he still looked much younger than his twenty-seven years, which meant he sometimes struggled to be respected on his first meeting with someone. He introduced himself to Lady Edwina before turning to Harriet. "I guess I shouldn't be surprised you're already on the case."

Harriet raised her hands in protest. "I was here seeing to a lame horse. Nothing more."

Van pulled his notepad and pen from his shirt pocket. "Did you notice anyone suspicious lurking about?" he asked Harriet.

"No." Harriet shook her head, but even she could hear the hesitancy in her voice.

"You must have seen Mr. Aubert leaving," Edwina insisted.

"Well, yes," Harriet admitted. "He left soon after Lady Castlegate went inside to see what he wanted." Harriet grimaced at the memory.

Van tilted his head, his brows knitting together as he studied her, as if he could read her thoughts.

Edwina made a sour face. "I knew exactly what the man wanted—to give my brother a proper earful. Not that he didn't deserve it, mind you. Maisie is no longer a free woman, and Clifford had no business trifling with her heart after all these years."

Van nodded. "You're referring to their exchange at the school reunion?"

"Yes. I'm afraid my brother was a little overwhelmed by the sight of Maisie. She has only grown more beautiful since he last saw her. I certainly couldn't blame Mr. Aubert for wanting to give Clifford a piece of his mind. But to steal from us—"

"I can't believe he'd steal anything." Harriet straightened, her certainty growing, despite what she'd seen. "He would have had to take the statue before you came into the room, but why would he? He thought he was going to get his chance to say his piece to your brother until you arrived."

"The elephant was there before he came this morning," Edwina insisted.

"When you saw him exit the house," Van said to Harriet, "was he carrying anything that could've concealed the statue?"

"It was about a foot high." Edwina showed them the height with her hands.

"He did lock a duffel bag in his trunk," Harriet conceded. "It wasn't small. Edwina would have seen him leave the house with it." She turned to the woman. "Didn't you?"

The question seemed to catch Edwina off guard. "I—I can't say I noticed. No."

"If he was making a sales call, he probably brought the bag as an example of his work. It was a nice-looking leather bag."

"He didn't show it to me," Edwina insisted, although given the mood she'd been in when she stormed the house, Harriet doubted the woman would have given him the chance.

"What kind of car was he driving?" Van asked Harriet.

"A compact silver Renault with his business name on the door."

Van immediately dispatched a BOLO—be on the lookout—for Pierre Aubert's car with instructions to impound it and its contents and to bring the driver in for questioning.

"Excellent." Edwina clapped her hands together with a little too much glee.

Harriet frowned at Van. "All of us just said that we didn't see Pierre Aubert with the statue. Before you hunt him down and treat him like a thief, shouldn't you speak to the staff and anyone else on the estate who might have actually seen something?"

"I plan to," Van assured her. "But if we're to catch the thief with the statue before he has a chance to hide or fence it, there's no time to waste."

"Except Pierre might not be your man."

"In which case, he should be happy to cooperate," Edwina said.

Harriet thought that, if she were Pierre, she wouldn't be too pleased if the family of the person who'd propositioned her spouse later sicced the police on her for daring to confront them about it.

"If you'll follow me," Edwina said to Van, her voice shifting from irritated to saccharine sweet, "I'll introduce you to my brother and show you the scene of the crime."

"I'm free to go?" Harriet asked as Van started after Edwina.

"Yes," Van said to her with a smile. "Thank you for waiting."

Harriet hurried through her remaining farm calls and raced into the clinic with no time to spare before her last appointment of the day.

Polly handed her a manila folder with Rover Wilcox's name on the tab. "He's here for his annual vaccinations. He and Nancy are waiting for you in the exam room."

Harriet handed Polly her bag. "Will you restock this while I'm with them, please? How long have they been waiting?"

"Less than five minutes. No worries. I told Nancy you were on your way from a farm call."

"Appreciate it." Harriet scanned the Staffordshire bull terrier's details in the file folder as she covered the short distance to the examination room and was relieved to see that there'd been no health concerns at the dog's annual checkup last year. Opening the door, she greeted Nancy and her solid, muscle-bound dog. Rover's entire rear end wiggled with delight at Harriet's arrival, and he eagerly kissed the hand she offered him to inspect. Staffies were a restricted breed in many countries. But while all dogs, like people, had unique temperaments, Harriet had never met a nasty Staffie. As with every dog breed, it was all in how the dog was raised.

Harriet stroked Rover's short, dark brown coat. "He's looking healthy. I see Polly weighed him and his weight is good for his size."

"It should be for how many walks he gets." Nancy grinned at her dog, who lapped up the attention. "He's brilliant company now that I'm retired, and he keeps me active."

Harriet gave Rover a full examination then administered his vaccinations. "There you go. He should be good for another year. But if you have any concerns, feel free to call me."

Nancy gathered up Rover's lead. "Rover, tell nice Dr. Bailey-Knight thank you."

Rover obediently woofed his appreciation.

Harriet laughed. "You're very welcome. What a smart boy you are." She bent down, gave him another rub, and then offered him a treat.

By the time Harriet rejoined Polly in the waiting room, Van had arrived to drive his wife home, since her car was in the repair shop.

"Have you found the stolen elephant yet?" Harriet asked him.

Polly's jaw dropped open. "Someone stole an elephant, and I'm only hearing about this now? How on earth did anyone sneak off with an elephant? I didn't even know anyone in White Church Bay owned an elephant. Is that legal?"

Van chuckled. "It's an elephant statue."

"You mean that giant one outside the Moorland Zoo? Thieves would have a tough time hiding that thing."

"No, this was a much smaller silver statue."

"That makes more sense. Who's the owner?"

"The Castlegates." Van gave her a rundown of the afternoon's events.

Polly snorted. "They think Pierre stole their statue? I wouldn't be surprised if Clifford orchestrated the whole charade to lash out at Maisie. You saw how annoyed he was Saturday night when she left the reunion after he made a fool of himself over her."

"I hardly think—"

"Or," Polly interrupted her husband, "he could've done it to frame Pierre and convince Maisie that he's unworthy of her in an attempt to win her back."

The notion sounded farfetched to Harriet, although she hadn't been at the reunion to witness Clifford's display. However, Polly's theory reminded her of something potentially significant. "It *was* Clifford who raised the alarm about the theft, even though Edwina went to the office first. It seems odd she didn't see anything wrong when Clifford noticed the elephant was missing right away."

"From the way she tells it, she was preoccupied with seeing Pierre out," Van said.

"I suppose," Harriet murmured. "Did you search the manor?"

"I advised the Castlegates to do so, since a staff member might have hidden it, intending to sneak it out of the house later. But I had no reason to think the Castlegates themselves fabricated the theft." Van rubbed his palm over his chin. "Even if I had, I could hardly accuse His Lordship of pinching his own silver."

Polly grimaced. "You're right about that. You might as well forget about passing your sergeant's exam if you get on the wrong side of the peerage."

"I didn't know you were studying for your sergeant's exam!" Harriet exclaimed. "That's fantastic."

"If I pass, it'll be fantastic." Van shook his head. "But I've got a lot of studying to do yet."

Polly gave him an encouraging hug. "You can do it, honey. You know the manual inside and out."

Harriet handed over Rover's records for filing. "Solve this case, and Lord Castlegate will probably recommend you for the promotion himself."

"Actually, we already have Pierre Aubert in custody, thanks to your noticing the duffel bag he had with him."

"But you said you didn't find the statue."

"Not on him, no. He had likely already sold or hidden it. What we did find in the bag was incriminating."

Harriet hugged herself, suddenly feeling more uncomfortable than ever about mentioning the bag. Thank goodness she hadn't commented on Pierre's furtive glances.

Van collected Polly's coat from the coat tree. "You ready to go? I need to report in at the office for half an hour or so after I drop you home."

"Don't keep us in suspense, Van." Polly slid her arms into her coat as he held it out for her. "What did you find?"

His fair skin flushed. "I can't say. But he had motive, means, and opportunity, which is enough for us to hold him for twenty-four hours before we charge him."

"Except if word gets out that he's being held, it could ruin his reputation and sink his business, even if he's completely innocent," Harriet protested.

Van's gaze dropped to the set of keys in his hand. "It can't be helped."

"What about granting him station bail?" Polly suggested. "You have the authority to do that."

"Not until after he's charged. And I'm afraid everything's already gone over my head. Once he's charged, I suspect he'll have to convince a magistrate to grant him bail."

"Surely that shouldn't be too difficult with such circumstantial evidence. I take it this would be his first offense?" Harriet asked.

Shifting his weight from one foot to the other, Van cleared his throat. "First time he's been caught."

"You sound as if the police have already decided he's guilty." Harriet planted her hands on her hips. "What aren't you telling us?"

"Don't stress over this." Van's tone reminded her of the one she used when attempting to calm a distressed animal. "When this goes to court, all you'll have to do is tell the magistrate what you saw, like you told me this afternoon."

Harriet gasped. "I have to testify?"

"It's routine. Any witness who makes a statement that supports the narrative the prosecutor is trying to establish could be called to the stand."

Harriet stared after them in horror as they left. The fact that Pierre had left the Castlegate home with a bag large enough to conceal the statue was circumstantial at best. It wasn't like Van to pin an entire case on something that flimsy. What else did he know?

CHAPTER THREE

The church emptied around her, but Harriet made no move to follow the departing parishioners, as the memory of Pierre's incriminating actions clawed at her thoughts.

"Lovely sermon, Reverend," someone chirped, their cheer jarring against the knot in Harriet's stomach.

She hoped Will didn't ask her later what she'd thought of the sermon, because she'd have to admit her mind had wandered. The sight of the vacant spot normally occupied by Maisie and her husband had set Harriet's thoughts zigzagging. Since Will had been at the conference Friday and Saturday, she hadn't had a chance to speak to him about the couple's plight.

At dusk the previous night, Maxwell had exploded in a barking frenzy at one of the windows that faced the drive. She'd hoped it was Will, home earlier than expected, but it wasn't. He didn't come in the door until much later. And it hadn't seemed fair to burden him with the news before bed. He was exhausted from the conference and the travel, and her own sleep had already been destroyed by the revelation that she'd be expected to testify against Pierre.

Perhaps it was for the best that she hadn't told Will yet. The news would probably have distracted him from his sermon. And, more than likely, he would have asked Maisie's permission to pray for them in church, which might have alienated Clifford.

The young lord's presence in church had been a pleasant surprise, since his father and sister had never shown much interest in it. Perhaps Clifford was different and had cultivated his faith during his years away from home. Of course, Polly had been more cynical about his reason for "putting in an appearance" as she'd put it. But if her theory was right, he'd made the effort for nothing, since Maisie had stayed away today.

Harriet and Will generally didn't talk much on the drive back to the farm after church. Sunday mornings tended to take a lot out of Will. He carried concerns about struggling parishioners as well as the occasional critique about his sermon. Harriet had learned to give him a little time to process things on the way home.

But today, she felt that the silence was heavier than usual.

"Are you okay?" she asked at last.

Will sent her a quick smile and squeezed her hand. "Just tired. The conference was good, but I didn't sleep well without you."

"Neither did I without you." The twinkle in his eyes warmed her heart as much as his words. But, hearing the fatigue in his voice, she hesitated to share the Auberts' situation before he had a chance to rest. Once home, she encouraged him to relax while she prepared lunch.

Although he'd normally decline the offer and help her anyway, today he didn't protest.

Seeing how tired he was, Harriet knew she'd made the right decision. But she'd have to tell him at lunch. The Auberts were members of their flock, and Will needed to know what was going on. He'd want to visit both Maisie and Pierre and offer them comfort and encouragement.

When Will still hadn't joined her at the table several minutes after she called him, she poked her head into the living room, certain she'd find him sound asleep in the recliner with Ash curled in his lap. To her surprise, he was on his cell phone.

"Lunch is ready when you are," she whispered.

He signaled that he'd only be a minute, so she retreated to the kitchen and got a head start on washing the dishes.

Will came in a few minutes later. "Sorry about that."

"Who were you talking to?"

"Alexandra Lennox, an old friend from uni who'll be in the area for the next couple of weeks. We're hoping we might get a chance to reconnect. We haven't talked in ages."

"A fellow pastor?"

"No, we met before I began my theological studies at Cranmer Hall. I'm not sure what she does now."

"Where is she staying while she's here?" Harriet filled Will's soup bowl and passed him the plate of sandwiches.

"She's renting a cottage in the lower bay." Will clasped Harriet's hand and said grace then tucked into his soup.

"Let's have her over for dinner one evening while she's here. Is she married?"

"What?" Will glanced up from his bowl, and Harriet repeated the question. "Oh. No, I don't think so. I never thought to ask."

"You seem to have a lot on your mind. Do you want to talk about it?"

He finished his lunch and took a sip of tea. "I'm sorry. I guess I've been distracted. What do you want to do this afternoon? It's not too chilly. Should we take a ramble?"

"That sounds like a great idea. But first I need to fill you in on what happened with the Auberts while you were away."

Will's brow creased, and she had the urge to reach up and stroke it smooth. Suddenly, the last thing she wanted to do was add another burden to his shoulders. But he would want to know.

The doorbell rang followed by Maxwell barking and two more bursts of the doorbell.

"Coming," Will called, hurrying to the front door.

Assuming the visitor was probably someone for him, Harriet cleared the table. Clients who wanted her services usually rang at the clinic door, even during non-business hours. Although most telephoned first.

A woman's distraught voice echoed through the house.

Harriet dried her hands and hurried to the door.

Maisie Aubert stood in the entryway, her wavy brown hair in disarray and her doll-like features marred by the tears streaming down her cheeks.

"Oh, you poor thing." Harriet swept past Will and wrapped a comforting arm around Maisie's shoulders. "Come and sit in the living room. I'll bring you a cup of tea."

"Her husband's been charged with stealing an elephant," Will said, clearly stupefied.

"I know." Harriet escorted the petite woman to the living room. "That's what I was about to tell you. It's a silver statue. Not a real elephant."

"And Pierre didn't steal it." Maisie sank into an armchair. "I don't know how they think he could. First, they held him without charging him, and Pierre assured me it was a mistake and would sort itself out. But now..." Her voice broke. "The police didn't even grant him station bail. Our lawyer says he'll have to wait until tomorrow and appear before a magistrate to request bail."

Will sat on the edge of the sofa. "How can we help?"

"You know Pierre. He's a good man." She accepted a box of tissues from Harriet and dabbed at fresh tears. "If you could vouch for his character to the police, maybe they would change their minds and grant bail at least. Pierre's worried about what this will do to his business. No one will ever trust him again if they think he's a thief."

"Start at the beginning and tell me what happened," Will said.

"I'll get that cup of tea." Harriet hurried to the kitchen while Maisie explained Friday's bizarre events to Will.

"I know Pierre would never steal anything," Maisie was saying when Harriet returned.

"If your husband is innocent, the police will quickly sort it out." Harriet handed her the tea.

"*If?*" Maisie squawked. "Pierre *is* innocent."

"Pierre *was* at the Castlegate estate around the time of the theft, paying what appeared to be an unsolicited call," Harriet said gently.

"How do you know so much about this?" Will asked her.

"I was there at the time, tending to a lame horse." Harriet regretted that she'd distressed the woman more.

Maisie shakily set aside her teacup after only a few sips. "There must be other potential suspects the police have overlooked. It's a big estate. Didn't you notice anyone else going in and out of the house?"

"Sorry, no. For the most part, I was in the stable. I happened to notice Pierre leaving, probably because Lady Castlegate made quite a scene when she learned of his arrival and then hurried to the house to 'deal with him,' as she put it."

"I heard they had a bloke from the halfway house working on a construction project there," Maisie said.

"I know you want to do anything you can to turn suspicion away from your husband, but you don't want to make unsubstantiated allegations," Will cautioned. "I've met all the halfway-house residents, and they seem to be sincere about making a fresh start. Most of the lads even join me for a weekly Bible study in their common room."

"My Pierre is a good man," Maisie countered, her face seeming to grow paler by the second.

"I know he is," Will said. "And I'll do whatever I can to help. What do you say we start by bringing our concerns to the Lord?"

As Will prayed, Maisie occasionally murmured her agreement between quiet sniffles. When Will concluded his prayer, Maisie said, "I don't know what I'll do if they don't let Pierre out. He's handling all this so much better than I am. I can't eat. I can't sleep." She stood as if to leave—and promptly collapsed back into the chair, her head lolling forward.

Harriet dropped to her knees beside the woman and checked her pulse and respiration. "She's fainted. Stay with her while I call Aunt Jinny."

Genevieve "Jinny" Garrett, a medical doctor in her early fifties, operated her practice out of her home, the dower cottage next door, but her car wasn't parked outside. Thankfully, she answered her cell phone on the first ring.

"I can be there in a few minutes," she said after Harriet explained the situation. "I joined my friends for lunch in town. But I'm finished, so I'll head straight over."

By the time Aunt Jinny arrived, Maisie had roused and accepted a few more sips of tea.

"Perhaps you could give us some privacy," Aunt Jinny said to Harriet and Will.

"Yes, of course." They slipped into the kitchen.

Ten minutes later, Aunt Jinny joined them. "Maisie gave me permission to share with you that it's happy news. From what she's told me, my guess is she's pregnant, possibly already four months along."

"She didn't know?" Harriet asked.

"She's suspected for a while but put off making an appointment because they've been disappointed before."

Harriet's heart sank. "How sad that Pierre can't be with her to celebrate."

"I've invited her to stay the night in my guest room rather than be home alone," Aunt Jinny said. "And I've assured her everything will look brighter in the morning, after Pierre's lawyer has his say in front of the magistrate."

They joined Maisie again in the living room. After hugs and congratulations were given, Will said, "We'll continue praying that the truth comes to light." He and Harriet walked Maisie and Aunt Jinny to the door.

The moment the door closed behind the pair, Will drew Harriet into his arms and held her close.

Tears rose to her eyes. "I wish I'd never noticed Pierre leaving the Castlegates'. Van said when the case goes to court, they'll want me to testify."

Will pulled back and met her gaze squarely. "Pierre and Maisie won't blame you for stating what you saw. He was let into the house, so he won't dispute the fact that he was there. I'm not sure why Van thinks your testimony would be necessary."

"I saw Pierre leave the house carrying a leather duffel bag that Edwina doesn't remember. I told Van I never saw the statue. I couldn't even tell if anything was in the bag. But he pretty much said that finding the bag in Pierre's trunk clinched their case against him."

"The statue was inside?"

"No. Something else incriminating was. But he couldn't, or wouldn't, tell us what. The worst part is that, as much as I want to believe Pierre is innocent, I can't shake the feeling he really was hiding something."

Will gave her a last squeeze and released her. "I should pay Pierre a visit."

"Now?"

Will's glum expression was apologetic. "We could go on that ramble first if you like."

"No, that's okay. I know you're tired. You should see Pierre while you still have the energy."

That night, Will shared a little of Maisie's personal history with Harriet. The poor woman had faced struggles most of her life, being brought up by a single mom because her dad had died in prison when she was a toddler. Yet Maisie had a magnetic, upbeat personality, and people seemed to enjoy being around her. Harriet had seen how hardworking and caring she was too. And her devotion to her husband was obvious. She hadn't shown a hint of doubt as to his innocence.

That unwavering loyalty was probably what triggered the dreams that plagued Harriet's fitful night—dreams of Maisie having to raise her child alone.

CHAPTER FOUR

Monday morning dawned as dreary as Harriet's spirits. Thankfully, by the time she dragged herself to the clinic, Polly already had it brightly lit and ready for their first arrival. "Rough night?"

Harriet recounted the events of the day before and her distressing dreams. "Maisie slept at Aunt Jinny's last night when this should be the happiest time of her life, with her expecting their first baby."

"She's expecting?"

Heat rose to Harriet's cheeks. "Oops, I probably wasn't supposed to mention that. But yes, she is. And I feel so bad that Pierre can't be with her."

"Here. Glad I brought this for you." Polly handed Harriet a to-go cup. "It sounds as if you need something stronger than tea to keep you going today."

Harriet wrapped her fingers around the to-go cup, soaking in its warmth, and took a sip of the strong coffee. "Thank you. You know me so well."

"If it's any consolation, you have a packed schedule this morning. That should take your mind off other things for a while."

"Sounds perfect." Harriet squinted past the still-empty waiting room and out the window to a copper-colored car turning in to the parking lot. "Who's our first client?"

"That'll be Janette Philbin."

"Gideon's owner?"

"That's the one. He's here for his annual checkup and vaccinations."

Harriet smiled. Wellness checks were the easiest appointments. She'd last seen Gideon in April when he had a persistent cough. But given the bounce in the golden retriever's step as he bounded toward the front door, he was eager to visit again.

Grinning, Harriet led Janette and Gideon into the exam room. But as she listened to Gideon's clear lungs, any hope that today's appointments would keep her mind off Maisie's situation were instantly crushed.

"Did you hear they've arrested that Frenchman for the theft of Lord Castlegate's silver statue?" Janette asked.

Harriet pulled the stethoscope from her ears. "I heard that, yes."

"It doesn't surprise me. He's French, you know. They lost respect for peerage. Overthrew their king, didn't they?"

"Hmm," Harriet murmured, continuing her examination of Gideon without bothering to point out that Janette was making those observations to someone who had been born and raised in America.

"I don't know what Maisie ever saw in him."

At that, Harriet could no longer hold her tongue. "I suspect, given that Lord Castlegate was the victim, the police feel pressured to produce quick results. But until the charges are proven in court, I'd prefer to withhold judgment. I admire Maisie immensely, and she believes in her husband's innocence."

"Well, she would, wouldn't she? Such a loyal sort."

Harriet decided to keep any further thoughts on the subject to herself. "Gideon appears to be in tiptop shape." She prepared his vaccination needles. "Do you have any concerns?"

"No, except I'll be glad when he gets past this chewing stage. My husband is tired of losing slippers to Gideon's insatiable appetite for gnawing things. And last week, it was one of his boots. We've resorted to shutting those in the closet when Ray takes them off."

"I'm afraid teething tends to continue until they're about a year and a half. You'll want to be diligent about hiding anything chewable for another six or seven months."

Janette sighed. "At least he'll outgrow it eventually."

"Yes, he should." Harriet quickly administered the vaccines without so much as a whimper from Gideon. "In the meantime, make sure he has plenty of chew toys to occupy him. That should help keep him away from your husband's shoes."

"Oh, we spoil him with toys, but there's something about the smell of Ray's slippers Gideon apparently can't resist." Janette exaggeratedly rolled her eyes, drawing a laugh from Harriet.

By the time Harriet saw Gideon and Janette out, two more clients were already waiting. Harriet snatched up the next file and led Dawn Rice to the exam room with her box of mixed-breed puppies in need of their first shots.

The elderly widow lived outside of the White Church Bay area but had always used Harriet's grandfather's services for her dogs. She was one of the most conscientious breeders Harriet knew, and her pups were always in high demand.

"I imagine you have a line of happy customers eager to welcome these adorable little fellows into their homes—as early Christmas presents perhaps?"

Dawn set the box of squirming brown-and-black speckled pups on the exam table. "Oh, yes. Now, did I hear that you married the pastor of White Church since I saw you last?"

"I did." Harriet lifted a puppy from the box to examine. "It'll be three months this week."

Dawn stroked one of the puppies still in the box. "My husband was never one to remember things like that. On our first anniversary he brought me a bouquet of wildflowers from the field after a farmhand asked him if he had something special planned for the evening." She laughed heartily. "I soon learned that if I wanted him to remember special dates, I needed to remind him. Men don't keep a calendar in their heads like we do."

Harriet fingered the silver star pendant she wore around her neck. Will had bought it for her for Christmas last year, when he'd told her how he felt about her. It had also been a commemoration of their adventure together in searching for the church's missing Christmas tree star and of his hope that they'd have many more adventures together. And what adventures they'd had already. She doubted she would need to prompt Will with reminders in the romantic-gesture department. If anything, she needed to start brainstorming what meaningful gift she'd give him to celebrate their first Christmas as husband and wife.

The rest of the morning continued in much the same way, her conversations with clients seesawing between her newlywed status and "poor Maisie."

When Mrs. Morris arrived for a checkup with her Great Dane, Socks, she seemed more interested in discussing the "Pachyderm Puzzle," as she'd dubbed the mystery of the missing silver elephant statue.

"I do feel sorry for Maisie," Mrs. Morris said solemnly when Harriet tried to switch the subject back to the Great Dane's condition. "I knew her mother, and a remarkable woman she was. I suppose it's no surprise, though, that Maisie followed in the dear woman's footsteps and married a man like her father. Funny how that happens even when the father is out of the picture from a young age. Poor duck."

"I wouldn't rush to judgment," Harriet replied. "The evidence against Pierre is entirely circumstantial. I've been involved in enough mysteries to know that things aren't always what they seem."

Mrs. Morris blinked in clear surprise. "You think he's innocent?"

"Only a fool would walk out of Lord Castlegate's home with a valuable statue, in broad daylight with eyewitnesses all around, especially when it was bound to be immediately missed. Don't you think?"

The older woman seemed to mull that over. "Hmm. And Pierre Aubert is no fool. But desperation can drive a man to desperate means. I heard—"

"I'm afraid I have a packed schedule this morning," Harriet interrupted. "Socks's heart sounds strong, so if you have no further concerns, I should move on to my next patient."

"Of course. I'm sorry. My mother always said I was a chatterbox. No, if you think the medicine is doing its job for Socks, we should be all set."

"It is. Continue with the same regimen, but if you notice any change in his condition, don't hesitate to call."

Harriet's next client, Mr. Foster, brought up the missing statue too. He lifted Chimney, his foxlike Shiba Inu, onto the examination table. "If I were on the case, I'd question the blokes living in that new halfway house. All of them have history. And I daresay any of them could've slipped into the manor and pinched the elephant."

Harriet opted not to comment on the theory as she examined the bump Mr. Foster had noticed on Chimney's eyelid. Will wouldn't be happy to hear that others shared Maisie's suspicions of the halfway house residents.

"Eyelid masses such as this are not uncommon in older dogs," Harriet said. "It doesn't appear malignant, but I recommend removal sooner rather than later. At this size, it would be a simple procedure under local anesthetic."

"Then let's deal with it right away."

"I'll let Polly know. We can probably arrange a surgery date within the week, if you like."

"Thank you." Mr. Foster lifted the dog from the table. "We don't want our boy to suffer, do we?"

"You've caught the mass early," Harriet assured him. "I doubt it's causing him any discomfort at this point."

When Harriet exchanged Chimney's file for the next one, Polly leaned close and whispered, "Is everyone prattling on about the elephant theft to you too?"

"Unfortunately, yes."

"I haven't encouraged it—honest. But I should have warned you. When something happens to one of the few nobles in the moors, it ranks up there with royalty scandals on the news scale."

"Except no one besides you has uttered a word against Lord Castlegate," Harriet said.

Polly squirmed, slanting a glance toward Miss Jane Birtwhistle, their last client of the morning. "Probably because some might consider such allegations slanderous."

"Ah." Harriet frowned. She'd never seen Polly nervous about what others might think of her opinions. She must have been one of Miss Birtwhistle's students before the schoolteacher had retired and devoted herself to caring for cats.

Jane Birtwhistle's newest acquisition—a feral cat with a serious case of ear mites—proved to be more challenging than the rest of Harriet's other clients of the morning put together. Anyone listening from outside the exam room would have thought she was torturing the poor animal. Not that Harriet could blame the cat. The ear mites had caused a secondary infection that had left the ear canal inflamed and painful. Plus, because it was feral, the cat wasn't used to being handled. Harriet had no idea how Jane had managed to catch the cat, let alone coax it into a crate to bring it to the clinic.

Since Polly was engrossed in a conversation on the phone when Harriet walked the pair back through the waiting room half an hour later, Harriet processed the payment then held the door open so Jane could keep both hands on the cat's crate. The generous heart of the elderly woman never ceased to amaze Harriet.

The sun had pushed aside the clouds and warmed the air considerably. Harriet filled her lungs, relishing the fresh autumn scent. Perhaps she and Polly should take advantage of the nice weather and eat their lunch in the garden.

Behind Harriet, Polly slapped down the phone. "This is unbelievable!"

CHAPTER FIVE

Harriet scanned the clinic's waiting room to ensure they were alone. "What's unbelievable?"

"The magistrate refused Pierre bail. They said he's a flight risk."

"Seriously?" Harriet clenched her fists. "If they're worried he'll return to France, they could just seize his passport."

"Exactly. It's ridiculous. And I'm sure if it were anyone other than *Lord* Castlegate's silver elephant that went walking, Pierre would've been on station bail by Saturday night—if he was charged at all."

Harriet eyed her friend. "You really don't like Clifford Castlegate, do you?"

Polly surged to her feet and busied herself straightening file folders. "Let's just say he wasn't the nicest kid in school."

"He was pleasant enough when I saw to Edwina's horse."

"I'm sure he was. He was always good at coming off as a total sweetheart in front of the teachers."

"I sense there's a story that involves you in there somewhere."

Polly rolled her eyes. "He started a food fight at lunch when we were about twelve, and *I* got caught retaliating, while he totally escaped punishment."

Harriet laughed at Polly's peeved expression.

"It wasn't funny at the time. The principal wasn't about to upset his parents, not when they were big donors to every fundraiser the school ever had. Meanwhile, my parents grounded me and canceled my first slumber party because of it."

"I can understand your resentment."

"Clifford can't get away with accusing someone unfairly this time. The stakes are so much higher here. You've got to clear Pierre's name."

"Me? That's his lawyer's job."

Polly wagged her finger at Harriet. "Those dreams of yours won't go away anytime soon with Pierre in jail."

Frustration over her own lingering suspicions that Pierre had been hiding *something* that day warred with Harriet's desire to see him reunited with Maisie. "Can't you convince Van to do something?"

"I've already talked to him till I'm blue in the face. But his superiors don't want him trying to prove Pierre's innocent when they've already decided he's guilty."

The clinic door opened with a jingle, and Aunt Jinny hurried in, her brow furrowed and her usual smile absent. "Have you heard the latest?"

"That the magistrate refused Pierre bail?" Polly said.

"Yes," Aunt Jinny said. "And I'm afraid they've likely uncovered a compelling motive for the theft."

"What's that?" Harriet asked. "You don't think he's guilty, do you?"

"I don't want to. Maisie is certain he isn't. But she did admit that the landlord for the storefront Pierre leases recently doubled the rent and they're struggling to make payments."

"Which gives the prosecutor ample reason to pin the theft on Pierre," Harriet concluded.

"We've got to at least try to do something to clear his name," Polly insisted. "Maisie doesn't deserve this. I went to school with her, and she's never had it easy. Even when Clifford was head over heels for her, his parents refused to acknowledge her. It's so unfair that when things are finally good for her—with a new husband and a baby on the way—that her life should be derailed again."

Aunt Jinny slapped her palm on the desktop. "I agree."

Polly and Aunt Jinny both lifted expectant gazes to Harriet.

"I don't see what I can do," Harriet told them.

"Find others with motive, means, and opportunity," Polly said. "Come on, you're an old hat at this by now. And you know if you don't at least try, and the charges stick, you'll feel doubly bad for the Auberts."

"We'll *all* feel bad." Aunt Jinny kneaded Harriet's shoulder. "But you do seem to have a special knack for getting to the truth."

"Exactly," Polly said. "So, the first thing we need to do—and when I say *we*, I mean Harriet—is examine the scene of the crime."

"And how am I supposed to do that?" Harriet indicated her outfit, covered in animal hairs. "Lady Edwina may be eager to call me to come see her horses, but I'm hardly fit to be ushered into His Lordship's office, especially now that their maid has learned not to leave tradesmen there."

"Good point." Polly tapped her finger on her lips. "I know. You could confide to Edwina how out of your depth you're feeling about being invited to speak at Lady Miltshire's brunch. Ask if she could share a few tips with you on how an American outsider might fit in.

How to greet people of different noble titles. The proper fork to use for what at dinner. That sort of thing."

Harriet squirmed. "Thanks for reminding me how ill-prepared I am."

"It'd be much simpler if you merely asked for a tour," Aunt Jinny suggested. "You can tell them you love touring manor houses, since you're from America."

"I have a better idea," Harriet countered. "Will plans to visit parishioners this week to solicit donations for the upcoming jumble sale to support the halfway house. I could ask him if I could go with him."

"That's a great idea," Aunt Jinny agreed. "You might start with the Castlegates by saying that a few townsfolk are suspicious of the men at the halfway house after the recent theft and that the support of such a prominent family in the community would go a long way toward putting them at ease."

"Then once you're in the door," Polly said, "you can *ooh* and *aah* over the place and ask for a tour."

"I don't know what you're so worried about," Aunt Jinny said. "You'll have Will with you, and that man could charm the birds from the trees."

Harriet sighed in resignation. "Okay, you win. I'll ask Will about it, and then I'll see what I can dig up—if anything."

By early afternoon, Harriet had completed her scheduled appointments for the day. She called her friend Claire Marshall, who worked in the church office. "Hey, is Will still around? I want to help him with collections for the jumble sale, but he's not answering his phone."

"Oh, I thought I heard it ringing. He must've left it in his office. He's showing Alex around the church. But he plans to leave soon to start today's collection rounds."

"Great. Don't let him leave before I get there, please. But don't say why. I'd like to surprise him."

Claire chuckled. "No problem. I'll make sure he doesn't leave without you."

"Thanks so much. I'll see you soon."

Polly gave her a thumbs-up. "Try to talk to as many of the Castlegate staff as you can. The help always see way more than the owners realize."

Ten minutes later, Harriet slowed the Beast when she spotted Will walking out of the church next to a very attractive woman. *That must be Alex, the old school chum.* When the woman paused at her car and leaned in for a hug, Harriet braked.

She smiled when she saw Will step backward.

But his evasive tactic didn't thwart Alex. She clasped his arms then bounced onto her toes and pecked his cheek. Will didn't reciprocate, but his answering smile was warm enough to hit Harriet with a jealous jolt.

She waited until Alex left before driving into the church's parking lot.

Will had already opened the church door, but at the sound of her vehicle he glanced over his shoulder, and his lips spread into a smile a hundred times more heartwarming than the one he'd given

Alex. He opened the passenger door. "This is a nice surprise. Is the rest of your afternoon free?"

"It is. I thought I might join you for the jumble sale collections."

"I'd like that. In fact, let's be optimistic about people's generosity in their donations and take the Beast instead of my car."

"No problem."

"All right. I'll fetch my jacket and let Claire know I'm leaving."

"Grab your phone too."

Will patted his pockets then grinned sheepishly. "I must've left it on my desk."

Harriet tapped her thumbs on the steering wheel as she waited for Will to return. Should she ask about Alex? Harriet trusted Will completely and didn't want him to doubt that for a second. But that didn't mean she wasn't curious.

The passenger door opened, and Will slipped inside. "It's a shame you didn't arrive a few minutes sooner. I could've introduced you to Alex. She stopped by the office to see if I could join her for lunch." He grinned at her. "And I remembered to tell her we'd have her over to the house for dinner one night once we sorted out a day that works with our schedules."

Harriet leaned across the console and kissed Will full on the lips. "Have I told you today how much I love you?"

He tapped his index finger on his cheek and shifted his gaze upward as if he was searching his memory. "Nope. Not today."

Harriet kissed him again. "Well, I do." She straightened. "Should we start with the Castlegates?"

"Sure. Returning to the scene of the crime, are we?"

Harriet's attention snapped from the road to Will.

"Don't act so stunned. I know how you can't resist a mystery."

Harriet huffed. "I can't help it if they fall into my lap. And I hate the idea that my testimony might help the prosecution throw the book at Pierre."

"I'm afraid he's not helping his case either."

"How so?"

"He's withholding information he says isn't relevant to the charges. He wouldn't even tell me what or why as his pastor. But it has clearly heightened the detectives' suspicions."

"You still think he's innocent though, don't you?"

"I do. What do you hope to learn at the Castlegate estate?"

"I'm not sure. Polly thinks we should talk to the staff, and Aunt Jinny thinks we should ask for a tour of the house. She said it might give us a better idea of how the thief might've gotten in and out of Clifford's office without being seen."

"I had a tour of the place the first year I moved back here, when Clifford's father was lord of the manor." Will glanced at her with a twinkle in his eye. "It's a fine example of Palladian architecture, and I'd love for my wife to see it."

"Perfect. Aunt Jinny was right. She said you'd know exactly what to say."

"Besides," Will added, a teasing note in his voice, "we could probably use the practice associating with the gentry. Sir Bruce is related to us somewhere on my grandmother's tree—Dad's mom—and I'm sure he'll want to take us to meet him the next time we visit. We'd better bone up on proper etiquette."

Harriet shuddered. "I prefer visiting people who accept us as we are."

Will nudged her arm. "I'm teasing. If he's family, he has to, right?"

"I don't know. I could ruin everything for your dad. I can see it now—Sir Bruce holding a white-glove affair, and I race in from a veterinary emergency, smelling like a barn and wearing rubber gloves instead. He could disown your father on the spot."

Will guffawed. "He'd be too charmed by your American accent to notice any breaches in etiquette."

"Let's hope we never have to find out."

CHAPTER SIX

Harriet stopped the Land Rover at the entrance to the Castlegates' driveway as a small black car drove out.

"I think that was Alex." Will spun in his seat for a second look. "I wonder what she was doing here."

"What brought her to White Church Bay?"

"She's gotten a research job in the area, counting endangered birds. Razorbills, I think she said."

"Interesting."

"I thought the two of you might enjoy comparing notes about your work with animals. She didn't get into specifics, but it sounds as if she's had an eclectic mix of jobs since graduation—all science-related, I imagine."

Harriet parked near the manor house. "I don't see Clifford's or Edwina's car, so unless they're both parked in the garage, we might be out of luck."

They walked to the front door, but no one answered the bell.

"That's strange," Harriet said. "I know they have a maid. Maybe she doesn't work Monday afternoons."

Will tried knocking.

A plump middle-aged woman, with her hair in a bun and a tomato-smeared apron tied at her waist, opened the door. "Hello,

Pastor. I'm sorry it took me so long to get to the door. What brings you by?"

"Hi, Rita. How are you?" Will extended a hand, and the woman shook it.

"Well enough, thank you."

Will introduced Harriet to the Castlegates' cook. Then he asked, "Are the Castlegates here, by any chance?"

"Miss Edwina is out riding. Master Clifford—I mean, His Lordship—had a meeting with his lawyer."

Will handed Rita one of his business cards. "I'm sorry we missed them. We were hoping they might have a contribution for the jumble sale the church is hosting weekend after next."

Rita slid the business card into her apron pocket. "I'll let them know."

"I appreciate that," Will said.

From somewhere in the house, Harriet heard a timer go off. "That'll be my pies needing to come out of the cooker. Nice to meet you, Harriet." Rita waved then closed the door without waiting for a response.

"Maybe we can try again on our way home," Will suggested.

They stopped at the house of the next closest parishioner, who generously donated three large boxes of clothes and a crate of old LPs.

"I wonder how many people still have record players," Harriet mused.

"They've been making a comeback for quite a while. I wouldn't be surprised to see a young enthusiast snap up this entire collection."

The residents of the next half-dozen places they stopped were equally generous.

After closing the Beast's back door on the growing stash of boxes, Harriet pulled her ringing phone from her coat pocket.

"Sorry to bother you," Polly said the instant the call connected. "The Harrisons have a horse that's poorly. Debra just called, and she's frantic. Sounds like it might be colic. I can text you the address."

"Yes, let them know I'll head straight there." Harriet ended the call and sighed. "I'm afraid I have an equine emergency I can't put off." When the address came through, she copied it into her GPS. "It's south of town, so I'll be driving past the church. Do you want me to drop you off so you can get your car? This call could take an hour or more."

"Perhaps you'd better. We can unload these boxes when you're finished."

Twenty minutes later Harriet arrived at the Harrison place and spotted a young woman in the pasture attempting to coax a prone horse to its feet. Harriet parked next to the gate. "I'm Dr. Bailey-Knight from Cobble Hill. Are you Debra? Is this the horse you called about?"

The woman nodded, and her eyes filled with tears. "Yes, I'm Debra. I found her like this when I got home about forty-five minutes ago. And she's not breathing right."

As she grabbed her bag from the back of her vehicle, Harriet took note of the sycamore tree overhanging the corner of the pasture and the large number of helicopter pods that carried its seeds scattered on the ground. "How long has your horse been grazing in this pasture?"

"Since about the middle of June."

"Do you supplement her diet with hay or anything else?"

"Not until winter. Should I be?"

"Let me examine her." Harriet listened to the young mare's breathing then managed to coax her to her feet. "There's a good girl." The horse's limbs trembled, but her pulse was close to normal, so hopefully the poison hadn't had a chance to affect the heart muscle.

"Is it colic?" Debra's voice quavered. "I've never seen it before, but I heard it can be quite dangerous."

At this point Harriet almost wished it were colic. "I'm afraid it's worse," she said. "We need to move her into a stall with fresh hay to eat." Harriet led the mare toward the barn.

"What's wrong with her?" Debra's voice rose.

A man rounded the barn and hurried to join them. Wrapping his arm consolingly around Debra's shoulder, he introduced himself as her husband, Roland. "We're not looking at colic, are we?" he asked.

"No, I believe she's suffering from hypoglycin-A poisoning," Harriet said. "It's also known as atypical myopathy."

"Poisoning? How?" Roland rubbed Debra's shoulder as she stifled a sob.

Harriet motioned to the helicopter seeds littering the pasture, then the tree they came from. "Sycamore seeds contain the poison, and there's no antidote. The best we can do is flush out her system and keep her hydrated to prevent further damage."

"I had no idea," Roland said.

Debra's face took on a sickly pallor. "We moved here just this last spring. No one warned us."

"Thankfully, she appears otherwise healthy, and you caught it early, so with dedicated nursing, the chances of recovery are good," Harriet reassured them. "If she was a pony or her breathing was any more labored, I wouldn't be as optimistic."

"I'll do whatever I have to do to take care of her," Debra said. "Day and night."

"You'll need to clear away the seeds before you let her graze in that pasture again."

"I'll take care of that right now." Roland raced off toward a small outbuilding.

Harriet helped Mrs. Harrison settle her horse in the stall and gave her detailed instructions on caring for the mare over the next few days. Once she was satisfied the mare was stable and Debra was sufficiently calm, she packed up with a promise to check in again the following day. "You might consider moving the pasture fence so the tree doesn't overhang it."

"If I know my Roland, he'll have that tree chopped down before the day's out. He won't want to risk this happening again."

Harriet nodded. There were several other trees that offered shade around the pasture, so removing this one might be the wisest choice.

On her way to her vehicle, Harriet saw that, as Debra had predicted, Roland and Mike Dane, a local handyman who'd helped Harriet get her own place into shape, were sizing up the tree with chainsaw and ropes in hand.

"I see you're not wasting any time. That's good." Harriet greeted Mike with a nod. "Still keeping busy, I see."

"I've been helping the Harrisons with repairs on the house."

"Don't know what we would've done without him," Roland chimed in.

Harriet grinned. "A lot of us around White Church Bay could say the same."

Mike's cheeks reddened at the compliments.

Roland excused himself to get fuel for the chainsaw.

"I heard you were at the Castlegates' when their statue was stolen," Mike said.

Harriet sighed. "Word sure gets around the village quickly."

"Ryker Williams was talking about it at Friday night's chamber of commerce dinner, sounding chuffed that the police were holding Pierre Aubert."

"Why should he be pleased about that?"

Mike waved away the question as if it was obvious to everyone. "Ryker's been griping for months that Pierre is poaching his customers."

"Do you think that's true?"

"I doubt it. But being French makes him an easy target. Folks want to believe the local bloke over the newcomer."

"Ah, yes." Harriet had experienced that as the new vet in town.

"Truth is, Ryker's never had the greatest delivery times. So anyone in a hurry likely gave Aubert a try."

"Interesting." Harriet mulled over this new information on her way to the church. When she got there, she texted Will, who hurried out of the office to help unload the donations. Then Harriet drove back to the clinic. Was Ryker merely reveling in his competition's misfortune? Or had he masterminded it somehow?

Polly paused her filing when Harriet stepped into the clinic. “How’s the Harrisons’ horse?”

“With extra nursing for the next week, I think she should be okay. I’m glad I didn’t delay going though, because it was a case of atypical myopathy, not colic.”

“Oh, I should’ve thought of that. Your grandad saw at least one case of that every autumn. I should send out an email blast to our horse clients reminding them of the danger.”

“That’s a wonderful idea.”

Polly jotted a memo on a sticky note and stuck it on the edge of her computer monitor. “Please tell me you got a chance to tour the manor house before I called.”

“I didn’t. Edwina was out riding, and Clifford was away.”

Polly glanced at the wall clock. “It’s still early. Why don’t you try again?” Her eyes twinkled. “You should check on their lame horse, anyway, don’t you think?”

“I might have another lead.” Harriet filled Polly in on Ryker’s vendetta against Pierre.

“All the more reason to return to the manor. Find out if Ryker was there that day.”

“He wasn’t. Not at the time of the theft, anyway. His car is covered with advertising for his business, so I would have noticed if it had been there.”

“Maybe he paid someone to help him.”

“I wondered that, but how would he have known Pierre would be there? I didn’t get the impression that either Edwina or Clifford was expecting him.”

"Only one way to find out. Pay the Castlegates another visit."

"No, what I should do is get back so Will and I can make dinner and figure out what we can cook for his old university friend later this week. Who, by the way, happens to be a woman."

"Am I sensing some rivalry?"

"Of course not. But I would like to make a good impression."

"I tell you what. I'll figure out a menu for your meal with the old uni friend. And if you're not back within the hour, I'll put your chicken legs in the oven for you for tonight's dinner."

"How did you know I planned to cook chicken legs?"

"I saw them thawing in your fridge when I needed more milk for my tea. Now go."

Against her better judgment, Harriet allowed Polly to shoo her out the door.

But by the time Harriet reached Castlegate Manor, both Edwina and Clifford had left for the evening. Harriet checked on Thunder, who nickered a greeting when she reached his stall.

A tall man strode into the stable. "Are you Dr. Bailey-Knight?"

"I am," Harriet confirmed.

"Alasdair Atkinson. I manage His Lordship's estate. I didn't realize you were coming in today."

"Merely a courtesy call to check on Thunder." Harriet stepped out of the stall and latched the door. "Has the excitement settled down around here since my last visit?" she asked casually, hoping Alasdair would prove to be a talkative sort.

"Yeah. They've made an arrest. But still haven't found the missing statue."

"I heard that. It's strange, isn't it?"

"If the police weren't so certain Aubert nicked the silver, my bet would've been on the lad helping build the gazebo in the garden."

"Oh?"

Atkinson smoothed his moustache as if debating whether he'd already said too much. "Brent is nice enough. But he has prior theft convictions. I overheard the detective say that's what landed him at the halfway house."

"Hard to believe he'd throw away his chance at a fresh start by risking stealing something from his employer," Harriet remarked.

"Maybe. But he spends an awful lot of time chatting with the maid, Louise, outside the servant's entrance. Could be he's just sweet on her. Or he could have other designs, if you know what I mean."

"You think he might've been angling for an 'in' into the house."

Alasdair shrugged. "It's what I'd do." He walked her to her vehicle.

After setting her bag in the back, she gathered her courage and said, "Is there a restroom I can use before I go?"

"Certainly. I'll take you to the house."

Perfect.

Alasdair brought her into the house through the servants' entrance, which opened into the kitchen where Rita was scrubbing the counter and muttering that the Castlegates had neglected to tell her they wouldn't be home for dinner.

When Alasdair told her Harriet needed to use the restroom, Rita waved her through, barely sparing her a glance.

"I'll leave you to it." Alasdair let himself out.

Harriet took full advantage of Rita's distraction and her own unfamiliarity with the house to open every door in her search for the bathroom. Behind the fourth door, she found a room that had to be Clifford's office. The rich scent of polished wood and aged leather with a faint whiff of pipe tobacco greeted her as she stepped inside. The walls were lined with dark oak paneling and adorned with portraits of stern ancestors whose gazes seemed to follow Harriet as she ventured farther into the room.

Two oversized chairs faced a grand mahogany desk, behind which was a tall window draped with ornate swags that framed a breathtaking view of the garden outside. Bookcases lined two walls, and knickknacks and figurines filled three tables along another. A tea trolley with half-filled cups and small plates containing only crumbs sat between two armchairs in front of a low fire.

Harriet stepped closer to examine the knickknacks. One of the tables had a large empty spot right in the middle. Was that where the silver elephant had been? She made a quick tour of the perimeter and saw that the windows were locked. Presuming they'd been that way last Friday, no one could have entered the room through one of them. Although the office wasn't far from the kitchen, where Rita had presumably been working at the time of the theft, Pierre would have easily been able to wander about the room unseen after Louise left him alone.

But could someone else have snuck in and out between the time he and Edwina exited, and Clifford discovered the statue missing?

Harriet shut the door behind her as she left the office and then found the bathroom so her ruse to get into the house wouldn't be an actual lie.

A few minutes later, on her return to the kitchen, she scrutinized the front door—also locked. But would it have been locked on Friday when everyone was home?

"Oh, there you are." Rita's voice made Harriet jump. Rita hitched her thumb over her shoulder. "Lady Edwina has a donation box for the church that you're welcome to take with you."

Harriet followed the cook, taking deep breaths in an attempt to return her heart rate to normal.

CHAPTER SEVEN

Dinner smells divine," Harriet said as she stepped inside the clinic. "Thank you for getting that started for me."

"No problem." Polly handed her a piece of paper. "And here are some menu ideas for your dinner with Will's mate, based on the food currently in your freezer."

Harriet scanned the list then gave Polly a hug. "You are a gem."

"We still need to figure out a dessert. I thought I might ask Doreen for suggestions tomorrow."

Doreen Danby was Harriet's closest neighbor, who also happened to be the best baker in town.

Polly put on her coat. "Did you learn anything new?"

"Maybe. Has Van said anything to you about the halfway-house resident who's constructing a gazebo at the Castlegates?"

"No. He's been annoyingly mum about the whole case. Was that the man Maisie thought the police should be questioning?"

"Yes. And the suggestion bothered Will. But I learned something more that could incriminate the guy. I'd like to talk to Will about it first though. Can I fill you in tomorrow morning?"

"Sure. Maybe I can coax more details out of Van tonight." Polly shot Harriet a wink then hurried out to her newly repaired car.

During dinner, Harriet told Will about the outcome of her emergency call and Will shared a few comical encounters from his afternoon.

"Gwen Higginbottom donated the most astonishing hat you've ever seen," he said. "It looks like something someone would wear in a Paris fashion show but never in real life. I had this overwhelming urge to keep it for us."

"What? Why?"

Will's eyes lit with amusement. "She said she wore it in London for a celebration of the Queen Mother's birthday twenty or twenty-five years ago. And I thought it would be the perfect hat for you next time we visit my dad."

Harriet laughed. "You're awful."

"I don't know. I think Dad would get a kick out of seeing you in an outlandish hat."

Harriet feigned a British accent. "I prefer not to dress above my station, thank you very much."

Will retorted in a scarcely understandable North Yorkshire accent. "I don't know, lassie. That accent of yours sounds right posh."

Harriet laughed so hard tears filled her eyes.

Standing, Will switched to a debonair accent, worthy of any nobleman. "Are you finished with your plate, my dear?"

"Why yes, kind sir. Thank you."

"I'll need to head out in half an hour for the weekly study at the halfway house," Will said in his normal voice. "I should be back in an hour and a half or so."

Sobering, Harriet took the serving dishes to the counter. "I wanted to talk to you about one of the residents." She filled him in on the estate manager's suspicions of Brent.

Will bristled at the intimation that a member of his Bible study group could be their thief. "Come to the study with me tonight and meet them. You'll see how absurd the suggestion is."

"I don't think they'd be comfortable having an interloper show up."

"Probably not," Will conceded. "But maybe you should visit with Louise. She's the housekeeper he's sweet on. You could catch up with her at the care home this evening. She volunteers to play the piano for their music nights."

"Brent told you about his interest in Louise?" Harriet couldn't keep the surprise from her voice. If the young man had dishonorable motives for seeking out Louise, surely he wouldn't tell Will about her. Would he?

"Yes. He seems quite taken with her. Talk to her and see for yourself."

"I'll do that," Harriet agreed. If she was going to cross Brent off their suspect list, she needed more than Will's opinion of him to go on. After all, their good opinion of Pierre hadn't been enough to convince the police.

As Harriet stepped into the care home's cozy common room, warmth enveloped her like a comforting embrace, a stark contrast to the chilly wind that had followed her through the door. The aroma of fresh coffee and sweet pastries filled her senses, but she resisted their temptation and settled into a seat at the back of the room.

Louise sat at the piano, and the gentle murmur of conversation faded as her fingers danced over the keys with an infectious enthusiasm. With her bright smile and lovely voice, she radiated a joy that soon drew in about thirty residents. The seniors' voices rose and fell in a happy chorus. Those who chose not to sing leaned forward in their seats, bobbing in time with the music. Harriet found herself humming along.

For the next half hour, the worries of the outside world faded.

To Harriet's surprise, at the end of the sing-along, a few residents were so eager to chat with her that she almost missed catching Louise before she left. Spotting the young woman heading for the door with her backpack on, Harriet apologetically excused herself and called after Louise.

Louise paused and cocked her head then glanced into her bag. "Did I forget one of my piano books?"

"No. I wanted to talk to you about Brent."

Her brow furrowed, and she took a tighter grip on her bag handle. "Has something happened to him?"

"No, no, nothing like that." Harriet motioned to the refreshment table. "Would you like a soda?"

"Sure. Orange."

Harriet snagged a can, handed it to Louise, and steered her toward a quiet corner. "I'm Dr. Harriet Bailey-Knight."

"The vet who married the pastor. I know. What's this about?"

"I hear you're fond of Brent?"

Louise's gaze turned wary. "We go out a couple of times a week. Why?"

"Is he a nice guy?"

"Very nice." A hint of defiance punctuated Louise's answer, as if she felt the need to defend the man, and Harriet wondered if Louise's parents or others had challenged her on her choice of boyfriend.

Harriet worded her next thought in the hope it would sound more conversational. "I hear he comes to the manor house quite often to see you."

"Who told you that?" Louise demanded. "Was it Rita?"

"I'm sorry. I didn't mean to imply—"

"Because she bends the rules too," Louise retaliated.

"You misunderstand me. I'm interested in whether you spoke to Brent outside the manor the afternoon the statue was stolen."

"I didn't have time, did I?" Her voice rose with indignation. "I was too busy looking for His Lordship and then fetching Lady Edwina. And then the police came."

The room around them went dead quiet, and curious gazes shifted their way.

Louise's cheeks reddened. "I don't suppose Rita told you she was on the phone with her boyfriend," she said in a lower voice.

"Oh?"

"The second I headed outside to fetch Lord Castlegate, she was. And Rita's boyfriend has had it in for Mr. Aubert ever since he opened his shop."

Harriet's interest rose. "Who's her boyfriend?"

"Ryker Williams." Louise's eyes flashed. The young woman clearly wasn't fond of the man.

"Did you hear what Rita said to him?" Harriet asked.

"No. I had to find His Lordship. But I'm sure she warned him that Mr. Aubert was there to score more business."

"Is that the reason Mr. Aubert gave you for his visit?"

"He didn't give me a reason. Just said he wanted to speak to Lord Castlegate." Louise took one more long gulp of her soda and tossed the can into a recycle bin in the corner. "Lady Edwina figured he was there to confront her brother about his attentions to Maisie."

"Is that what she said?"

"More or less. I wasn't listening in on purpose, you understand. She was talking so loudly that no one could help but overhear." Louise twisted her fingers around the strap of her bag, clearly anxious to escape. "With how Ryker goes on about his competition, it stands to reason Rita would assume Aubert was making a sales call."

Harriet thought she needed to set one thing straight. "I should tell you that Rita wasn't the one who mentioned your conversations with Brent to me."

"Oh." Louise ducked her head and stuffed her hands into her jacket pockets.

"Do you think it's possible Rita colluded with her boyfriend to steal the elephant so Pierre would be blamed?" Harriet asked.

Louise shook her head vigorously. "No way. Rita would never do that. She's worked for the Castlegates for years and is as loyal as they come. No one could ever convince her to steal from them."

"Even if it was just for a short time?"

"Not even then." Louise set her lips in a firm line.

Harriet's hopes deflated.

"I can't say the same for Ryker though," Louise added.

Interesting. Could Ryker have somehow set up Pierre to take the fall for the theft? But if not Rita, who would he get to hide the statue?

At the risk of upsetting Louise again, Harriet ventured one more question about Brent. "Did you happen to let Brent into the house at any time Friday afternoon?"

"Of course not. Never. Why would I do that?"

Harriet wanted to believe the young woman, but a line from *Hamlet* instantly whirled through her thoughts. *The lady doth protest too much, methinks.* Harriet made a mental note to have Polly urge Van to find out whether Brent had ever been granted admittance to the house.

She hated to think ill of a man she'd never met. But if he was a seasoned thief and had been in the house before, he would know how to get in and out quickly and unseen. Given how long it had taken Rita to answer the door that afternoon and how distracted she'd been when Alasdair brought Harriet in later, it was unlikely the cook would have paid much attention to any comings and goings Friday either. Someone could have slipped in and out through the front door then taken off through the field, out of view of both the stables and the back garden.

And it sounded as if Ryker Williams had plenty of motivation to be that someone.

CHAPTER EIGHT

The next morning, Harriet found Polly and Aunt Jinny chatting over their teacups in the clinic. "No clients this morning?"

"Not for half an hour." Polly poured Harriet a cup and beckoned her to join them. "So, what's the scoop?"

Harriet recounted what she'd learned about Ryker Williams's potential motive. "Except I can't figure out how he could've made the elephant disappear."

"An inside man?" Aunt Jinny suggested.

"Or woman," Polly said. "He's dating Rita, the Castlegates' cook."

Aunt Jinny shook her head. "I've known Rita a long time. There's no way she would snatch the elephant for Ryker, boyfriend or not."

"That's exactly what Louise told me," Harriet said.

"Okay, but could he have persuaded her to hide it so it people couldn't find it?" Polly's eyes gleamed with the glint of a new theory.

"You mean long enough for Pierre to get arrested and jailed?" Harriet suggested.

"Exactly." Polly set her teacup on the table. "And convince his customers to switch allegiances."

"Right," Harriet mused. "Because even if the statue was 'found' later"—she used air quotes—"it wouldn't convince everyone of

Pierre's innocence. The damage to his reputation would be permanent. A lot of people think where there's smoke, there's fire."

"It's an interesting theory," Aunt Jinny agreed. "But I still can't see Rita consenting to frame an innocent man, even if only for a few days."

"Louise said that too," Harriet said. "She was quite defensive of Rita once I told her that Rita wasn't the one who informed me of her frequent conversations with Brent, the halfway house resident who's building the new gazebo."

"That's what you wanted to talk to Will about?" Polly guessed.

"Yes, and he was the one who urged me to talk to Louise. She, of course, believes Brent is innocent. But if Ryker is our instigator, as seems most likely..."

"You think he convinced Brent to do his dirty work?" Polly asked.

Harriet shrugged. "I hate the idea of casting suspicion on another potentially innocent person."

"Do the Castlegates have any kids visit the house?" Aunt Jinny asked. "You know how my grandchildren love to rearrange my knickknacks when they visit. Perhaps one of their little visitors hid the elephant."

"I didn't see any children around when I was there. I believe some come to the estate to ride the horses, but they would've been in school at the time the elephant went missing."

"Is it possible the statue disappeared before Pierre got there?" Aunt Jinny asked.

"Van says no," Polly chimed in. "Pierre hasn't said much, but apparently, he admitted to picking it up and examining it when he was waiting in the parlor for Clifford."

Harriet paced the waiting room. "How are we supposed to clear Pierre if we can't come up with any other plausible suspects?"

"Maybe we should come at it from a different angle," Aunt Jinny said. "Maybe instead of trying to figure out how someone else could have done it, we need to concentrate on reasons why Pierre couldn't have done it. Isn't that what reasonable doubt is all about?"

"I would think they already have plenty of reasonable doubt," Harriet said. "It's so unfair that they're keeping him in custody on so little evidence. It's purely circumstantial."

Polly glanced at the clinic door. "Actually," she said in a low voice, "Van did say that there are details about the bag they found in Pierre's car boot that suggest it was used for nefarious purposes."

Harriet stared at her. "That must be what Will was talking about when he said that Pierre is withholding information and it isn't helping him," she said.

"Probably. Van insisted he's not at liberty to elaborate on the nature of any of it, aside from saying that Maisie didn't know anything about the bag."

"Then it isn't Pierre's, surely," Aunt Jinny reasoned. "It must belong to a client."

Polly nodded. "You're right. And doesn't that say something about Pierre's character that he wouldn't want to incriminate a client by revealing that person's name?"

"Seems a reasonable conclusion to me," Aunt Jinny agreed.

"Well, if the motive we've assigned to Ryker Williams doesn't shed enough reasonable doubt on the case against Pierre, maybe we can drum up enough with my theory that Clifford Castlegate set him up," Polly said.

Aunt Jinny shook her head. "No barrister will cast aspersions on Lord Castlegate without solid evidence."

Harriet sighed. "I think we need to speak to Pierre before we do anything else. Perhaps he saw something he doesn't realize is significant to the case."

"Maisie has a checkup with me this morning," Aunt Jinny said. "She'd probably like to go with you. Maybe you could encourage her to ask him why he's not telling the police what he knows about the bag when doing so would help his case. It might even get him out on bail."

Harriet shrugged. "Sure. It's worth a try. Ask her to come see me after her appointment."

Later that day, Harriet approached the jail's stark, gray building, uneasiness growing in her with every step. Inside, the fluorescent lights cast a harsh glare on the sterile, white walls. The clang of a metal door reverberated through the corridor, a grim reminder of the reality Pierre faced. An officer directed Harriet and Maisie to wait in an equally grim room, its windows secured with heavy iron bars that cast menacing shadows across the pitted marble floor.

Harriet sat at the metal table in the center of the room while Maisie paced like a caged animal. The distant echo of children's laughter from the playground across the street felt hauntingly out of place.

The door opened, and a guard escorted Pierre inside. He wore the same clothes Harriet had seen him in four days ago, and his face was a mask of worry and fatigue. The sight brought a lump to Harriet's throat.

Maisie wrapped her arms around her husband, resting her cheek against his chest, and the guard gave them a few seconds before clearing his throat.

When Pierre sat across the table from them, Harriet winced at the sight of how much he'd aged in a few short days.

"Thank you for bringing Maisie to see me," he said to her.

The injustice of the situation squeezed Harriet's heart like a vice, leaving her feeling uncomfortably powerless despite the hope she'd given Maisie.

"Pierre, whose bag did they find in your car?" Maisie pleaded. "Harriet thinks if you tell the police, your cooperation might convince them to grant you bail."

"It won't," he said, his voice low and strained. "They'll twist whatever I say. The police will always believe people like the Castlegates." He emitted a frustrated sigh. "This is my punishment for trying to do a good deed."

"What do you mean?" Maisie asked.

"Nothing. Forget I said anything." He clasped his wife's hand. "I'm sorry, love."

"I can't forget," Maisie wailed. "I want you home. I know the bag isn't yours. Just tell them whose it is."

He stroked his thumb across her hand but didn't lift his gaze to meet hers. "It isn't any of their business. It wasn't used to conceal the missing elephant, so its owner is irrelevant to their investigation."

"But the police believe that you carried the elephant out in that bag, don't they?"

"The statue was on the table when I left. If it hadn't been, Lady Edwina would've noticed when she had me leave, wouldn't she?"

Harriet nodded, although Edwina had been so upset about Pierre's presence that she probably hadn't been paying attention to her surroundings. "Did you see anyone else in or around the house as you left? Or did you notice something different from when you first arrived?"

"I saw the maid and Lady Edwina. That's it."

"Think hard. Was there a coat on a hook in the entryway that wasn't there before? A hat? Anything?"

Despair flickered in his eyes as he met Harriet's gaze. "Nothing important."

"I wish you'd let me be the judge of that. I've helped the police solve a few mysteries. You'd be surprised how the most seemingly inconsequential clue ends up cracking a case wide open."

Pierre snapped his mouth shut, and Harriet couldn't help but wonder if he knew he had such a clue and didn't want to share it.

She couldn't think of a single good reason why he wouldn't—if he was innocent.

"Time's up, ladies," the guard announced.

Maisie assured Pierre she wasn't giving up and that everyone was praying. When Maisie stepped into the hallway, Harriet asked the guard if she might have a few minutes alone with Pierre.

"You're the vet who took care of my daughter's kitten a while back, aren't you?" the guard asked, studying her. "My daughter's name is Marcie, and her kitten's name is Cleo."

"That's me," Harriet said. The kitten had come in with a respiratory infection but had made a full recovery with treatment.

The guard considered it then nodded. "Just make it fast."

"Certainly."

Pierre observed her warily.

"I'm trying to help you," Harriet told him. "But for Maisie's sake, if you had anything to do with the statue going missing, you need to come clean now. You clearly have reason to be angry with Clifford, given his abominable behavior at the school reunion. Maybe your lawyer could argue mental duress."

Pierre flinched. "I didn't go to the Castlegates because of that. I didn't even know about their relationship until the maid left me in the office and I saw their school yearbook open on the desk to a photo of them together. The caption said something about 'most likely to run away together.'"

That sounded an awful lot like he would have had a motive. And in the passion of the moment…

"But it doesn't matter," he insisted, his voice filled with conviction. "It's probably for the best the police think that's why I was there."

"So why did you really go?"

"To talk to Clifford, like I said. With the best of intentions. But Edwina would have none of it." Pierre stood, making it clear that the interview was over. "Believe me. It's better for everyone if the true reason for my visit doesn't come to light."

"Even if that means they throw the book at you?" Harriet pressed. "Somehow I don't think Maisie would think that's better for either of you."

But Pierre walked away from her and said to the guard, "I'm ready to go back to my cell now. Thank you for the visit, Doc. Please look after my wife for me."

CHAPTER NINE

Outside the jail, the drizzle mirrored Harriet's dreary mood. She'd wanted to give Maisie hope, but her conversation with Pierre had only raised more doubts. And Maisie must have guessed as much, because the hopeful expression she'd flashed when the guard escorted Harriet to where she waited had quickly dissolved into resignation. They trudged out the door and opened their umbrellas to shield themselves against the insidious damp.

"Harriet?" Will hurried across the street, a pastry bag in hand and Alex trailing behind him. "I didn't know you were in town. Visiting Pierre?" Will acknowledged Maisie with a sympathetic nod.

"Yes, we were hoping he might've seen something that would point us to the real thief and clear his name."

"Goodness." Alex's eyes widened. The redhead shivered in a stylish olive-green waxed coat. While it might be keeping her dry, it clearly wasn't keeping her warm.

Will made introductions.

Harriet shook the woman's cold hand. "Nice to meet you."

Alex returned the nicety, her tone as icy as her skin.

"Excuse me," Maisie cut in. "I need to pick up something from the store. I'll be right back." She hurried away.

Harriet longed to escape with her. The briny tang of the sea air competed with the scent of decaying leaves and the musty odor rising from the centuries-old cobblestone, doing nothing to lift her spirits.

She offered Alex as warm a smile as she could muster. "Will tells me you're here to count razorbills."

"Razorbills. Yes. Elusive little birds."

"Indeed." Harriet chuckled. "I imagine they'd be a rare sight this time of year." And at more than a foot in height, she wouldn't characterize them as "little." She ignored that and said, "They generally nest in our seaside cliffs from about March to July."

"Of course, yes." Alex adjusted the hood on her jacket then balled her hands into the ends of her jacket sleeves. "At this point, I'm scouting out potential nesting sites and plotting the scope of the investigation."

"Investigation?"

"Research investigation."

"I see." Although Harriet wondered how she was keeping notes, since Alex didn't appear to be carrying anything for that purpose. Perhaps she was taking photos and dictating audio memos with her cell phone.

Will held up his pastry bag. "I was buying a treat for Pierre from the Happy Teacup when I ran into Alex. I suppose you're just coming from a visit with him." To Alex he added, "Harriet has a talent for solving mysteries."

Alex's gaze sharpened. "Sounds like a dangerous hobby."

Harriet bristled at her demeanor. Although, if Harriet had to be out in awful weather to scope out nesting sites, she supposed she'd be ill-tempered too.

Will wrapped his arm around Harriet's shoulders and kissed the top of her head. "I must confess, her methods have given me a few gray hairs."

"It's not as if I'm hunting down murderers. I'm merely searching for clues the police might've missed."

"Nevertheless," Alex countered, "one never knows what a criminal might resort to in order to avoid being caught."

Harriet gritted her teeth. Not because Alex was wrong, but because of her condescending tone, as if Harriet hadn't sense enough to exercise caution.

Spotting Maisie approaching, Harriet snatched the opportunity to shut down the conversation. "I need to go, but we'll have more time to chat when you come visit our home."

"Yes, I'm looking forward to it."

Harriet managed a smile, though she doubted it was convincing.

Will kissed Harriet's cheek. "I'll see you tonight."

Harriet and Maisie walked in silence to the parking lot. Given Pierre's reticence, Harriet's optimism about clearing his name was fading fast. She unlocked the Land Rover's doors. "Perhaps your best course of action is to plead your case with Lord Castlegate and ask him to drop the charges."

Maisie groaned.

Harriet's heart ached for her. Maisie and Pierre were anticipating the birth of their first baby, what should be a very happy time, and instead Maisie was drowning in fear that her husband might be imprisoned for the first several years of their child's life. "If Clifford still cares about you," Harriet said softly, "he should hate to see you suffering this way."

Maisie sucked in a deep breath and seemed to make an effort to pull herself together. "Maybe. But I'm not thrilled with the idea of throwing myself on his mercy. Or about the assumptions people are bound to make about Pierre if the true culprit isn't exposed." Maisie yanked open the Beast's door. "I think I'd just like to go home."

Harriet started her vehicle, mentally scrambling for other avenues she could try to clear Pierre's name. She didn't dare question Brent herself, but not because of Alex's warning. Although, if there was a suspect she thought might take desperate action to avoid capture, an ex-con would be at the top of her list.

Harriet drove slowly through the streets toward Maisie's homestead on the outskirts of town. "What can you tell me about Ryker Williams?"

Maisie shrugged. "Not much. I know he doesn't like Pierre. But I don't think it's personal. He probably just doesn't appreciate the competition."

"Yes, that's the impression I've gotten from others as well." Harriet drummed her thumbs on the steering wheel. "The way I see it, that gives him the strongest motive for stealing the elephant."

Maisie crinkled her nose. "How do you figure? For all his complaining, I don't think Pierre's shop has hurt Ryker's business that badly. Besides, even if it has, one statue won't solve any cash-flow problems in the long run."

"Ah. But they might if selling the statue and pocketing the money wasn't his end goal."

"What do you mean?"

"What if his goal was to frame Pierre for the theft?" The more Harriet considered Polly's theory, the more it seemed the best fit—if they could identify Ryker's man or woman on the inside. "It's like you told Will and me the other day," she continued. "Ryker may not succeed in getting Pierre locked up for long, but the suspicions alone could severely impact Pierre's business."

"I'd like to know why the police are so interested in knowing who owns the leather bag they found in the boot of his car. And I don't understand why he won't even tell me whose it is."

Harriet bumped her palm to her forehead. "I can't believe we didn't think of this sooner. Why don't we go to your husband's shop and search his records?"

Maisie wrung her hands in her lap. "I hate to search for the owner's name behind his back."

"Even when knowing the name might help?" Harriet respected Pierre's sense of honor, but if he was staying silent to protect the owner's identity at the cost of his own reputation and freedom, that owner must have something truly unsavory to hide. And shouldn't the bag's owner at least know what that silence was costing Pierre? If he were half as honorable as Pierre, he would go to the police himself and find out why they were so interested in his duffel bag.

"Okay, let's try." Maisie rummaged in her purse and drew out an oversized key as Harriet hung a U-turn to take them back into town. "We might still come out empty-handed," Maisie warned. "Pierre doesn't always take a name for repairs. Sometimes he just gives the customer a ticket they can bring in later to claim their item."

"You know what doesn't make any sense?" Harriet asked.

"What?"

"If customers normally come by his shop to pick up their items, why would Pierre have the bag with him in his car? And why would he take it with him into the Castlegates' house?" She couldn't believe she hadn't thought to ask that question of Pierre. "Surely if it belonged to Edwina or Clifford, Edwina would've taken it from him before shooing him off."

"You're right. That is odd. Unless there was something unique about the bag's design that he'd wanted to show Clifford, and maybe offer to make him something similar."

"Does he create his own designs?"

"All the time—shoes, clutches, wallets, bags, even saddles. His father and grandfather before him were all leatherworkers. He told me the first toys he can remember playing with were little dinosaurs his father stitched out of leather."

"That's so awesome." Once Pierre was released from jail, maybe she'd commission him to make some for her cousin's twins. Harriet parked at the shop and prayed that they'd find a sales slip with the duffel bag owner's name.

"That's strange," Maisie murmured as she climbed out of the Beast.

"What?"

"The display in the front window is messed up. Pierre usually leaves rearranging the displays to me. I should've come by sooner to check on the shop and contact any customers who might be anxious about reclaiming their items." Maisie turned her key in the lock but struggled to open the door. "It's stuck."

"Let me try." Harriet turned the handle and leaned her shoulder into the door, but it barely budged. "It feels like something's blocking it. Maybe a box fell over in front of it?"

"Pierre doesn't usually stack anything near the entrance." Maisie braced both hands on the door beside Harriet and helped shove.

The door abruptly gave way, bringing them toppling inside with it.

Harriet staggered, trying to regain her balance. She was so busy watching where she stepped that she didn't register what they'd walked into until Maisie let out a strangled cry.

CHAPTER TEN

Harriet's breath caught in her throat. She'd never seen a place so callously trashed. Shelves once lined with beautifully crafted leather purses and bags of every description had been overturned, the stock scattered. The computer was destroyed, and file folders and their contents lay torn and shredded on the floor. Even the coffee carafe had been shattered, shards of glass peppering the countertop.

Maisie slumped to the floor. "Why would anyone do this to us?" she managed to eke out in between sobs.

Harriet helped her to a chair, murmuring in a vain attempt to comfort her. She surveyed the room, trying to make sense of what she was seeing. A random act of vandalism? Retaliation for Pierre's perceived attack on one of the town's own?

Or something more sinister?

"Can you tell if anything's been taken?" Harriet asked. They needed to report this to the police. But since the police currently held Maisie's husband for a crime she was convinced he didn't commit, Harriet doubted Maisie would want them there.

Maisie wiped her eyes. "I'm sorry. I'm not usually one to cry. But lately..."

"You have every reason to cry. There's nothing for you to apologize for."

Maisie checked the cash register. "There's no money here. But Pierre might've taken it when he locked up last Friday. He might have wanted to make the deposit before he went to the manor. I can check with him later or ask at the bank and see if he did that." She gingerly stepped around the purses and luggage scattered on the floor and matched a couple of shoes to their mates.

"You probably shouldn't move anything until the police have a chance to examine the scene."

Maisie stiffened.

"I know they're not your favorite people right now. But we need to report this. With any luck, a security camera in the area caught the culprit on video." Harriet scanned the ceiling corners. "You don't have any security cameras?"

Maisie shook her head. "It never felt necessary in a town like White Church Bay."

Harriet drew her into a warm hug. "Don't worry about this mess. After the police have done what they need to do, I'll ask Will to arrange for volunteers from the church to put things right for you."

Blinking away fresh tears, Maisie nodded. "Yes. Thank you."

Instead of calling the emergency line to report the break-in, Harriet called Van on his cell phone and explained the situation. "Given the suspicions whirling around Pierre since his arrest, I figured you'd want to handle this personally," she told him. "There's bound to be a connection."

Van thanked her and promised to be over right away.

As Harriet disconnected, she realized there was one thing she'd like to search for before Van arrived. "Maisie, if Pierre made a record of the duffel bag owner's name, where would that be?"

Maisie helplessly motioned to the battered computer and the pile of confetti on the floor that had presumably once been their printed records.

"Does Pierre keep copies of his computer records on another device or in a cloud storage?"

"I have no idea. I manage the farm, and he manages the shop."

If Pierre knew why they were asking about a backup, he probably wouldn't give them the information. Then again, maybe he wouldn't assume that was why they went to the shop. Given the state of the place, asking if his records were backed up off-site would be a natural question.

A few minutes later, Van arrived as promised, with another officer in tow. Van introduced her as Officer Winters. While he asked detailed questions about who had keys to the place and so on, Officer Winters dusted for prints and took photos of everything. She reported that the door's lock exhibited telltale scratches, indicating that it had been picked.

Something about Van's questions niggled at Harriet, but she couldn't quite put her finger on why. Then as he did one last walk-through before releasing the scene so they could straighten up, she realized what it was. He knew how things had been arranged before the break-in—as if he'd been there recently.

While Maisie was occupied with Officer Winters, Harriet tugged Van aside. "Did your people do this to the shop?"

"Of course not."

"But you've been here since Pierre's arrest, right?" The redness creeping up his neck gave him away. "You searched the place."

Van averted his eyes and shrugged.

"Why? What did you think you'd find?" As soon as the question was out of her mouth, she knew the answer. They'd been after the name of the bag owner too. Thankfully, Van hadn't seemed to put two and two together and didn't suspect her reason for being at the shop.

"We had a legally executed search warrant, and that's all I can say about it."

Harriet nodded, confident she already knew the answer. "Do you think this is a random break-in? A coincidence?"

"No."

"So you believe this is connected to your investigation into the missing statue."

Van shook his head, his expression apologetic. "You know I can't comment on that. I'm sorry."

"I understand. But if you don't think the break-in was random, then someone was either looking for something or wanted to send Pierre a message. Don't you think?"

"Was there some part of 'I can't comment' that you didn't understand?" Van's tone rang with amusement.

"I'm sorry. You know me. I'm thinking out loud," Harriet said. "We know you think the owner of the duffel bag in Pierre's car is connected somehow, though Pierre insists that he or she isn't. Yet he won't even share the owner's identity with Maisie. And he wouldn't tell us why he went to see Clifford Castlegate. In fact, he said it was probably better if you thought it was to have it out with him over Maisie."

Van's head tilted. "He said that to you?"

"Yes. So what if this vandalism was meant as a message to Pierre to stay quiet?"

"Quiet about what?" Van asked.

"I don't know. The bag's owner, perhaps? Do you think that person used it for something illegal?"

Van scowled at her. "You know I can't tell you. Do you want me to lose my job?"

"Of course not. I just want Pierre to be treated fairly. You and I both know if the statue belonged to anyone else, Pierre would be out on bail already—if he was charged at all. The evidence is completely circumstantial."

"Unless Pierre talks or we get evidence that shows he's not involved, my hands are tied."

"Why?"

"Because despite the legitimate questions raised by this break-in, the evidence for the elephant theft still points to Pierre."

Across the room, Maisie dropped the box she'd been returning to a shelf, her face deathly pale. Clearly, she'd overheard.

"I think we have everything we need. We're going to go. See you later, Harriet. Mrs. Aubert, we'll be in touch." Van and Officer Winters left the shop.

Harriet called Will and explained what had happened. "Do you think you could arrange for a couple of volunteers to help Maisie clean up?"

"Sure. Mike Dane is here fixing a few of the seats in the balcony. Let me ask him." Will must have put his hand over the speaker, because Harriet heard him talking to someone in muffled tones in the background. Then he came back on the line. "Mike and I will be right over."

In the meantime, Harriet began helping Maisie straighten up. But a call from Polly about a dog with a paw problem cut short

Harriet's contribution to the cleanup effort. After Will assured her that he would see Maisie home, Harriet left the three of them to it and headed for the clinic.

"Joe is waiting in the exam room with Murphy," Polly said as Harriet stepped through the door.

"Got it."

The black lab's sorrowful whine quickened Harriet's step.

She let herself in the door and saw that the dog had already been outfitted with a cone to stop him from licking his wounds. "You poor thing. No wonder you're feeling so sorry for yourself." Harriet washed her hands at the sink then made a proper fuss over the dog. Since Murphy had boarded with her in the past, they were already good friends. "Did he have a tussle with a wild animal?"

"We're not sure. My wife first noticed him licking his paw last night. We probably should've called round first thing this morning. But he seemed content with Julie's nursing—warm compresses and the like."

Harriet carefully examined the inflamed paw, which was warm to the touch. "I'll insert a drain, which should provide Murph some immediate relief, and we'll start him on a course of antibiotics. Julie can continue with warm compresses a couple of times a day, as well as clean around the drain. Sound good?"

"Whatever you think is best."

Harriet called Polly into the room to assist, and they soon had Murphy far more comfortable than he'd been when he had arrived. "Keep an eye on it. If it grows worse instead of better, call me right away." Harriet typed the instructions for the antibiotics into the computer so Polly could print a label. "Polly will get Murphy's medication for you." Harriet ruffled the fur at the dog's neck. "I'm afraid you'll need to keep that collar on for a while longer, Murph. But you'll start feeling better real soon."

Joe hoisted the dog into his arms with a grunt. "We certainly don't underfeed you, do we, Murph?"

Harriet hurried ahead to open the car door for him.

Joe carefully laid Murphy on the back seat then shook Harriet's hand. "Appreciate your cutting short your other errands to see to him."

"It was no problem at all."

Polly came out with Murphy's medication. "Here you go," she said to Joe. "I tucked the instructions in the box."

As she and Harriet returned to the empty waiting room, Polly said, "Tell me everything. Considering how long you were gone, I'm assuming you managed to coax all sorts of clues out of Pierre."

"Sadly, we got nothing." Harriet caught Polly up on everything that had transpired.

Polly whistled when she was done. "Whoever trashed the shop must have been furious with Pierre."

"That was my first thought too."

"But?" Polly knew her well.

"What if the person who owns the duffel bag trashed the shop?"

"Why would they? Because the shop was closed, and they couldn't pick it up?"

"That's one possibility. But I was thinking about Pierre's reluctance to share the owner's name. What if that has nothing to do with protecting the person's privacy and everything to do with protecting himself and Maisie from retaliation?"

"Retaliation for what? Pierre didn't tell the cops the owner's name."

"This could have been a warning that much worse would happen if he does."

"No wonder he doesn't want to talk. This client must be super shady." Polly gasped. "You don't think he'd go after Maisie, do you?"

Alex's warning outside the police station replayed in Harriet's head. "We need to focus on solving the theft and not on uncovering the duffel bag's owner, which Pierre insists isn't connected."

"You think the police are barking up the wrong tree?"

"Considering that's why they have Pierre sitting in jail, yes. Ryker Williams seems like our strongest suspect."

Polly opened her file drawer and walked her fingers straight to the *W*s. "Walker, Wallace, Wiley, Williams. Here we go." Polly withdrew a thin file. "Ryker has a three-year-old dog. And guess what? He's due for annual vaccinations. I think I'll call him and schedule an appointment."

CHAPTER ELEVEN

Harriet, love, it's Gordon."

Adjusting the temperature on the oven for their evening meal, Harriet smiled at her father-in-law's thick Scottish accent. His lilting intonation evoked a sense of belonging that made the distance between them feel a little smaller. "How are you doing?"

"Smashing. I won't keep you long, as I imagine you're about to have tea."

"No problem. It isn't ready yet." She began setting the table one-handed. "What's up?"

"I've been trying to ring Will on his mobile, but he's not answering. Is he home yet?"

"No. He's helping a parishioner get sorted after a break-in."

"In White Church Bay?" Distress punctuated Gordon's exclamation. "Nasty business. What's this world coming to?"

"It is disturbing. Can I help you? Or do you want me to have Will call you when he gets home?"

"No need, love. It can wait. You'll be wanting to settle down to a quiet evening."

"Nonsense. We love chatting with you." She finished setting the table and sank into a kitchen chair to give him her full attention. "With my parents living halfway around the world and you in

Scotland, we cherish every opportunity to reconnect." A pang in Harriet's chest reminded her that this Thanksgiving would be her first without her parents. At least she'd see them for Christmas. Perhaps this year she wouldn't make a big to-do about Thanksgiving, since the Brits didn't celebrate the American holiday anyway.

"Did Will tell you I was going to Fetlar to visit Sir Bruce's estate?" Gordon asked. Sir Bruce was the older gentleman he'd recently befriended and then discovered they were distantly related.

"Yes. Have you set a date? Will thought you might go in the spring when the wildflowers will be blooming."

"I've already been." Gordon's voice grew animated. "Sir Bruce needed to see to a few things there and asked me if I'd like to go with him. Lovely chap. He chartered a private yacht for us."

"Experiencing how the other half lives, huh?"

He chuckled. "I suppose I am."

From the island of Muckle Roe, where her father-in-law lived, it was only a short drive across an interisland bridge to Mainland, the largest island of the Shetland archipelago. But traveling from there to Scotland proper took a full day or more, so she imagined that traveling by road and interisland ferries from Muckle Roe to the island of Fetlar would take at least a few hours. Skirting the islands on a yacht at sea sounded much more fun. As her father-in-law chronicled his trip with Sir Bruce, the affection and pride in his voice for both the man and the islands they called home were obvious.

"Why doesn't Sir Bruce live on Fetlar anymore?" Harriet asked.

"I'm afraid he needs more care than he can get there. Only sixty people live there now, despite it being one of the largest islands by landmass."

"At more than double that population, Muckle Roe must seem like a thriving metropolis," Harriet teased.

Gordon laughed heartily. "You're a cheeky one."

"Does anyone live on the estate now?" With so few people on the entire island, she couldn't imagine how an estate of any size could be maintained.

"Yes, a caretaker and his wife. Sounds as if they operate it as a B&B during the summer months. Sadly, that seemed to be news to Sir Bruce. The poor chap suffers memory lapses, and I'm not sure how much say he has in the estate's affairs anymore."

"I'm sorry."

"Don't be. He seems happy. He lives in a good care home with a private suite of rooms. The nurses call him Sir Bruce and show him a good deal of deference. But he doesn't demand it. He's like an ordinary bloke by all accounts."

That was oddly reassuring. Ever since her father-in-law had learned he was related to the baronet and invited her and Will to meet him on their next visit, Harriet had been having silly nightmares of meeting him in an outlandish hat and curtsying all wrong. "Is he a member of the titled peerage?"

"He's a baronet by birthright, but not one of those lords that sit in the parliament's upper chamber. I'm still researching the title's history. Wondering if it might date back to James III when he married Princess Margaret of Denmark and brought our islands into the realm as part of her dowry."

"Oh, I remember reading about that." Harriet had been fascinated by how great swaths of land could change national affiliations by virtue of a royal marriage or decree. Her heart warmed at

Gordon's enthusiasm. Historical research was clearly an enjoyable hobby for him.

Her oven timer beeped, and Gordon said, "Sounds as if your cooker's calling. I won't keep you."

"It's been lovely chatting with you, Gordon. Call anytime."

At the clinic the next morning, Harriet was already powering on the office computer and overhead lights when Polly dashed in.

"I have news," Polly exclaimed, shedding her coat. "I was talking to my brother last night. It turns out that he plays darts with the Auberts' landlord. You won't believe what he said."

Harriet laughed. "Well, don't keep me waiting."

"*Ryker* was the one who convinced Pierre's landlord to raise his rent."

"Really?"

Polly held up her hand. "Really. My brother says Ryker wanted to make it more difficult for Pierre to undercut his prices. I guess he figured if Pierre's rent got raised, he'd have to charge his customers more to be able to afford it."

"Interesting." If it was true, the tidbit certainly bolstered their theory that Ryker had somehow orchestrated Pierre's frame-up.

Later that morning, Harriet eased into a chat with Ryker about the recent theft as she examined his dog—an adorable Scottish terrier with a mischievous personality, if the way he tried to nibble her stethoscope was any indication.

"This is a lovely collar your dog is wearing," she observed. The dog's name, Scamp, was imprinted amid a whimsical flourish of forest creatures and trees.

"Made that myself," Ryker boasted, his chest puffing with obvious pride. "Custom leather dog collars and horse bridles are my most popular pieces."

"You're a leatherworker like Pierre Aubert?"

Ryker snorted. "Not in the same class at all, my dear. My business has served the people of White Church Bay and surrounding villages for nigh on seventy-five years, ever since my grandfather started it."

"That's quite a legacy." She didn't bother to mention that Pierre came from a similar family of leather craftsmen. "But you must have been shocked to hear of Pierre's arrest. I understand his work is well respected too."

He sniffed with obvious disdain. "I wasn't the least bit surprised at the news. I never trusted the man."

"Why not?" Harriet kept her focus on Scamp, hoping his owner didn't notice her cringe at his belligerent gloating.

"From the moment Aubert moved here, he was working the angles. He talked my mate into renting his storefront at an absurdly low rate on the pretext he'd handle all the necessary updates himself."

"Your friend must've thought it was a fair exchange."

"At first. But that was almost two years ago. And the daft bloke hadn't raised the rent since, even though the amount Aubert was out of pocket for the few improvements he made would've been compensated for by the low rent long ago. My mate was losing money hand over fist."

"I see." Harriet readied the dog's vaccine. If Ryker's friend wasn't inclined to raise Pierre's rent, why should Ryker interfere? Harriet wanted to believe his motive was to eliminate the competition. But a defense lawyer would no doubt argue he was simply looking out for his friend's best interests. Harriet might believe that herself if Ryker wasn't so obviously hostile toward Pierre.

Harriet administered the vaccine. So far, she hadn't learned anything the police could act on, so she opted for the direct approach. "I guess you'd be happy to see Aubert's business fold then? As a result of his arrest, I mean."

Ryker shrugged. "I don't make a habit of wishing ill on fellow businessmen, even my so-called competition. But Pierre is a different sort. If you know what I mean."

"Sorry?"

"He doesn't respect the lines."

"The lines?" Harriet didn't have to feign confusion, since she honestly had no idea what he meant.

"The scoundrel was poaching my clients," Ryker blurted, his face reddening and the veins in his neck bulging.

Harriet hid her eagerness for him to elaborate by bending over Scamp and rubbing his ears. "Do you think that's why he visited the Castlegates the day of the theft? To try to poach His Lordship's account from you?" She looked up with what she hoped was casual interest on her face.

Dropping his gaze, Ryker smoothed his shirt, his lips contorting as if he'd swallowed something sour. "Yes, because I saw Edwina leaving Aubert's shop one day last week."

"How upsetting."

Harriet scrambled to make sense of the observation. Edwina hadn't given any indication she'd paid Pierre a visit prior to his appearance at their house. Had it been to give him work, as Ryker clearly assumed? Perhaps she'd taken him business as a peace offering for the scene her brother had made at the school reunion—or she'd merely gone to apologize. No, that couldn't be right. Pierre claimed he didn't know anything about Clifford and Maisie until he arrived at the estate.

"It surprised me. I can tell you. But the French accent is popular with women, from what I understand. I doubt her brother would entrust his business to the man."

"I recall someone mentioning you date their cook, Rita. I imagine she puts a good word in for you whenever the opportunity arises."

He chuckled. "I doubt she has many such opportunities. But she's as supportive as they come in other ways."

In other ways?

"The fact is that I've personally supplied the family since Edwina was a child, long before Aubert came here and set up shop."

"So, seeing Edwina at Aubert's shop must've felt like quite a blow," Harriet concluded, setting Scamp on the floor.

"Sure. Made me realize I might need to step up my game."

"I see. Well, it's been lovely chatting with you. Scamp is in perfect health. So unless something changes, we'll see you again in another year."

Harriet waited until Ryker had settled his bill with Polly before joining her at the front desk. She invited the sole client sitting in the waiting area to go ahead to the exam room before sharing with Polly.

"Did you get enough for me to put Van onto him?" Polly said.

Harriet sighed. "As far as I'm concerned, he all but confirmed our theory that he framed Pierre. He certainly had motive, and even intimated Rita was *very* supportive of him, which I took to mean she would be willing to hide the statue for him."

"Giving him means and opportunity." Polly lifted the phone receiver. "I'll ring Van and tell him."

Harriet shook her head. "There's no point. We still have no proof."

CHAPTER TWELVE

Wednesday morning flew by with little time to dwell on how they might secure solid proof against Ryker and Rita. Dr. Gavin Witty, another area vet, called to ask Harriet to fill in for him at a local farmers' auction while he was laid up with a sprained ankle. With Polly's assurance that she could reschedule the day's appointments, Harriet agreed. She'd filled in a few times at the auction since moving to Yorkshire and found the venue an enjoyable change of pace from her usual routine.

She'd heard horror stories about farmers drugging animals before the sale to disguise an injury or ailment, or thieves trying to pass off stolen animals as their own. At an event like this, being the final word of authority sometimes required walking a fine line between opposing interests, but thankfully all the exchanges were amiable today.

By the time Harriet returned to the clinic in the early afternoon, Polly had cleared their docket for the rest of the day. "That's a nice surprise." Harriet helped herself to a cup of tea from the pot behind Polly's desk. Noticing a plate of scones sitting next to the pot, she exclaimed, "And so are these! Are they from Doreen?"

"Yes, and they're delicious, as usual. She experimented with pumpkin spice especially for you. She's playing with potential recipes for your dinner with Alex."

Harriet sampled a bite. "Doreen's such a sweet woman, and these are so good."

"She doted on your grandad's sweet tooth. And I for one am grateful she didn't stop when you took over." Polly snatched a corner of Harriet's scone and popped it into her mouth with a grin. "I thought I should leave the last one for Will."

"He'll appreciate your thoughtfulness, I'm sure."

The bell over the door jingled, and a bedraggled Maisie scurried in.

"Is there a problem at the farm?" Harriet abandoned her tea and scone and moved to grab her vet bag. "You should've called."

"No, I'm not here about the farm." Maisie patted uselessly at a smudge on her barn coat. "I guess I should have changed first, but it didn't occur to me. I was doing the chores and thinking about Pierre, and I realized you were right, Harriet. I need to throw myself on Clifford's mercy."

Harriet wavered, uncertain whether to respond with "Good for you" or "Are you certain?"

"Will you go with me?" Maisie pleaded.

Harriet opened her mouth but found herself speechless.

"I hate to think what the town gossips would say if word got around I'd been to Clifford's house alone."

"That's a good point." Polly raised an eyebrow at Harriet.

"Of course I'll accompany you," she said. How could she pass up an opportunity like this?

Both women freshened up before heading to the Castlegate estate. Cutting a sideways glance at the lovely woman in the passenger seat, Harriet realized how right Maisie had probably been about the potential for wagging tongues if she'd paid this call alone.

Maisie fiddled with her coat zipper. "His car is here." Her voice wobbled.

"Relax," Harriet urged. "Approach him as an old friend, and I'm sure he'll see your side of things and want to help."

Maisie took a deep breath and held it longer than Harriet would have thought possible, before blowing it out. "Okay, I'm ready." She reached for the door handle. "Let's do this."

When Clifford opened the front door and saw Maisie, his eyes lit up. "What an unexpected pleasure. Please come in."

"Herbert's not on door duty anymore?" Maisie asked.

"Our old butler? No, he retired years ago, and Dad never replaced him. We've learned to answer our own door—at least when the housekeeper isn't around," Clifford added with a wink.

Harriet toed off her boots in the entryway and noticed a designer handbag lying on the floor next to the grandfather clock.

Clifford didn't offer them a tour of the extravagant house. It sounded as if Maisie had been there frequently before Clifford's father doused the flames of young love.

Instead, Clifford led them straight to his office. He motioned for them to sit in the chairs in front of his desk. Rather than taking his seat behind the desk, however, he pulled a chair up near Maisie's. He offered them refreshments, which Maisie declined, so Harriet followed suit. Given how Maisie's hands trembled, she was probably wise not to risk trying to hang on to a teacup.

Clifford shifted his knees so they almost touched Maisie's and began with typical niceties, utterly ignoring the elephant in the room. Or, more to the point, the elephant missing from the room.

But Maisie launched straight into her reason for coming. "Clifford, one word from you, and I know the police would release Pierre until the trial."

"Or better yet," Harriet interjected, "you could ask them to drop the charges against him altogether."

Clifford sliced a glare at Harriet then leaned forward and cradled Maisie's hands in his own. "It breaks my heart to see you working so hard to keep your little holding afloat when I once promised to give you the world. Maybe still could, if things were different," he added in a murmur.

"I love Pierre," Maisie replied. "He's a good and honorable man. I know he didn't steal your statue, and I'm sure the trial will exonerate him. But I don't know if I can bear waiting that long." Her voice cracked on the last word, but she gathered herself and said, "I can't manage both the farm and the shop by myself. And Pierre's arrest is destroying his reputation. Horrible people have vandalized the shop."

Alarm flashed in Clifford's eyes. "That's dreadful. Not while you were there, I trust."

"No. But who knows what they might do next?"

Harriet nodded her agreement as Clifford shot her another narrow-eyed glance. She couldn't decide if he was annoyed by her presence, or believed that she was behind Maisie's request.

"Let's hope it was a random act." Clifford stroked his thumb over the back of Maisie's hand. "I'm so sorry. You don't deserve any of this."

"It's been hard to take," Maisie admitted. "I know the police need to do their job. And because you're a titled lord now, they're no doubt even more eager to nab a suspect in your case. But believe me. They have the wrong man."

"I assure you I didn't use my position to pressure them."

Maisie's expression softened. "So you'll speak to the police about releasing Pierre?"

Clifford let go of her hands and straightened in his chair. "I'm afraid having the charges dropped may not be that easy."

Maisie stiffened. "But it's your statue that's missing. The police will listen to you."

"You could say you don't wish to press charges," Harriet added.

Clifford shook his head. "The statue was bequeathed to my sister, not me. So the decision would be hers."

"Surely if you asked her," Maisie pleaded. "It would mean so much to me if you would do this." She twisted her hands in her lap then lifted her chin. "You see, there's something else I haven't told you."

His eyebrows lifted. "Oh?"

"I'm expecting. And I don't want the baby to grow up the way I did."

Clifford ducked his head, his gaze shuttered. "I understand." His voice sounded truly pained.

Maisie reached for his hand and clutched it like a lifeline. "Will you speak to Edwina then?"

"I will. But don't get your hopes up," he cautioned. "Edwina was ridiculously fond of that silly statue. She's very sentimental about that sort of thing." He motioned to other knickknacks in the room. "Heirlooms from grandparents and such. Not to mention, the statue is valuable."

"But isn't it insured?" Harriet asked.

"Yes," he acknowledged without tearing his gaze from Maisie's, although Harriet didn't miss the irritated twitch in his jaw. "However, I could see the insurance company refusing to pay if we decline to press charges."

Maisie flinched.

Clifford squeezed her hand. "I know it's not what you hoped to hear, my dear. I promise I will talk to Edwina. But I'm concerned that if we ask the police to drop the charges, the insurance company will assume we are in cahoots with your husband."

Maisie yanked her hand from Clifford's. "Pierre did *not* steal your elephant!"

"Shh," he soothed, the way a parent might console a hurting child. "I know you want to believe that. You might even need to believe that. I'm not heartless. I still care for you. I'm haunted by the fact I could have ever believed you gave up on us."

Harriet stared at him, unable to believe what she was hearing.

"After our exchange at the school reunion, I dug out my father's old journals and read through the entries for the months after he sent me away to boarding school. He wrote that he'd paid to have your letters confiscated at the school so that I'd never know anything about them, and the same was done with the letters I tried to mail." He rubbed the back of his neck. "I should've realized he'd do something like that. I should have snuck into town to mail my letters. If you'd had a computer, I could have—"

"We can't change what's done," Maisie said.

"No, sadly," Clifford conceded. "But I do promise I will do my best to put this entire matter to rest. In the meantime, would you let me buy you dinner? Something tells me you haven't eaten a proper meal since all this happened."

"I can't." Maisie's gaze shot to Harriet.

"Everyone will expect Maisie at tonight's prayer meeting," Harriet chimed in. "Since Pierre's situation is our primary prayer concern at the moment."

"I see. Of course."

Maisie pushed to her feet, signaling her readiness to leave. But hoping to at least clear up the duffel bag mystery, Harriet said, "Have the police talked to you about the bag they found in Pierre's car?"

Clifford blinked in obvious surprise. "I don't know what you're talking about."

"The day of the burglary, I saw him leaving with a bag that the police seem to feel proves Pierre is guilty."

"Oh. Yes. They said the statue was no longer in it."

"They have no proof it ever was," Maisie grumbled under her breath.

"That doesn't make sense to me," Harriet said. "Pierre says it belongs to a client. But why would he bring another client's bag to your house?"

"Perhaps to show me a sample of his work. I understand that he had asked to see me before my sister told him to leave."

"But it wasn't his work," Maisie interjected. "The police showed me a picture of the bag, hoping I'd know how Pierre came by it, and I'm certain it isn't one of his designs."

"And surely he would've told the police if he'd brought the bag to show you," Harriet said. "As it is, he's refusing to tell them who it belongs to."

Clifford shrugged. "Afraid I can't help you. I didn't see the thing."

"Could it have been Edwina's?" Harriet asked. "Perhaps a custom order that didn't meet with her satisfaction?"

"She said nothing to me about giving Aubert any business. She certainly didn't act as if she wanted anything to do with him, as I'm sure you recall." Clifford had the grace to flash Maisie a contrite expression. "I'm sorry. Nothing personal, my dear."

Maisie folded her arms without responding.

"That's strange, because Ryker Williams mentioned seeing Edwina at Pierre's shop last week," Harriet said.

"I'm sure he's mistaken. We've faithfully taken our business to Ryker Williams's shop for as long as I can remember." Clifford again shifted his focus to Maisie and apologized.

Not wanting to put Maisie through another moment of this torment, Harriet let the matter drop and said goodbye.

Given how Edwina had acted when she heard Pierre was at the house to see Clifford, it hadn't seemed as if she had any outstanding business with him. Her visit to Pierre's shop had more likely been to apologize for her brother's behavior. Then again, she didn't seem like the type to do that either.

Besides, Pierre said he didn't know about Clifford and Maisie when he went to the manor. Maybe Edwina had simply gone into the shop out of curiosity—to take a gander at her brother's competition if he was serious about winning back Maisie's affection.

Harriet was pleased to see the support expressed by their church family at the prayer meeting that night. True, some refrained from outright affirming Pierre's innocence, but since they didn't know him that well, Harriet could understand their doubts. The fact that DC Van Worthington, a trusted member of the congregation, had arrested Pierre, a relative newcomer, no doubt contributed to their hesitation.

At least their uncertainty didn't stop them from wanting to help Maisie through this stressful time. None had the leatherworking skills necessary to help keep Pierre's shop open while he awaited trial, but several people offered other types of assistance, such as filling two coolers with freezable meals.

Maisie was near tears most of the evening. When she expressed her gratitude, Will said simply, "This is what family does for one another."

As people filed out of the meeting, Rita rushed in against the flow. Thankfully, Maisie had accepted an offered lift home from her neighbor and been one of the first out the door, because the first words from Rita's mouth were, "I didn't touch the elephant."

Her declaration snagged the attention of the attendees still lingering behind, so Will quickly ushered her into his office. Harriet followed without waiting for an invitation.

Will shut the door behind them and motioned for Rita to sit. "I assume you're talking about the statue stolen from the Castlegate home?"

"Yes."

"Why did you feel the need to come here to tell me you didn't touch it?"

"Because people are saying I hid it to help Ryker ruin Pierre's reputation." Her voice cracked with emotion. "I'd never do such a beastly thing."

Will shot Harriet a questioning glance. But she hadn't discussed her suspicion with anyone besides Aunt Jinny and Polly. Neither of them would have said anything.

But then Harriet remembered one other person she'd discussed the theory with—in a somewhat public place, where who knew who might have overheard. Not everyone in a care home was hard of hearing after all. And anyone who'd caught snippets of her conversation with Louise might have repeated them to others.

Will consoled Rita over how unfair it felt to be falsely accused of something, adding, "There's a lot of that going around."

Rita's eye twitched. "You mean Pierre Aubert?"

"I do."

"I know my Ryker doesn't like him. And he's far too pleased over his being locked up. But he didn't set him up like folks have been saying."

"I haven't heard anyone suggesting such a thing." Will spared Harriet another glance, and she was suddenly grateful she hadn't had the chance to share that particular theory with him.

"I'm afraid someone could have overheard me speaking with Louise at the care home about the theft," Harriet admitted. "Your name came up, since you were working at the manor at the time of the theft. I'm very sorry for the distress this has caused."

Rita sniffed. "Louise knows I'd never do such a thing."

"And she said so, I assure you. But perhaps our eavesdroppers didn't hear that part. Regardless, I shouldn't have been having that conversation in such a public place. Please forgive me."

As Rita studied Harriet, she pressed her lips together so tightly the color drained from them. Finally, she said, "Yes, of course. I can't imagine how much worse the poor Auberts must feel if Pierre is truly innocent."

"We're praying the truth comes to light," Will said. "If you saw or heard anything that might help the police in their investigation, please don't hesitate to call them."

"I was in the kitchen the whole time, so I didn't see anything. Louise told me on her way outside to fetch His Lordship that Pierre had come." Rita fiddled with her scarf. "I admit I did call Ryker to tell him. I assumed Pierre was there to discuss business and thought Ryker would want to know." She lifted her gaze to Will's. "But I didn't tell the police that."

"You were afraid how it might sound?" Will suggested gently.

Rita shrugged. "It's no secret that he dislikes Pierre. But Ryker never came to the house. He couldn't have taken the statue. That's why I didn't say anything."

Will nodded. "Nevertheless, if people are whispering about this, DC Worthington is bound to hear about it too. And it would be better if he heard it from you first, don't you think?"

Rita's nose scrunched, as if the suggestion had put a bad odor in the air. "I suppose so."

"Good." Will stood and motioned them both to the door. "I believe you might find DC Worthington at the police station. His wife mentioned he was working late when she came to tonight's prayer meeting."

"All right. Better to get it over with, I suppose."

Harriet dragged her feet as they headed out, not eager for the discussion Will was bound to initiate about the dangers of her sleuthing. Not the physical danger Alex had mentioned, but the danger to people's reputations and the resulting stress it might cause.

But what about the stress the Auberts were enduring? Questions needed to be asked if they were to get to the truth.

The sun had long since dipped below the horizon, leaving the sky a deep indigo dotted with stars. The faint sound of laughter and chatter drifted from a cluster of young people crossing the street. Rita must have walked to the church, since she too set off on foot.

Will caught Harriet's hand in his. "I'm proud of you for owning up to your possible part in the gossip against Rita."

Harriet flinched. "It's scary how a few well-meaning questions can have such unsettling consequences. I feel bad for her."

"I think she'll feel better after she admits to Van the information she withheld."

"Do you think it will help Pierre's case?"

"I'm not sure. Ryker may have motive, but they can't place him at the scene."

Harriet sighed as they strolled across the parking lot. "That's what I told Polly."

The Land Rover sat alone in the lot under the glow of a flickering streetlamp. A piece of paper flapped in the breeze under its windshield wiper.

"What do you suppose that is?" Harriet asked.

"Well, I know it's not a parking ticket." Will reached for the folded page. "Someone advertising something, I imagine."

"A lost pet, maybe." Harriet leaned in close as Will unfolded the page. But when she read the message scrawled across it in jagged red letters, fear knotted her throat.

Asking too many questions can be hazardous to your health.

CHAPTER THIRTEEN

When Harriet stepped into the clinic Thursday morning, the sharp scent of disinfectant ricocheted her thoughts back to the words scrawled on the note left on her windshield: *hazardous to your health.*

They'd dropped the note at the police station, for what good it would do. The officer who wrote up the report acted bewildered by her questioning Pierre's arrest when, in his opinion, the case was solved. To Harriet, the threatening note proved the true thief was worried she might expose him.

After catching Polly up on what had transpired the night before, Harriet said, "Will's worried about my safety. I'm just plain mad."

"No kidding," Polly said. "Van must not have heard about your bringing in a note. At least he didn't mention it when he got home."

"I'm thinking Clifford is behind it. I really dislike bullies."

"Hold up." Polly paused in the process of pouring herself a cup of tea. "I thought we suspected that Ryker framed Pierre."

"I did. But since he was happy to complain about Pierre and answer my questions, I can't see why he'd threaten me afterward."

"Unless Rita complained to him about what people were saying," Polly suggested.

"I suppose," Harriet conceded. "But I'm fairly certain I caught Clifford off guard when I asked him about the duffel bag and why Edwina visited Pierre's shop."

"Why do you think that?"

"First, he denied knowing anything about a bag until I pressed the matter. Then he seemed in a hurry to dismiss any possible connection between the bag and him and Edwina. Van hasn't mentioned anything else about the bag to you?"

"Not a peep."

Harriet flipped the sign on the clinic door to Open with a little too much force. "If we knew why the police were so interested in the bag, it might help us figure out how to clear Pierre's name."

"Sounds as if you've come around to believing my original theory that Clifford wants to sideline Pierre so he can win back Maisie. But I don't see how that has anything to do with the bag's owner."

"Then why would Clifford act so clueless about it?"

"He was probably perturbed that you were questioning him, especially if he's guilty."

Harriet gritted her teeth. "How are we going to prove it?"

"It'll be tricky. Like you said, if he's behind that threatening note, he's a bully. And he has the power to be a dangerous one." Polly grimaced. "I have a bad feeling that when Van hears about the note, he'll be warning us off too." She shrugged into her coat. "I'll be right back. Ida has a brilliant recipe for butternut squash that would be lovely for the big dinner."

Harriet groaned at the reminder of the upcoming visit from Alex. She made a mental note to ask Will if he'd confirmed a night and time. "Want me to go instead?" She wouldn't mind checking on her grandfather's art gallery and visiting with the gallery's manager, Ida Winslow.

"That's okay. Our first client isn't due for twenty minutes." Polly motioned to the stack of file folders as she strode to the door. "Why don't you see what you think of the roasted veggies recipe I printed out for you last night? I have it in one of those folders." She ducked out the door.

"You're a sweetheart," Harriet called after her. As she thumbed through the pile in search of the recipe, a folder fell open on the floor. *Castlegate Burglary* was written on the folder's tab. Harriet chuckled. *Leave it to Polly to create a file for our theories.* She gathered the papers that had spilled out of the folder, and a stray note caught her attention. The barely legible scrawl seemed to be a description of what the police had found in Pierre's trunk, including a brown leather weekend bag containing *an ingeniously concealed secret compartment.*

Harriet gasped. *When did Polly find that out? And why didn't she mention it? No wonder Pierre's silence raised Van's suspicions.* Harriet scanned the other pages in the file with a sinking feeling. The file wasn't Polly's. It was a police file. When Polly rushed out of the house that morning, she must have also grabbed Van's file along with the one for the recipe. Sure enough, the folder beneath it held the printout of instructions for roasted vegetables.

She slapped the police file shut and glanced out the clinic window. Van would be upset if he found out she'd read his file, especially with how much he'd stressed that his superiors were insisting on radio silence.

As she set the folder back on Polly's stack, she couldn't help feeling annoyed. The folder was disappointingly sparse for such a significant case. Then again, she supposed it was a routine burglary, and not a particularly large one at that. In fact, the only thing that made this one stand out was the victim—Lord Castlegate. Never mind that they'd turned Pierre's life upside down over it.

At the sight of a figure nearing the door, Harriet quickly straightened the file folders and focused her attention on the recipe Polly had brought in for her.

Will let himself in the door, and Harriet's heart thumped.

"Will," she exclaimed, her voice sounding suspiciously like the proverbial cat that ate the canary, even to her own ears. "I thought you were working on your sermon at the church this morning."

"I was about to leave when Alex called. She can't make dinner Friday, so I was thinking maybe I could suggest that she come tonight. But I wanted to check with you first. What do you think?"

Harriet breathed a secret sigh of relief that Will was too preoccupied to pick up on her uneasy demeanor. "Tonight would be just fine," she said, trying for a more normal tone.

"Are you sure? If we don't have time to cook something, I'd be happy to pop over to the grocer's and pick something up. Maybe a rotisserie chicken?"

"No need. Polly has masterminded an entire menu for us." Harriet motioned to the page sitting on the desk, ignoring the guilty twinge over the police file she'd inadvertently seen before he came in. "I wouldn't want to disappoint her."

"If you're sure you've got time today. I've got meetings all afternoon, or I'd help."

"I'm sure, though I hope I don't regret it."

Will laughed. "I'm sure whatever you make will be brilliant. But if an emergency derails your day, don't hesitate to call me. I can always pick something up, even at the last minute if need be."

"It'll be fine," Harriet assured him. There was no way she wanted to serve takeout to a possible former flame of his.

Thankfully, she had a light workday, with no farm calls scheduled. Nevertheless, the morning raced by with back-to-back office appointments.

Polly must have sensed Harriet's growing anxiety about meal prep. As Harriet handed her the file from their last appointment of the morning, Polly said, "Good news. I was able to reschedule your late-afternoon appointment, so we're done for the day."

"Seriously?" Relief washed over Harriet at the reprieve.

"Doreen says she's making an extra-special dessert for you, and I'm ready to be your sous-chef and personal gofer for the afternoon."

Harriet pulled Polly into a grateful hug. "What would I do without you?"

Polly laughed. "Serve takeaway?"

"Bite your tongue!" Harriet shed her lab coat, snatched up the recipes Polly had printed for her, and hurried to the kitchen. Everything else would have to wait until after dinner—even the theft she knew more about than she was supposed to.

CHAPTER FOURTEEN

Three hours later, Harriet ticked another item off the to-do list she'd written out. "The roast is in the oven, the potatoes are peeled, the root vegetables are chopped, and Ida's squash dish is ready." She checked the time and felt herself getting a bit antsy despite all they'd accomplished. "Are you sure Doreen knows I need the dessert for tonight?"

Polly added a glass to a tray already filled with gleaming silverware. "Don't worry. She'll be here." She scooped up the tray and headed to the dining room. "Let's set the table."

"Right." Harriet grabbed the napkins, teacups, and saucers. As Polly set out the glasses, Harriet arranged the forks on the left and the knives and spoons on the right.

"Slow down," Polly cautioned. "You want this to look just right, don't you?"

Harriet frowned at her place setting. "Did I do it wrong? Does the dessert spoon go at the top? I can never remember."

"Yes, dessert spoons and dessert forks both go at the top." Polly adjusted the angle of the dinner fork a fraction. "And make sure everything's lined up evenly with the plate edge. It's all about symmetry. Then"—she shifted the glass—"the water glass sits above the knife. And if you want to be extra fancy, you put a small side plate on the left for bread."

Harriet gasped. "I don't have any nice bread. Do you think I should run to the bakery and pick up a loaf?"

"No, you'll be fine without."

Harriet followed Polly's instructions, carefully aligning the silverware. "I don't think I've ever paid this much attention to the table before. Next, you'll be telling me to iron the serviettes."

Polly grinned. "I would if you had linen ones."

Harriet laughed. "Then I'm glad I don't. All this fuss is starting to convince me that I'm going to make a major faux pas at Lady Miltshire's brunch on Saturday."

Polly chuckled. "You'll be fine."

Harriet stepped back and admired the effect. "Anything else before I set fire to the roast?"

Polly swatted her with a dish towel. "Don't even joke about that. The beef smells divine. But remember to give it fifteen minutes to rest after you take it out."

"Yes, ma'am." Harriet gave Polly a mock salute. "I'm so nervous about hosting Alex. I feel like I'm hosting royalty."

"You'll do wonderfully," Polly said. She squeezed Harriet's arm. "Just keep calm, ask her lots of questions about herself, and remember—she's here to catch up with Will and get to know you, not to inspect your house or critique your table manners."

"Thank goodness."

The doorbell rang, and Harriet's stomach lurched. "I hope that's Doreen, not Alex arriving early."

"Yoo-hoo! It's me," Doreen called from the hallway, having let herself in.

"We're in the kitchen," Polly responded.

Doreen bustled in carrying a cardboard box. "Sorry I'm late." She set the box carefully on the counter. "When Polly said you needed an extra-special dessert, I thought a Battenberg cake with a fun flavor twist would be perfect."

"Oh, thank you, Doreen," Harriet said, meaning it with all her heart.

"Don't thank me yet. We still have to assemble it." Doreen opened the box, and Harriet's heart sank at the sight of strips of cake, a tub of what looked like chocolate pudding, and something resembling a ball of clay. "Polly, find us an oblong plate to set this on when we're done. Harriet, grab a rolling pin. You have marzipan to flatten."

So that was what the ball was. Harriet fished the rolling pin out of a drawer. "You don't think this is all a bit too much? It's only Will's friend, after all."

Doreen laid a gentle hand on Harriet's shoulder. "Think of this as a practice run. If you can host your hubby's old mate without a hitch, Lady Miltshire's brunch will be a walk in the park. What do you know about it so far?"

"Lady Miltshire said it won't be a formal sit-down affair. The food will be served buffet-style with tables set around the room so people can move about and mingle."

"That's perfect," Polly said, selecting two serving plates from the cupboard. "You'll want to circulate before you speak so you can get a feel for people's interests. It'll make addressing them later feel more natural."

"But don't hover by one table for too long," Doreen advised in between instructions to Harriet, who was rolling out the marzipan into as neat a rectangle as she could. "Move from group to group with a smile and a few friendly words. Lady Miltshire's crowd will expect charm, a touch of wit, and for you to feel comfortable with them."

Harriet pictured herself mingling in a room full of elite people she barely knew. The word *comfortable* didn't fit. She gnawed her bottom lip. "So I should focus on light conversation?"

"Yes. Avoid controversial topics at all costs," Polly advised. "You can always comment on the decor or the food, which are bound to be lavish. Compliments go a long way with Lady Miltshire's set, and it makes people feel at ease."

Doreen chuckled. "Compliments go a long way with everybody. And remember, if you can get someone laughing, it'll make the whole group warm to you. As the guest speaker, you'll already have their attention. Some clever repartee will help them feel you're one of them."

Harriet smoothed her apron, feeling her confidence lift. "I have plenty of comical pet stories."

"Excellent." Doreen handed Harriet the chocolate filling to spread over the marzipan. "Most of the guests will likely be animal lovers who will enjoy those."

"Then when you take the floor, try to bring in something charming or amusing you heard from a guest," Polly suggested. "People love to feel they're part of the moment. It makes the whole room feel connected."

Doreen began placing the strips of orange and chocolate cake on the marzipan, while Harriet joined them with more filling until they formed a beautiful checkerboard pattern, which they then encased in the marzipan.

Doreen added a finishing touch of candied orange and shaved chocolate to the top of the cake. "There, it's all ready. Chocolate-orange Battenberg cake."

"Thank you so much, both of you." Harriet took a deep breath and felt the last of her tangled nerves loosen their stranglehold.

The oven timer chimed, signaling it was time to add the vegetables to the roast.

Polly gave her a hug. "We'll skedaddle before Will gets home. Have fun."

Five hours later, with the afternoon a distant blur, dinner behind them, and dessert plated and ready to serve, Will declared the meal perfect. Harriet couldn't have been more pleased with how smoothly the evening had gone so far, if she ignored her jittery insides.

Although, she was somewhat heartened to realize that their guest seemed as nervous as she was. At first, Alex had appeared at ease. She'd admired the old estate and beautiful property. She'd won the approval of Ash and Maxwell, if not Charlie, who continued to watch her suspiciously from under a corner table.

But the more Harriet asked Alex about her research project, the more she hedged. In fact, if Alex weren't an old friend of Will's,

Harriet might be inclined to seriously doubt her story. It had crossed Harriet's mind more than once that the woman's true motive for being in White Church Bay might be to reconnect with Will.

Regardless, too many of Alex's comments about her research project didn't quite ring true. In the interest of being a good host and not humiliating the woman, Harriet resisted the impulse to challenge her.

Harriet carried the plates of Battenberg cake to the table, and Will brought the tea tray.

Alex gasped. "Did you bake this?"

"I'm afraid I can only take credit for helping to assemble it. Our neighbor actually made it."

"How marvelous. Battenberg cake is my favorite. But I've never had it in chocolate and orange flavor." Alex tasted a forkful, and her eyes brightened with pleasure. "Delicious. Like those chocolate oranges I've always loved." She launched into a "remember when" recollection with Will from their college days, which leached a bit of the satisfaction Harriet had felt at the woman's initial reaction. But Alex's story was funny. Harriet could easily picture the cunning cat finding the chocolate orange Alex had been saving for exam time and batting it about the house like a toy.

Harriet eyed Charlie and Ash and shook her finger at them. "Don't you two get any ideas," she said playfully.

They moved to the living room with their second cups of tea, with Ash and Maxwell leading the way and Charlie stalking behind them.

Alex set her purse on the floor by her feet and perched on the corner of the settee with her saucer and teacup in hand. "I don't think he likes me." Alex jutted her chin toward Charlie, who once again took up sentry duty under a corner table and stared at the guest.

"Charlie is a she," Will said. "Harriet's grandfather named all his cats Charlie, male and female. One less thing to remember, he used to say."

Alex rolled her eyes. "I should've realized. It's a wonder I passed biology."

Harriet chuckled politely. As much as she didn't want to admit it, she had to wonder if some of the ill will she was feeling was prodded by a little green-eyed monster. And she didn't mean the furry one crouched under the table.

As Harriet sipped her tea, listening to Will and Alex reminisce about their university days, her gaze wandered about the room. Between establishing herself in the veterinary practice and getting married, updating her grandparents' old home hadn't been high on her priority list. This room was like a time capsule frozen in the charm and quirks of the 1980s when her grandmother was still alive, while the decor and content of some of the other rooms dated back even further to the days of her great-grandparents. As a child, Harriet remembered this room always having the faint scent of wood polish and a hint of lavender from dried bouquets arranged in an old vase that must have reminded Grandad of his beloved wife and Harriet's grandmother, who died before Harriet was born.

The faded floral wallpaper still brightened the room, while the thick, beige carpet added a feeling of warmth, along with the old fireplace that partitioned the dining area from the living room. Mismatched photos and a few of Gran's knickknacks still graced the mantel, including a diorama that Harriet's dad had made as a child. Bark formed the platform, while pinecones acted as trees and a teasel with googly eyes resembled a giant hedgehog. Harriet smiled at the memory of how Dad would fondly graze his finger over the hedgehog whenever they visited, no doubt remembering his late mother's delight with the love-filled gift.

Nestling into the overstuffed armchair, Harriet caught herself before tucking her feet under her. What a faux pas that would be if she did the same at Lady Miltshire's event. She smiled to herself at the absurd thought as she set her teacup on the heavy oak coffee table.

Harriet endeavored to interject the odd comment or question into the conversation, if for no other reason than to practice making small talk before Saturday. As she'd expected, Will responded by seamlessly including her in the conversation.

Maxwell, on the other hand, was apparently bored with the whole affair. He pushed his nose into Alex's purse, knocking it over and spilling half the contents.

"Maxwell, no! I'm so sorry, Alex." Harriet dropped to her knees to pull Maxwell away and help corral the items. She reached under the settee for a wayward lipstick tube and found a surprising business card as well. "'Auberts' Luggage, Paris,'" she read. "How interesting. We have a leatherworker here in White Church Bay who came from Paris, whose name is also Aubert."

Alex snatched the card from Harriet's hand. "I doubt they're related. Aubert is a common name." She focused on rearranging the contents of her purse until she managed to close the zipper. "I had this zipper repaired at the shop when I was in Paris. I probably should've bought a bigger purse."

"I know what you mean," Harriet agreed. But she was certain Pierre must be related to the person Alex had gotten the business card from. Maisie had said that his father and grandfather before him were leatherworkers in Paris. Why would Alex deny it? She was still pondering that question when her phone vibrated in her pocket. "Excuse me," she said. "I need to check to make sure this isn't a veterinary emergency."

"The trials of being a 24/7 practice," Will quipped to Alex as Harriet stepped into the entryway to answer the call.

Maisie's caller ID appeared on Harriet's screen. As soon as Harriet connected the call, the other woman spoke a mile a minute. "Please, can you come over right away? My chickens—it's an emergency."

"Of course. I'll leave immediately." Harriet disconnected, only then realizing she hadn't asked Maisie for symptoms. She hoped the items she kept in her medical bag would suffice. She stepped back into the living room. "I'm sorry. I have a client with an urgent situation. I need to leave." She extended her hand to Alex, who stood to return the offered handshake. "It was wonderful to meet you. I apologize for having to cut out early. Perhaps we can get together again before you leave."

"That would be lovely."

"I'll see you to the door, Alex," Will said. "I like to accompany Harriet on her evening calls whenever I can. You understand."

"Of course." Alex slid her arms into her coat as Will held it out for her. "Thank you both for a beautiful evening. And thank you, Harriet, for that delicious meal."

"Hold on a minute." Harriet dashed into the kitchen and quickly wrapped a large section of the Battenberg cake for Alex to take home with her. "Here, take this to enjoy tomorrow."

Alex gave Harriet an unexpected hug. "You *are* a treasure." To Will she added, "You're a lucky man."

With a wide smile, Will wrapped his arm around Harriet's shoulders. "Don't I know it," he said.

Minutes later he and Harriet had changed into barn clothes and were hurrying out to the Land Rover.

"I didn't expect you to come too," Harriet said as they sped off for the Aubert farm with Will at the wheel. "You haven't seen your friend in a long time."

"That's true, but I will always prefer the company of my wife to that of anyone else."

Harriet's heart lightened. After tonight she was confident that the green-eyed monster wouldn't rear its ugly head again.

"Park near the barn, please," Harriet instructed as they pulled up the lane at the farm.

Will did as she asked then grabbed her bag before climbing from the Beast.

Their breaths formed clouds as they jogged to the barn, and a strange uneasiness settled in Harriet's chest. Something was wrong.

A biting chill wrapped around the farm like a menacing shroud. Shadows danced across the front of the barn, cast by the glow of a single yard light. A faint mist curled above the ground, mingling with the scent of damp earth and the ever-present odor of ammonia.

Will reached for the door handle. "The barn is dark."

"She might have the red lights on inside so we won't disturb the birds' sleep," Harriet murmured, suddenly more grateful than ever for Will's company.

An eerie stillness blanketed the yard, which in the daytime would be alive with the cluck of hens and flapping of wings.

The front door of the farmhouse burst open, the metal screen door clattering against the outside wall. Light spilled onto the porch, silhouetting Maisie standing in the doorway. "Forgive me for lying. They might've been listening."

CHAPTER FIFTEEN

Grateful Will had accompanied her to the call that apparently *wasn't* a vet emergency, Harriet hurried across the farmyard to join Maisie on the porch. "*Who* might've been listening?"

"The police." Maisie glanced from side to side as if an officer might jump from behind a bush any second.

Harriet shot Will a worried look.

"What's going on?" he said, his tone stern. "Why did you call Harriet here on false pretenses?"

"I'm sorry." Maisie ushered them inside. "I didn't like to say over the phone why I really wanted you to come. There's someone here I want you to meet."

Someone Maisie couldn't mention over the phone for fear the police would find out? A chill shot down Harriet's spine.

Maisie led them into the kitchen, where a dark-haired man with a neatly trimmed beard waited.

He wore a slim-fitting cashmere sweater atop crisply pressed chinos and a quiet air of sophistication that would have seemed less out of place at Castlegate Manor than this snug stone cottage. He held out his hand and said in a thick French accent, "I'm Jacques Aubert. Pierre's older brother."

Will then Harriet shook his hand. *Is this the same Aubert who owns the Paris shop Alex visited?* His calloused fingertips surprised her, suggesting he was no stranger to hard work despite his elegant appearance. "I didn't realize Pierre had a brother." She searched Maisie's eyes for confirmation.

"We've been estranged for some time," the man said softly, his words heavy with sorrow.

"Their falling-out was what prompted Pierre to leave Paris and move to White Church Bay," Maisie explained.

"The fault was entirely mine," Jacques clarified. "And I fear I'm to blame for Pierre's current troubles as well."

Harriet's jaw slackened. "How?"

Jacques motioned to the chairs around the kitchen table. "Please, may we sit?"

Harriet and Will settled into chairs while Maisie fetched the teapot and two more cups and saucers.

"I read online that Pierre was arrested for theft," Jaques continued. "But I know he would never steal anything."

"How can you be sure?" Will countered. "By your own account, you haven't seen him in several years."

"I just *know*," Jaques insisted. "I'm here to clear his name. And make amends." He winced then added in scarcely more than a whisper, "No matter what it costs me."

Maisie set a cup of tea in front of Harriet. "Jacques thinks he knows why Pierre is keeping mum about the duffel bag."

"Oh?" Harriet returned her attention to Jacques again.

"I think my brother wishes to protect Maisie and perhaps...others."

"What makes you think that?" Harriet asked as Maisie sank into the chair beside her.

Jacques showed them a recent news report on his phone.

Harriet gaped at the article about a traveler caught transporting a large amount of cash in a leather bag *with a secret compartment.* Later investigation uncovered that the man was moving funds in an elaborate money-laundering scheme. No wonder Van had been so cagey about the other reasons the prosecution had opposed bail. Her heart thudded in her chest at the reminder of what she'd read in Van's file. Between her appointments and preparing dinner for Alex, she'd forgotten all about her breach and the info she'd gleaned.

Despite her actions being an innocent mistake, she should probably tell Van what she'd done and hope it didn't compromise their friendship.

"I'm certain the police suspect Pierre of being part of this money-laundering operation," Jacques said.

Which would explain why Van's higher-ups demanded he keep a tight lid on the investigation.

Will's brow creased. "Why would they think that?" His focus swung to Maisie. "The two of you rarely travel abroad, right?"

"We've hardly been out of town since our honeymoon," Maisie confirmed. "But the police seem fixated on finding out more about the bag they found in Pierre's boot. Jacques wants to visit him tomorrow." A whisper of hope lightened her tone. "He thinks he can convince Pierre to tell them who owns the bag."

Returning his attention to Jacques, Will tilted his head curiously. "Why do you think you'll be able to do that?"

"I'll assure Pierre that I can guarantee he and Maisie won't suffer any…" He momentarily lifted his gaze, apparently searching for the right word. "Repercussions."

"How can you be so certain?" Skepticism laced Will's tone.

"I'd rather not say." Jacques's lips twitched into the faintest of smiles. "For your own protection, you understand?"

"No, I *don't* understand."

Jacques patted the air, which seemed to only enflame Will's exasperation. "Don't worry. I know these people. We have an understanding."

Harriet shuddered. How did he expect them not to worry after admitting he had an understanding with criminals who used money mules to move cash? The only people she knew of who did that were members of organized crime. "Why are you telling *us* all this?"

Jacques covered Maisie's hand. "Maisie told me about the note left on your vehicle last night."

Harriet's attention snapped to her friend. "How did *you* hear about that?"

Maisie recoiled. "DC Worthington mentioned it when I went in to see Pierre earlier. I assumed the detective hoped it would prompt me to share whatever he imagined I've kept from him."

Harriet frowned. If Van thought some mafia type left the note on her vehicle, he'd be warning her off the case even more.

"No matter." Jacques stirred a sugar cube into his teacup, as if they were casually discussing an upcoming sports event rather than a showdown with nefarious criminals who might actually follow through on threatening notes left on windshields. "I asked Maisie to invite you here so I could assure you that you needn't worry about any of this any longer."

Were they telling her she was off the case?

Jacques reclined in his chair and sipped his tea. "I'll take care of everything for Maisie and my brother moving forward."

Harriet stared at him. By rights, she supposed she should be relieved Maisie no longer pinned her hopes on Harriet proving Pierre's innocence. But Jacques didn't come close to giving her the same warm fuzzies he'd apparently instilled in Maisie.

They chatted a while longer without learning anything more then said good night.

As Harriet and Will walked to their vehicle, she said, "Did you have an uneasy feeling about leaving Maisie alone with that man too? How do we even know he is who he claims to be? By her own admission, this is the first time she's met him."

"Surely she's seen Pierre's family pictures and would recognize him that way. I could see a family resemblance." Will opened the Beast's passenger door for Harriet. "I'm more concerned about the kind of people Jacques knows. They must be serious, to make him so certain he can 'guarantee' Pierre and Maisie's safety."

Harriet shuddered. "I was thinking the same thing. I don't even want to know how he knows those people, let alone why he thinks he can trust them. Because we're talking organized crime here, aren't we?"

"I think so."

"Let's pray he's not fooling himself."

"And Maisie," Will added soberly.

CHAPTER SIXTEEN

The next morning, Harriet paced the clinic floor, waiting for Polly's arrival. Will hadn't minced words about his wish that Harriet leave the matter of Pierre's connection with the stolen elephant statue to the police to sort out. But she had one more obligation to fulfill before doing that—coming clean with Polly's husband about inadvertently seeing his file.

And before she could do that, she needed to be sure she wouldn't land Polly in hot water for bringing the file to the office yesterday.

"Hello, early bird," Polly chirped, sweeping into the clinic, sounding as bright and cheery as the sunshine outside. She swept off her jacket hood and spun around, flinging loose her dark hair, which sported new white and blue streaks. "What do you think? My brother is a huge Manchester United fan, so I thought I'd torment him by sporting the Leeds United team colors before Saturday's match."

"Cute." Harriet chuckled. She didn't follow the UK's soccer tournaments, which they called football over here, any more than she'd followed American football games. But the fervor among fans seemed to be every bit as strong. "What does Van think?"

"He doesn't care." Polly hung up her coat, flashing a huge grin. "He says whatever makes me happy makes him happy."

The detective constable was still as utterly smitten with his wife as he'd been from the first time Harriet had seen them together. She cleared her throat. "Speaking of Van."

Polly flapped a hand at her. "Oh no, you don't. I want to hear all about your night. What did Alex think of the dinner? What's she like? Did you impress the socks off her?"

After glancing at the clock, Harriet poured Polly a cup of tea. Deciding there was enough time before her first appointment, she welcomed the momentary reprieve. "Alex loved the dinner. And Will's comments made me sound like God's gift to the kitchen."

Polly smirked. "More like God's gift to him, I'm sure."

"Yes, he was very sweet. But let's hope he doesn't start expecting gourmet spreads to become a regular thing."

"Not with your schedule. Besides, he was a bachelor for how many years? I'm sure anything fancier than sandwiches count as gourmet to him."

"Are you kidding? The church ladies used to spoil him with meals and desserts."

"Never mind Will. What was Alex like?"

"Very nice. I'm honestly not sure how she landed the research project though. She doesn't seem to know much about birds. And something else was weird." Harriet frowned, recalling Alex's dismissal of the business card Harriet found after Maxwell's antics. Then again, she could have been straining to contain her annoyance with the dog.

"Well?" Polly pressed.

"Maxwell felt the need to demonstrate what a terrible pet disciplinarian I am, despite my being a vet."

"What did he do?"

Maxwell rattled into the clinic through the adjoining door to the house, apparently having heard his name.

Polly wagged a finger at him. "Were you a naughty boy at dinner last night?"

"He and Ash warmed up to Alex right away. Charlie was the one who didn't want anything to do with her."

"That's not like Charlie." Polly squatted next to Maxwell and scratched his neck. "Your sissy usually loves everyone, doesn't she, sweet boy?"

"Not last night," Harriet said. "Charlie took to planting herself in the corner of whatever room we were in and not taking her gaze off Alex for a second. At one point, I had to shoo her away because she was making even *me* uncomfortable. Then Maxwell tipped over Alex's purse and spilled the contents all over the floor."

Polly burst into laughter. "Way to go, Maxwell."

"It wasn't funny. I was mortified."

"Let's hope you've gotten in your quota of dealing with animal antics at that dinner, so everything goes without a hitch at Lady Miltshire's tomorrow."

Harriet shuddered at the reminder. Lady Miltshire's guests would be far more chic than Alex, and no doubt schooled in etiquette rules not even Polly had heard of.

"Poor thing. You look scared to death." Polly stood up and gave Harriet a hug. "You'll do great. Don't worry." As if realizing Harriet would prefer to talk about something else, Polly moved behind the desk and opened the day's appointment schedule on her computer screen.

"Uh, there's something else I need to discuss with you before anyone arrives," Harriet said.

Polly tapped two more computer keys then gave Harriet her full attention.

Harriet caught herself squirming. "Um, yesterday morning, when you popped over to the art gallery to pick up Ida's recipe, I accidently happened upon Van's case file when I was looking for the recipe you printed for me."

"Oh, yes, I grabbed it by mistake. By the time I noticed and called him, he had driven himself to distraction trying to figure out where he'd put it."

"I'm sorry. I should've told you right away, but then Will came in to say we were having Alex over for dinner, and everything else went out of my head."

"It's no problem." Polly returned her attention to the computer, and the printer whirred into action. "Might've done Van some good to fret over where he'd put it. He'll remember to be more careful with files he brings home in the future."

Surprised by Polly's nonchalance about the whole thing, Harriet second-guessed her impulse to come clean. Had Van been so relieved to get the file back that he hadn't considered someone might have looked at its contents? Or didn't he care? "Did Van ask you if you read the file?"

"No. Why?"

"You didn't read it then?"

Polly grinned. "No, I was kind of preoccupied with making sure your evening went off without a hitch. Remember?"

"Yes, because you're the best friend ever." Harriet heaved a huge sigh. "Whereas I did something I shouldn't have."

Polly blinked, but said nothing, apparently not making the connection to Harriet's questions about Van's file.

"I read it," Harriet blurted. "But honest, when I realized what it was, I stopped."

Polly chuckled. "Look at you so worried. It's no biggie. Van's not going to slap the cuffs on you or anything. And if he gets miffed, I'll remind him how many times we've helped him solve cases."

Harriet shook her head. "You didn't register the name on the case file, did you?"

"No." Polly's eyes widened. "Was it Pierre's? What did it say?"

Harriet gritted her teeth. "Are you sure you want me to tell you? I don't want you to feel like you have to keep a secret from Van. I plan to tell him I saw the contents, but I wanted to make sure I wouldn't get you in trouble for bringing the file here."

Polly waved away Harriet's concern. "Tell me. Did you learn something we can use to crack the case?"

A chill sluiced through Harriet's veins at the thought of what mafia types did to people who stuck their noses where they didn't belong. "Not so much that as about why we need to leave the investigation to the police."

Polly's frown said she'd need more convincing.

Harriet filled her in with the barest of details about their introduction to Jacques the night before. Then she revealed what Van's file said about the secret compartment found in the leather bag. "Only I didn't realize *why* that was such a big deal until last night, when

Maisie's brother-in-law showed us the article about a traveler caught using a secret compartment in his luggage to transport a huge sum of cash. The police said it had to do with laundering money."

Polly gasped. "The police must think Pierre is connected to whatever organized crime ring is using travelers to move their money."

"His brother implied as much. He also all but said he has some kind of relationship with whoever Pierre is worried about." An involuntary shudder rippled through Harriet's limbs. "I don't like the sound of that at all. But Maisie is optimistic Jacques can help Pierre, and they've told me not to concern myself with it anymore."

Polly winced. "I guess not, if we're talking organized crime. We don't want to mess with that. I can ask Van to stop by when he's in the area this morning, if you like."

Harriet worried her lip. "As much as I'd like to have the conversation over and done with, having a detective constable show up here might raise unnecessary suspicions."

"Nonsense. Everyone knows Van is my husband. They'll think he's popped by to see me."

"The locals all know that. But we don't know who else might be watching."

The pen in Polly's hand stilled, leaving a small inkblot. "Oh. I see what you mean." She scanned the day's schedule. "You have a full forty-five minutes between your last morning appointment and the farm call. I could ask Van to meet you somewhere. You wouldn't want to be seen going into the station either."

"I'm not sure which would be worse—being seen going into the police station or being seen openly talking to a police officer at a local diner."

"How about at the church? Is Will there today?"

"Yes, he has volunteers coming in to set up tables in the parish hall so we can start organizing donations for the jumble sale."

"Perfect. I'll ask Van to meet you there."

It was Harriet's turn to give Polly a hug. "You're the best. Thanks."

Harriet returned to the clinic after a couple farm visits.

"Van called to say he had a nice chat with you," Polly said.

Shrugging out of her heavy coat, Harriet sighed. "Yes, but as far as he knew, Jacques hasn't been in yet to clear Pierre's name as he'd promised Maisie. Since the police didn't find any proof at Pierre's shop that the bag they confiscated from his car belonged to a client, Van isn't optimistic that he'll be cleared unless he starts cooperating."

"But you told him what Jacques told you?"

"Yes. And hopefully Van has since heard from him too." Harriet took off her beanie and shook out her hair. "Maisie said they'd go in this morning. I should've asked her to call me afterward. How much time do I have before Mrs. Lawson's appointment?"

"Twenty minutes."

"Okay, I'll go to my office and try calling Maisie now."

"Good plan."

Sitting behind her desk, Harriet tapped her pen on the chair arm as the call rang. Maisie's voice mail kicked in. Harriet disconnected without leaving a message. Hopefully, Maisie would call back.

In the meantime, Harriet reviewed her medical logs from her two farm visits to reassure herself they were thoroughly completed. Once she'd caught up on all her paperwork, she gathered everything into a neat stack and took it to Polly's desk for filing or posting.

The small waiting area was still empty.

"Any news?" Polly asked.

"I got Maisie's voice mail." Harriet handed the paperwork to Polly. "But I caught up on these."

"Great. I imagine Mrs. Lawson will be here any minute."

Harriet strolled to the window and peered down the driveway. "She's usually punctual."

"I was thinking the same thing. Do you want me to give her a ring in case she's forgotten?"

"Give her a few more minutes. I don't want to make her feel bad if she's merely running late." Harriet paced the waiting area.

Polly chuckled. "Want to talk about it?"

Harriet jolted to a stop. "Talk about what?"

Polly waved her hand back and forth, mimicking Harriet's pacing. "You clearly have something on your mind."

"Just anxious for news about Maisie and her brother-in-law's visit to the jail. I had the impression they intended to go in first thing this morning. The fact they didn't makes me worry that maybe we were too trusting to leave Maisie alone with Jacques last night."

"Do you want me to call Van and ask him to call around to her house?"

"Would you?"

"Sure. I'll tell him to check first if they've been in since you spoke with him, okay?"

"That would be terrific. Yes, please."

The clinic door burst open, catching them both by surprise. Mrs. Lawson rushed in with her aging spaniel behind her. "I'm so sorry I'm late." She pressed her hand to her chest, clearly trying to catch her breath. "There's been a horrible hit-and-run in town. Someone struck a pedestrian then just drove off."

Harriet's heart stuttered. "Was the person hurt badly?"

"They must've been," Mrs. Lawson said. "A helicopter came. Doesn't that usually mean the victim has to get to the hospital faster than an ambulance could get them there?"

"Oh, dear," Harriet murmured.

"It happened right outside the police station too."

"The police station?" Harriet's gaze shot to Polly. Dozens of people would be in and out or passing by the station every hour. The likelihood the victim was Maisie or Jacques—

"I got stuck in a long line of traffic, not realizing what happened," Mrs. Lawson continued. "Then when they rerouted us, I'm afraid I got all turned around."

"That's all right," Polly assured her.

Harriet nodded. "You go ahead and take Boots into the examination room. I'll be with you in a moment." She steadied herself, pretending to focus on the dog's limp as he walked the hall beside his mistress. When the pair finally disappeared into the room, Harriet spun toward Polly, "When you call Van, see what you can find out about the hit-and-run."

Polly picked up the phone receiver. "On it."

During the spaniel's examination, Harriet moved on autopilot, her thoughts far from the room. The unease that had brewed in the back of her mind all day intensified, threatening to boil over if she didn't hear from Maisie soon. Maisie, who'd said she was going to the police station with her brother-in-law today. Maisie, who should have called by now to let her know how the visit had gone. Maisie, the one Pierre had implied could be in danger.

Harriet's fingers stilled against the dog's fur. "Did...did you happen to see whether the hit-and-run victim was a man or woman?" she asked Mrs. Lawson, her voice barely above a whisper.

Mrs. Lawson shook her head. "I wasn't close enough to see much of anything. I only learned why traffic was stalled because the chap behind me wandered up the line of cars to ask what was going on."

"I see." Harriet forced herself to focus on Boots. Jumping to conclusions wouldn't help anyone, she reasoned. But reason couldn't stop the anxiety clawing at her chest.

She needed to finish the exam, but part of her was already plotting her next move. If Polly couldn't reach Van, they could call Will at the church. In fact, if he'd heard about the accident, he might already be at the scene. "I'm so sorry, Mrs. Lawson. Could you excuse me a minute?" Harriet hurried to the front desk. "Did you talk to Van?" she asked Polly.

"Went straight to voice mail. I've been on hold with the main line ever since. People must be inundating the police station with calls."

"Try calling Will. If we can't get in touch with anyone, I'll run into town as soon I'm finished here."

"Will do." Polly disconnected, and Harriet returned to the exam room.

A few minutes later, she had Boots settled with a new medication for his hip pain. She walked with him and Mrs. Lawson to the front desk.

"Will wants you to call him," Polly said quietly before seeing to Mrs. Lawson's invoice.

Harriet bid goodbye to Mrs. Lawson then slipped into her office to make the call.

Will answered on the first ring. "I'm on my way to Whitby to the hospital. Jacques and Maisie were involved in an accident outside the police station."

"Is Maisie okay?"

"Only Jacques was struck, but she's in shock, so they loaded them both into the helicopter." Will's voice sobered. "Jacques is in bad shape."

Harriet's throat dried. "How bad?"

"Bad enough to bring in a helicopter."

"Do the police have anything to go on? To track down the driver, I mean."

"The details are still sketchy. But they're searching for a black pickup."

"Did the accident happen before or after Jacques and Maisie went into the station to see Pierre?"

"Before. I think."

Harriet grimaced. The timing was too coincidental for comfort. "So, someone who didn't want Jacques speaking to Pierre could've deliberately targeted him."

"Let's not jump to conclusions."

"You heard Jacques last night. He made it sound as if Pierre had good reason to keep his mouth shut. And Jacques clearly overestimated his influence on these guys."

"Or it was simply an accident," Will said firmly.

Harriet clenched her fist. "There's no way this was an accident. It's too much of a coincidence to believe that. And if someone is willing to do something like this to keep the truth from coming out, who knows what they'll do next?"

CHAPTER SEVENTEEN

Later that evening, Harriet scowled at her reflection in her bedroom's full-length mirror. She should be at the hospital, keeping vigil with Will and Maisie at Jacques's bedside—not trying on outfits. "Remind me. Why did I agree to speak at Lady Miltshire's fundraiser?"

"Because it was an honor to be asked." Polly wrinkled her nose at Harriet's outfit—the sixth she'd tried in the last fifteen minutes. "Lord Miltshire invites dozens of members of his club to his annual pheasant shoot, so you can be sure Lady Miltshire will have invited their better halves to her charity brunch."

The invitation had surprised Harriet until Lady Miltshire shared that it was a fundraiser in support of rehoming retired racehorses. Then her asking a vet to give the keynote speech made sense. But given how passionate Lady Miltshire sounded about the cause, Harriet prayed she didn't let the woman down.

"And this will be a great opportunity for you to hone your gentry skills," Polly teased.

"You and Will are both incorrigible. I make one comment about being worried about making a spectacle of myself when meeting Sir Bruce, and the two of you never let me forget it."

Polly grinned. "You know I'm teasing. Be yourself. Lady Miltshire doesn't strike me as the type of person who has much patience for anyone who puts on airs."

"Then remind me again why I'm trying on every outfit in my closet to decide what I should wear."

"Because it's fun."

Harriet rolled her eyes. "For you, maybe." If Polly hadn't volunteered to help her pick out what to wear, Harriet would have settled for her black cocktail dress. Sure, it was a decade old, but it was a classic. Harriet held up the dress Polly had set aside without even bothering to see it on her. "Mom always said a girl couldn't go wrong with a black cocktail dress."

Polly snorted. "For an evening affair, maybe."

Ignoring her protest, Harriet donned the dress and gave it a twirl.

Polly pressed her lips together and studied Harriet from various angles. "It's not bad. With a tweed blazer and the right accessories, we could probably make it work."

Harriet frowned. "I'm not wearing any heels higher than an inch. I'll be nervous enough speaking in front of all those posh Londoners without worrying about twisting my ankle."

To Harriet's relief, they eventually settled on a comfortable skirt and blazer, and Harriet spent the rest of the evening *trying* to rehearse her speech. Rehearsing should have been easier with Will still at the hospital, but Harriet found her mind continually straying there too.

Will finally arrived home at half past nine with the grim news that Jacques remained unconscious. A friend had taken Maisie home and volunteered to stay the night with her.

"Has anyone told Pierre about his brother?" Harriet asked.

"I don't think so," Will replied. "I asked Maisie if she wanted me to, but she's too petrified to tell Pierre what his brother wanted to say to him, since clearly Jacques can't even protect himself, let alone her and Pierre."

"So she doesn't think it was an accident either?"

"She claims the driver deliberately swerved at Jacques."

"Then surely the police will offer her and Pierre protection, especially if he helps them."

"I don't know. I'll try to speak to Van in the morning." Will took Harriet's hand, his gaze empathetic. "How are you doing? Nervous about tomorrow?"

She shrugged. "I've been too worried about Maisie to be nervous. So thanks for reminding me that I should be."

Will chuckled and kissed her temple. "You'll have them eating out of your hand like every ornery horse you've ever been called to treat."

"Maybe if I picture the group as a herd of horses, I'll feel right at home."

"There you go."

Driving the Beast up the Miltshires' lane past the guests' gleaming row of parked cars on Saturday morning, Harriet realized her first mistake. At the very least, she should have borrowed Will's Kia. She could almost picture the Bentleys, Rolls Royces, and Aston Martins sneering at her well-used Land Rover as she puttered past. The only vehicle older than hers was a vintage Austin-Healey polished to a mirrorlike gleam.

Thankfully, the shooting party had already set out in their pursuit of pheasants, and Lady Miltshire's guests were no doubt gathered inside the manor house. However, to avoid embarrassing her host should someone arrive late, Harriet drove around to the stables to park then legged it to the front door.

A staff member greeted her and led her to the drawing room. The spacious room was aglow with late morning light streaming through the tall windows that offered an exquisite view of Yorkshire's rolling hills, while the fire crackling in the hearth added an unexpected air of coziness.

Along one wall, a long table covered in crisp white linen was set with delicate china, crystal glasses, and more silverware than Harriet knew what to do with. Vases filled with fresh-cut flowers, no doubt from the estate's conservatory, were artfully arranged between platters of food. The scent of baked scones, buttery croissants, and rich coffee mingled with the aroma of smoked salmon, while an array of quiches and fruit tarts rounded out the selections. A well-dressed waiter approached her and held out a tray filled with a selection of sparkling fruit juices.

Harriet chose a delicate flute of orange juice. Holding it like a shield, she fortified herself with a deep breath and faced the guests clustered about the room.

The glamorous women from London's upper crust were dressed in elegant yet understated attire, no doubt considered the latest in high-end country chic—burgundy wool dresses, tailored tweed blazers, and silk scarves draped over their shoulders. Their jewelry, although not ostentatious, hinted at old money, with discreet diamond studs and gold bracelets that spoke volumes without shouting.

Harriet fiddled with the top button of her brown herringbone blazer, wishing she'd opted for a simple gold chain necklace instead of the string of pearls with matching dangly earrings. She suddenly felt like an unsightly nag in a room full of thoroughbreds.

Besides Lady Miltshire, the only women Harriet recognized were Lady Edwina and Mrs. Lillian Hammond, a local estate agent whose daughter was an avid horsewoman.

"Nasty business, that theft of yours," Harriet overhead Lillian say to Edwina.

"Isn't it?" Edwina exclaimed. "Can't trust tradespeople these days." She fluttered her hand and added pretentiously, "I suppose we never could."

Lillian stiffened, clearly finding the sentiment distasteful. She spun to greet Harriet. "Lovely to see you here, Harriet. I'm looking forward to your presentation."

Harriet thanked her, but before she could say more, Lillian flitted off to another cluster of women, leaving Harriet standing alone with Edwina. Forty-eight hours ago, she would have jumped at the prime opportunity to encourage Edwina to have the charges against Pierre dropped. But after what had happened to Jacques, not to mention his theory about organized crime's connection, Harriet found herself reluctant to poke the bear.

"How's Thunder doing this morning?" she asked instead.

"Not much better yet. But at least no worse." Edwina sipped her juice as her gaze drifted over the various cliques around the room.

"That's something anyway," Harriet said banally, all the while mentally kicking herself for letting her fears override her desire to champion Maisie's cause. Nothing ventured, nothing gained, she reminded herself. "Any developments in your burglary investigation?" she asked, deciding that playing dumb was the safest route.

"Nothing. Aubert is refusing to cooperate with the police. I've resigned myself to the likelihood that the statue will never be recovered."

"I'm sorry. Your brother mentioned that it had been your grandfather's and was quite special to you."

Edwina cocked her head, surprise flashing in her eyes. "You spoke to Clifford?"

"Yes. I visited him with Maisie. He didn't tell you?"

Her countenance brightened. "No, he didn't," she said in a tone that sounded far more gleefully intrigued than affronted. "Does Maisie wish to rekindle their friendship?"

Harriet faltered. Edwina had been annoyed with Clifford when they'd last talked, and her change in attitude threw Harriet off-kilter. "No, nothing like that," she mumbled. "Maisie loves her—"

"I'm sorry." Edwina's gaze strayed to a group of women across the room, and she squeezed Harriet's arm. "Would you excuse me? I just spotted someone I've been eager to meet."

"Of course. It's been nice chatting—"

Edwina hurried off before Harriet's words were out of her mouth. So much for that. The chat confirmed one thing at least—Clifford hadn't even attempted to convince his sister to drop the charges against Pierre. Which might support Harriet's initial theory that he'd been the author of the note left on her windshield mere hours after their chat. But dallying with organized crime? Why would someone of his stature risk it? Nothing added up in this case.

Scanning the room, Harriet suddenly felt as restless as a squirrel in a roomful of terriers.

Lady Miltshire rescued her, drawing her into conversation with a trio of women discussing the finer points of dressage—an equestrian sport that looked much like ballet, but one Harriet knew little about. Nevertheless, she managed to occasionally interject an intelligent word or two when it came to a horse's health or abilities or what stressed them.

Excusing herself from the group, Harriet helped herself to a few of the delicacies as she strained to stop rehashing Edwina's words in her mind. Lady Miltshire, however, soon noticed Harriet's solitary state and bustled her toward another group of women. They were talking about fashion, a topic completely out of Harriet's depth.

Then Lady Miltshire moved Harriet on to a pair of elderly women discussing a hip issue in one of their dogs. Finally, a subject Harriet could sink her teeth into. Forgoing the last of her scone, she gave them a rundown on possible causes and treatments. "Although the condition can't be cured, intervention can greatly improve your pet's quality of life."

The dog owner beamed her gratitude at Harriet. "Thank you so much. I'll consult my veterinarian about it at once."

The conversation lulled, and Harriet excused herself to refresh her plate. But before she reached the banquet tables, a ruckus erupted at the far end of the hall.

A small whippet had slipped into the room and was now darting about, barking enthusiastically at anyone who dared cross its path.

Harriet hurried toward the troublemaker. "Come here, you little scamp," she called, breaking the decorous atmosphere.

In a wild chase that would have made any greyhound envious, Harriet zigzagged around tables, hair flying as she dodged a startled woman holding a teetering teacup and saucer.

"Is that Dr. Bailey?" she heard someone whisper, and her face heated. Of course, that could have been from the combination of the sprint and her woolen blazer.

Finally, with a deft move honed from years of wrangling all kinds of animals, Harriet scooped up the dog. "Gotcha!" She felt a triumphant grin spread across her face. Her heart pounded from both the excitement and the sudden realization that every eye in the room was on her.

Lady Miltshire approached with the elegance of a swan gliding across a lake, her expression amused. "Well done, Dr. Bailey-Knight. I see you have a way with spirited pets?"

Blushing, Harriet cuddled the small dog now happily licking her face. "Oh, you know, just a typical day at the clinic." A staff member relieved her of the wayward animal, and Harriet straightened her blazer. "Of course, as much as I love animals, I must admit that today I'd hoped to master the finer points of social expectations at such gatherings."

Laughter erupted from a few nearby guests, and Harriet began to relax.

"Fear not, my dear." A twinkle lit Lady Miltshire's eye. "If you can manage a lively whippet, I daresay you've already mastered more than most." She daintily clapped her hands to draw the attention of the rest of her guests. When silence fell over the room, she invited Harriet to the podium as the others made themselves comfortable in the plush armchairs arranged around it.

Harriet's relief at the reprieve from making small talk was soon dwarfed by another wave of panic as she gazed at the politely smiling faces. Even the way the women sat and sipped their refreshments screamed a refinement she didn't share.

Meanwhile, she was supposed to speak about the need to rehome retired racehorses to a group of women who likely owned horses more valuable than her entire practice. No pressure.

"Ladies," Harriet began, her voice a touch higher than she'd intended. She cleared her throat and tried again, imagining the familiar comforting smell of hay and barns instead of the delicate scent of expensive French perfume. "Lady Miltshire has asked me to speak to you this morning about retired racehorses. As you know, these majestic creatures give their all on the racetrack. But after their careers come to an end, many of them don't have much to look forward to."

She paused, and Lady Miltshire encouraged her with a soft smile. Of course *she* was perfectly at ease. This was her world, these were her friends, whereas Harriet's world involved much more mud and far fewer crystal flutes.

She forged ahead. "I've worked with several retired racehorses, and I can assure you they're far from done after their last race. They simply need a safe, loving place to call home." Harriet imitated Lady Miltshire's smile, hoping it appeared warm and not nervous. She must have said something right, because the women were surprisingly attentive.

Feeling braver, Harriet said, "Imagine these horses enjoying their golden years in a lovely country paddock." She was trying to sell it for Her Ladyship, but she wasn't sure these women even visited their own paddocks, let alone thought about what might live in them.

Harriet continued with her rehearsed speech, feeling braver and more sure of herself as she went along. The women showed concern when she spoke of the plight of neglected racehorses, and twenty minutes later she hoped she'd done enough to open their pocketbooks to aid Lady Miltshire's worthy cause.

Remembering Doreen's suggestion, she added, "Of course, the real challenge with horses—especially after they retire—is getting them to follow doctor's orders. I mean, if I had a pound for every horse that actually agreed to go easy on the sugar cubes, I'd be broke."

A low chuckle circulated the room.

Harriet smiled and wrapped things up on a high note. "Lady Miltshire has been a champion of this cause. We hope you'll consider joining us to help these horses have the futures they deserve."

A hum of agreement arose followed by polite applause.

As Lady Miltshire traded places with her at the podium, Harriet carefully picked her way to an empty chair. Sinking into the seat, she blew out a breath, happy to have survived without spilling anything on herself or knocking over the crystal. She sincerely hoped her father-in-law wouldn't ask her to host a party for Sir Bruce the next time they visited. The thought of being expected to make intelligent conversation while arranging smoked salmon on silver platters made her feel like she was about to break out in hives.

She'd much rather stick to what she knew best—animals and barns—rather than trying not to trip over herself in a room full of silk scarves and elite manners.

CHAPTER EIGHTEEN

I SURVIVED! Harriet texted Will forty-five minutes later after managing to extricate herself from the gathering.

Will immediately called her. "How'd the talk go?"

"Surprisingly well. I didn't make any major faux pas, and Lady Miltshire is pleased with how many pledges came in."

"I'm not surprised." Not a hint of teasing colored his warm declaration.

"Thank you." Hearing voices in the background, she said, "Are you at the hospital?"

"The parish hall. I'm heading out soon with one of the van drivers to collect more donations for the jumble sale. Are you heading to the house?"

"Only to change. Then I'll come help with sorting. Is Polly there?"

"Yes." Will chuckled. "I'm sure she'll be eager to hear a play-by-play of your entire morning."

When Harriet arrived at White Church, the parish hall, usually used for tea gatherings and church meetings, was filled with the smell of old books, freshly laundered clothes, and dust from forgotten attic treasures. The long wooden tables set up around the perimeter were organized into artful displays with clothes at one end of the hall and general paraphernalia at the other. However, plenty of tables in the center of the room were still piled high with mismatched stacks of clothing, bric-a-brac, and household items, all waiting to be organized.

The room was abuzz with quiet conversation as the volunteers attended to their assigned tasks. Polly stood in the center of the action, sleeves rolled up, sorting through a pile of donated goods with Doreen Danby.

"How can I help?" Harriet asked, joining them.

Polly beamed a welcome. "Help me check these winter coats for missing buttons and broken zippers while you tell me *every* detail of your time at Lady Miltshire's."

"Me too," Doreen said.

Harriet exaggeratedly swiped her hand across her forehead. "I'm just glad it's over."

Polly laughed. "Why? What happened?"

"What didn't happen? One of the guests brought along a whippet of all things, and the dog caused quite a scene."

"Of course you took it in hand," Polly guessed.

Harriet nodded. "I did catch the whippet, which seemed to impress Lady Miltshire's guests." In hindsight, Harriet had to admit that balancing poise and authenticity hadn't been as difficult as she feared.

Doreen grinned. "I wish I'd seen that."

By the time Harriet had relayed the rest of the brunch's highlights to Polly and Doreen, they'd finished sorting through the stack of coats and moved on to folding linens.

At nearby tables, other parish members stacked kitchenware or sorted children's toys. Their quiet conversations ran the gamut from the upcoming sale to tsking over recent events in town, including the theft, Pierre's subsequent arrest, and the fact that the hit-and-run driver was still at large.

The only people who worked in silence were the young men arranging furniture in an artful array in the far corner.

Harriet tilted her head in their direction. "Who are those fellows?"

"They're the blokes from the halfway house." Doreen held up an ancient pair of roller skates. "Aren't these adorable?"

Harriet's attention strayed once more to the men. They seemed to be working diligently. One caught her watching him and gave her a shy smile before ducking his head to focus on tightening a chair leg.

"I spoke to a couple of them earlier," Doreen said. "They're happy to be included and more than willing to help, since the sale's proceeds will go toward fixing their leaky roof."

Harriet nodded, encouraged by the sense of shared purpose in the air despite the differences in background and circumstances of the volunteers, especially given the aspersions some had cast at the young men following the Castlegate burglary.

The door blew open, and several men lumbered in, carrying more boxes. The guys who'd been arranging furniture hurried to assist. Outside, the wind howled and the sea mist rolled in, a chilling reminder that despite the friendly atmosphere in the parish hall, all was not well beyond its walls.

Polly whispered to Harriet, "We really need to focus on who took that statue and where it is now. From what Van hinted last night, the police are concentrating more on that bag they found in

Pierre's car than they are on the elephant. If we can figure out who took it and where they've stashed it, it might go a long way in getting them to believe him."

Harriet wasn't sure the police would believe Pierre, elephant or no elephant.

Polly must have taken her silence for agreement. "Have we eliminated Louise's boyfriend as a suspect?"

"She claims he didn't go into the house on the day the statue went missing."

"So," Polly concluded, "assuming he didn't sneak in when she wasn't looking, that leaves Ryker and Clifford as our prime suspects."

"Except Ryker was nowhere near the house, and Rita says she didn't help him."

"Was there anyone else around?"

Harriet conjured a mental image of the people she'd seen about the place that morning. "The groom was out in the stable with me the entire time. And Edwina was there. I imagine the estate manager was around too, although I didn't see him."

"Where was Clifford?"

"According to Edwina, before he wandered into the barn and asked after her horse, he was in the garden with Brent, discussing the gazebo construction."

Polly mulled over the information out loud as she folded children's shirts. "If we eliminate Pierre as a suspect, the statue had to be on the estate when Van arrived to investigate. Because no one else left, right?"

"Right."

"But no one could find it. Or so they claimed."

"No surprise there," Doreen chimed in. "The number of hiding places on such a massive estate could keep the police busy looking for days."

Polly smirked. "Or Clifford hid the thing in his safe. It's the one place he could be confident no one else would be able to look."

To Harriet's surprise, one of the halfway house residents sidled up to them. "If I nicked it, I'd stash it in a vehicle on the estate and fetch it later."

"That's a brilliant idea," Polly exclaimed.

"Surely the police would've searched all the vehicles," Doreen countered.

Polly gaped at Harriet. "Except yours. Because Van let you leave as soon as he finished questioning you, right?"

"W-well, yes," Harriet stuttered.

Polly held her palm out to Harriet. "Give me your keys."

Harriet's stomach jolted. "I'm pretty sure I would've noticed an elephant in my truck."

But would she? The Beast had been unlocked the entire time she'd been tending to Edwina's horse. And it hadn't been in her line of sight. Recalling that Edwina had changed her clothes before coming back to the barn, Harriet figured that Clifford would have had time to slip out of the house unseen for a few minutes.

She gave her head a hard shake at the crazy notion. "Even if the thief stashed the statue in my vehicle, it's been more than a week since the theft. Surely whoever stole it would have retrieved it by now."

Polly looked very pleased with herself. "Maybe someone tried. Remember you said Maxwell went crazy barking at the window Saturday night and you couldn't figure out why?"

Harriet's pulse quickened. "You think Maxwell heard someone prowling around outside?"

"It could have been someone trying to get the statue back, and it would also explain how the thief knew which vehicle was yours in the church parking lot Wednesday night."

"That's true," Harriet admitted. "But if he already retrieved the statue, what's the point of looking in there now? What do you expect to find?"

"Evidence. The only time you leave the Beast unlocked is at a house call. So if the statue isn't there and there's no evidence the lock has been jimmied, we can assume Maxwell scared the thief off Saturday night and they weren't able to try to get into your car. That would narrow the retrieval opportunities to the handful of farm and house calls you made this week." Polly grinned triumphantly and hustled out of the hall.

Harriet trailed after her. "That's assuming the statue was ever stashed in my vehicle."

Polly examined the area around the Beast's door locks first. "I'm not seeing any scratches." She unlocked the back door with the key then searched under all the seats. Nothing. Next, she examined the locked boxes containing veterinary equipment. "This padlock has scratches that could be from someone taking picks to it."

Harriet gulped. It was the box she stored the portable X-ray machine in—a box she'd had open at the Castlegate farm. She unlocked it. Within minutes, she and Polly had half the contents pulled out.

"I don't think he would've been able to fit the statue in here," Polly said. "Unless he took some of your stuff out and returned it *after* he'd retrieved the statue."

Frowning, Harriet rearranged the items in the box the way she liked them. "I definitely would've noticed if stuff had been moved or if it was missing when I repacked my equipment before leaving the farm."

"Hold on." Polly tilted her head and shifted the box. "What do we have here?" She plucked a woman's kid leather glove from behind the box. "Is this yours?"

Harriet examined the glove. "Maisie probably dropped it when I took her to see Clifford."

"I've never seen her wear anything that fancy," Polly said.

"Her husband is a leatherworker. Of course he'd make her nice gloves."

Polly pulled out her phone. "Only one way to find out." She texted a photo of the glove to Maisie with a query. Within moments, she had a reply. "It isn't Maisie's."

Scrunching her nose, Harriet shoved the glove back into Polly's hand. "You better take it. The owner must've doused their hands with perfume or hand lotion before putting it on. The smell is giving me a headache."

Polly sniffed the glove. "So all we have to do is figure out who uses this fragrance."

Harriet shook her head. "More than likely the glove fell out of one of the donation boxes Will and I collected. A thief wouldn't be foolish enough to remove her glove and leave it behind."

Polly handed Harriet the keys. "I suppose you're right." They headed inside, and Polly gave the glove to one of the women arranging the table filled with hats and scarves and mittens. "If you come across a glove without a mate, this might be it."

"Right." The woman took the glove and added it to a stack of orphaned items.

Polly appeared loath to admit defeat. "Just because we didn't find any evidence doesn't mean the thief didn't use the Beast to get the elephant statue off the estate." She steered Harriet back to where they'd left Doreen. "The thief could've hidden it under one of the seats where you wouldn't have noticed it. Have you seen any strangers or out-of-place vehicles around any of your vet calls since then?"

"The guy would have to be pretty brazen to follow me onto a farm where anyone might see him." Remembering Clifford's reaction to her questions when she visited with Maisie, she added, "But I think you might be onto something with the safe idea."

Polly pondered a moment before nodding. "The trouble is, if Clifford hid the statue in his safe to frame Pierre, there's no way he'll open it for us."

Doreen smiled. "Maybe we could get someone else to open it," she said.

Harriet frowned. "What do you mean? Who?"

Doreen handed Polly a box of tousled trousers to fold. "Why not ask Edwina to open it?"

"But why would she?" Harriet asked. "What possible reason could we give her? Do we just walk up to her and say, 'Hello, Lady Castlegate. We think your brother, the lord of the manor, stole your statue and you'll find it in the safe'?"

Polly laughed. "I don't think we need to be that blunt," she said. "But think about it. Edwina believes Clifford wants to get back together with Maisie, so she's got to be aware that he has a plausible motive to frame Pierre. I don't think it would take all that much to convince her that he might have stolen the elephant himself."

"But what if she doesn't believe us?" Harriet still thought it was a crazy idea. "And even if she did, why would she let us see inside the safe?"

"Oh, that's easy," Doreen said. "I know Edwina Castlegate well enough to know that if you challenge her, she'll do whatever it takes to prove you wrong. She'd take the opportunity to rub it in your faces. Of course, if the statue is in the safe, then she won't be happy to be the one who's wrong."

"I hear what you're saying," Harriet said. "But is there a way we can get her to open the safe without accusing Clifford of anything?"

Polly turned to Doreen, who raised her hands in exasperation. "I came up with the idea of Edwina opening the safe. It's your turn."

Polly's brow furrowed in concentration as she continued folding clothes. After a minute or two, she brightened. "I know. We could appeal to her family pride. I could tell Edwina about the novel I'm reading, and how for generations the patriarch of the family kept a secret document hidden away in the family safe that revealed a forgotten branch of the family tree."

"Sounds like an intriguing story," Harriet said, although she wasn't sure where Polly was going with it. "It's like how Will's dad has discovered an unknown noble branch in his family tree."

"Right. You could mention that and ask Edwina if they have any documents in their safe that reveal a forgotten branch of the Castlegate family that they're keeping hidden from the world."

"Even if there are such documents, why would she admit that?" Harriet asked. "She'd just deny it."

"Of course she would." Polly's eyes gleamed. "Then all we need to do is suggest that a 'true lady' would have nothing to hide and would open her safe."

Harriet arched an eyebrow and laughed. "You've come up with some crazy ideas in the last eighteen months, my friend, but that's one of the craziest."

Polly frowned. "It sounded better in my head."

Harriet stifled another laugh, even as she felt a pang of guilt that they could make light of the situation when Pierre was sitting in jail and his brother was still unconscious in the hospital.

Polly folded her arms over her chest. "Well, we'd better figure something out," she said. "One way or another, we need to see inside that safe."

CHAPTER NINETEEN

The Crow's Nest was alive with chatter and laughter as Harriet, Will, Polly, and Van stepped inside, hoping to claim a table before the Saturday evening crowd got any thicker. Scanning the room, Harriet steered her group to an empty booth near the fireplace. The warm glow of amber lights spilled over the table and the scent of woodsmoke mingled with the hearty aromas of roast beef and shepherd's pie.

"I feel like having a steak and kidney pie tonight," Polly said, not bothering to read the menu the server handed her.

"That sounds good," Van agreed. "Make that two."

"Make that three," Will chimed in.

Harriet closed the menu and handed it to the server. "I'll try the scampi. With tea, please."

"I'll have tea as well," Polly said.

"Fancy a game of darts while we wait for the food?" Will asked Van as the server set down a bowl of potato chips, or crisps as they were called there.

"Sure. You girls want to join us?"

"That's okay, you go on," Polly said for them both.

When the pub door swung open with a gust of cool air, Polly froze.

Harriet peeked over her shoulder to see who'd captured Polly's attention.

Lady Edwina stood at the entrance with a tall, striking man at her side who looked every inch the out-of-towner—maybe even a royal once removed. He wore a tailored coat and carried himself with an air of confidence. Edwina linked arms with her date and guided him to a table by the window.

"Can't say I've ever seen her here," Polly muttered. "She usually holds court somewhere with more prestige."

Isla Hammond, a young horse enthusiast with a freckled face and cheery disposition, approached their table with their teapots and cups. Isla's horse, Jasper, was one of Harriet's patients.

Harriet greeted her with a warm smile. "I didn't know you worked here. I just saw your mom this morning at Lady Miltshire's."

"I just started a couple weeks ago," Isla told her. "This is one of the few weekends I don't have a competition, so I offered to fill in for a friend." Isla tracked Polly's gaze across the room. "Lady Edwina? Here?" She sounded surprised to see the woman. "Isn't this a bit, um, rustic for her tastes?"

Edwina laughed at something her date whispered in her ear, her perfectly manicured fingers resting lightly on his arm.

"Maybe she's trying to be more down-to-earth?" Harriet suggested. Even as she said it, she recalled Edwina's clear efforts to be exactly the opposite at Lady Miltshire's earlier that day while conversing with London's elite.

"Down-to-earth?" Isla chuckled. "Not from what I've heard. According to my mate, after our last horse show in Boroughbridge,

Edwina went straight on to Harrogate for the full spa treatment at the Turkish Baths. Then the next day she apparently tore through the high-end boutiques like they were going out of style."

Polly's gaze snapped from Edwina to Isla, a glint of interest in her eyes. "Wow. That's not a cheap weekend."

Isla leaned closer as if sharing a scandalous secret. "Tell me about it. And you should see her horse tack—all brand-new, top-of-the-line stuff."

"Sounds as if she's consoling herself over the pain of her father's death by spending her inheritance," Polly mused.

"I don't think so. I overheard her griping that her father refused to give her a penny more than her monthly allowance, and her brother's no better now that he's taken over the purse strings." Isla tucked her serving tray under her arm. "I figure she must be awfully persuasive with her dates, because there's no way her allowance could cover all that boutique shopping, plus spa days, horse shows, and dining at the nicest restaurants."

Harriet's mind flicked back to the designer bag she'd noticed in the entryway during her visit with Maisie to the Castlegate estate. The entire Castlegate stable had seemed upgraded as well, with new pristine saddles and bridles, all high-quality leather and gleaming silver hardware.

A burst of laughter erupted from the group playing darts next to Van and Will as Isla moved away to tend to another table.

But as if her thoughts had traveled in a similar direction to Harriet's, Polly remained fixated on Edwina, who animatedly chatted with her date, gesturing in a way that drew attention to her glittering jewelry.

"Wonder if the diamond bracelets were a gift from him," Polly murmured.

"He looks as if he can afford them." The pieces were ostentatious yet elegant, a blend that suited the persona Edwina seemed eager to project.

Isla's mother happened by and paused at their table. "Harriet, lovely to see you again. I thoroughly enjoyed your presentation this morning."

"Thank you."

"I saw Isla stop by your table. Did she tell you how well she and Jasper did in their last dressage competition?"

"She didn't." Harriet mentally kicked herself for not asking Isla how Jasper was doing.

"She doesn't like to toot her own horn," Lillian said proudly. "But she brought home a blue ribbon in her level."

"That's brilliant," Polly exclaimed.

"Yes, excellent," Harriet agreed. "We'll be sure to congratulate her when she returns with our meals."

Edwina's tinkling laughter carried across the room, and a knowing smile played on Lillian's lips. "You two appear to be as interested in our Lady Edwina as I am. Although I can't say I envy her these days."

"Why not?" Harriet asked.

Lillian adjusted the silk scarf knotted neatly at her throat. "Lord Castlegate has asked me to handle the sale of the estate. Once it goes through, I'm afraid she'll have to learn to budget her allowance. As I understand it, besides a few specific bequests such as the grand piano, several pieces of artwork, and her mother's jewelry, a monthly allowance is the only other provision her father made for her in his will. The estate itself was left to Clifford."

"And Clifford wants to sell it?" Harriet's voice rose in surprise. She peeked Edwina's way, hoping she hadn't overheard the question.

"You didn't know?" Lillian slanted a conspiratorial glance around the bustling pub. "He engaged my services a few weeks ago. Says he's returning to London as soon as he can shift the place."

Polly sat up straighter, confusion shadowing her eyes. "Selling Castlegate Manor? I thought he was set on staying to win Maisie back."

Lillian let out a knowing chuckle. "Didn't we all after the scene he made at the school reunion? But I asked him the next day if he wanted to cancel the listing, and he said no. Categorically, in fact. He's rather keen to put all the fuss with Maisie behind him." Lillian studied his sister again. "Which means Edwina will lose her cushy, rent-free home and the stable for her horses. If she plans to keep up this lifestyle, she'll either need to snag herself a wealthy husband or figure out how to stretch her allowance." Lillian fluttered her fingers and went back to her table.

Polly seemed almost disappointed. "There goes our theory," she muttered. "If he's set on selling, then why frame Pierre? Maybe I had the motive right, but the wrong person."

Harriet snatched a chip. "I don't follow."

"What if Edwina isn't happy about Clifford selling the estate? I mean, she wouldn't be, right? Like Lillian said, if Clifford leaves, Edwina will suddenly have to spend a significant chunk of her allowance on her own living arrangements and her horses' room and board."

"What are you saying?"

"Instead of Clifford being the one who fit up Pierre, what if Edwina did it to give her brother a reason to stay in White Church?"

"You mean, to rekindle his relationship with Maisie."

"Yes. Be her champion when her husband turns out to be a thief. And, more to Edwina's advantage, not sell the estate."

Mulling over the theory, Harriet snuck another peek at Edwina, who was now tossing her hair back in laughter. "It's not entirely far-fetched." Harriet mentally reviewed the afternoon of the theft. "Edwina didn't come out of the house until several minutes after Pierre left. She would've had time to hide the statue before her brother went inside. The timeline makes sense."

"What timeline makes sense?" Will slid onto the bench seat beside her.

"Please tell me you two aren't still batting around theories about this duffel bag business," Van added, sliding in beside his wife.

"No, we were discussing the missing elephant timeline," Harriet countered.

"Which has nothing to do with the bag," Polly said, keeping her voice low. She explained their theories that the statue never left the premises or had been stashed in Harriet's Land Rover to be retrieved later. "We're leaning toward it never left the house. Think about it," she added. "Where is the one place no one would think to look for it, and also the one place where the servants couldn't hide it or find it?"

Will and Van exchanged glances, but neither hazarded a guess.

"The family safe," Harriet said. "It's probably hidden in Clifford's office behind a painting or something."

Will's head bobbed from side to side, his lips pressed together in contemplation. "It's a good theory."

Van sighed. "It may be, but I have absolutely no basis to request a search warrant for their safe."

"And simply asking to be shown the contents of a lord's safe would be awful for your career," Will added.

"Not necessarily." Harriet explained why Edwina had catapulted to the top of their suspect list. "If Edwina did hide the statue there without Clifford's knowledge, he'd have no qualms about opening the safe."

Van shook his head. "He'd be insulted to have his integrity questioned by a lowly DC."

"Harriet and I could ask to see inside," Polly suggested.

"No!" Will and Van said at the same time.

"Until this whole mess is sorted," Van continued more softly, "it's better you stay away from the Castlegate estate altogether."

"I can't do that," Harriet said. "I'm treating their lame horse."

Will reached for Harriet's hand under the table and folded it inside his. The warmth of his touch soothed the tension triggered by Van's warning.

"Stick to the barn then," Van said, "and don't discuss anything but the horse."

"You don't think the duffel bag has anything to do with the Castlegate theft, do you?" Harriet asked.

"As you well know, Pierre is our prime person of interest," Van said, clearly pained to have to remind her. "And as the situation with Pierre's brother has made clear, nosing about anything to do with him could be dangerous."

CHAPTER TWENTY

Sunday morning, news came from the hospital that Jacques was conscious. Harriet called Maisie to ask if she'd like them to drive her to see him after church.

"I'm afraid my morning sickness is too brutal for me to go anywhere," Maisie said, only she sounded worse than ill. Her tone sounded truly fearful.

Harriet couldn't blame her for being nervous about being seen visiting Jacques after witnessing the horrible scene Friday morning. "Is there anything we can do to help?" she asked. "Organize a meal train for you, or arrange for a few volunteers to help with chores?"

"Thank you, but no." Maisie's words trembled. "I'm not keeping much down these days, and having chores to do is a welcome distraction."

"Okay, but if you need anything at all, don't hesitate to call, all right?"

"I will. Thank you. You've been so kind." Maisie said goodbye and ended the call.

Harriet's heart ached for the woman. This should be a time of happy anticipation for her. Instead, fears of what the future might hold continued to mount.

After church Harriet and Will ate a quick lunch at home then headed to Whitby Hospital to visit Jacques. Harriet's hand tightened around Will's as they rode the elevator to Jacques's floor. The doors opened, and they scanned the numbers with accompanying arrows on the opposite wall. The buzz of the fluorescent lights made the ambience of the otherwise quiet hallway feel somehow unsettling. And the flicker of concern beneath Will's calm demeanor was unmistakable.

Turning right as the arrows directed, Harriet spotted a police officer stationed outside a room at the end of the hall. "Is that Jacques's room?" she whispered to Will.

"I think so."

The sharp-eyed officer watched them approach, posture rigid and businesslike.

Unease prickled Harriet's neck. Van hadn't mentioned police involvement when he'd talked about Jacques's condition last night.

Will slowed his step. The stairwell door opened, and at the sight of a familiar figure veering toward the officer, Will pulled Harriet into an empty room.

"What's Alex doing going to Jacques's room?" Harriet hissed.

"Beats me." Will's brows knitted as he peeked past the doorframe.

Alex's unexpected arrival in White Church Bay around the same time as the Castlegate burglary suddenly seemed more than a little suspect. She exchanged a few words with the officer, who moved aside. She entered Jacques's room without a backward glance, leaving Harriet and Will to bide their time.

"Strange she'd be here," Harriet murmured, unable to shake the image of the business card that had tumbled out of Alex's handbag when Maxwell upended it the other night. She'd explained it away, but Alex's presence in White Church Bay this particular week was too coincidental.

"Very strange," Will agreed, his voice threaded with a faint ripple of suspicion.

When Alex returned to the hallway, Harriet and Will jerked back into the shadows of the empty room, but she must have glimpsed the movement, because her footsteps slowed as she neared their door.

Harriet's pulse quickened even though they'd done nothing wrong.

Alex started when she saw them. "Will, Harriet." She forced a smile. Her gaze darted to the police officer, and her voice lowered. "Didn't expect to see you here."

"Small world, isn't it?" Harriet said.

Alex gave a dismissive laugh then muttered something about needing to return to her research and strode off.

"This is getting weirder by the minute." Harriet squeezed Will's hand and tilted her head toward Jacques's room. "You ready?"

The officer's gaze flicked to Will's clerical collar as they approached. Will pulled out his identification and presented it. The man took his sweet time scrutinizing the ID then finally approved their admission with a brisk nod before shifting to stand sentry in the doorway, where he could presumably both observe them and keep an eye on the hall.

Jacques lay in the hospital bed, still and pale, the hum of monitors filling the silence. His face was bruised and swollen. But the bruises weren't what held Harriet's gaze—it was the metal handcuff securing his right wrist to the bed rail.

Will inhaled sharply, and Harriet suspected his questions matched her own. Jacques was the *victim* here. The guard's presence was understandable. In fact, she'd taken it as an encouraging sign that the police acknowledged that the driver hadn't struck Jacques by accident. So why on earth was Jacques handcuffed?

Will turned to the guard. But before he could say a word, Harriet tugged his hand and met his eyes with a subtle shake of her head. The guard, the handcuff, even Alex being here—they didn't know enough yet to ask the right questions, and prying could make the situation worse.

Will seemed to understand, offering her a slight nod as he swallowed his words.

They both returned their attention to Jacques, their unspoken questions hanging heavy in the air.

Jacques's eyes blinked open at Will's gentle greeting. "Pastor, how is Maisie?"

"Worried about you and Pierre, but she wasn't injured."

"*Bon.*" Jacques closed his eyes once more, his features relaxing.

"Did you see who struck you?" Harriet asked.

Jacques shook his head without opening his eyes.

"Why are you handcuffed?" Will asked.

Slowly, Jacques rolled his head sideways and faintly tugged his shackled wrist. But an infinitesimal shrug was his only response to Will's question.

Will stepped closer to the bed, effectively blocking the guard's line of sight of Jacques, and lowered his voice. "The woman who left your room a moment ago—do you know her?"

Jacques shifted uncomfortably, the handcuff clinking as he adjusted his position. "A customer of mine from Paris, yes." His accent thickened with hesitation. "We met some months ago."

"How did she know you were here?"

"Said she heard about my accident. She was curious if I had family in the area. I thought she was only being polite. Perhaps I was wrong?" His gaze shifted from Will to Harriet, his brow creasing. "Why do you ask?"

"The timing of her arrival in town feels a little too convenient," Harriet said. "She told us she came to White Church Bay to research rare birds. Yet she came to the hospital to see you—a virtual stranger who once repaired her purse." Even as Harriet spoke, she wondered if stating the observation aloud was a mistake. How did they know they could trust Jacques any more than Alex?

Jacques exhaled, wincing as he shifted again. "She said she heard about Pierre's arrest and recognized the surname, wondering if he was related to me. I told her I came here to help him."

"How did she respond to that?" Will asked.

Jacques's already pale skin lost what little color remained, making the dark circles under his eyes stand out. "She wanted to know if I had evidence that would clear him. She was insistent."

Will's jaw tightened. "What did you tell her?"

A troubled expression clouded Jacques's face. "Very little. Now that you mention it, her story did seem dodgy."

No kidding. Harriet recalled Alex's abrupt dismissal of the possibility Pierre was related to the Aubert family of the business card in her purse. Now she was here asking Jacques about it? "Did she mention anything about the hit-and-run?"

Jacques rattled his cuffed wrist, his expression hardening. "No. But I'm thinking she knows more than she's letting on."

Will's brow furrowed. He slanted a glance toward the guard and lowered his voice even more. "Do you think she may be connected to whoever ran you down?"

Jacques's gaze lifted to theirs, his eyes sharp despite his weakened state. "What do you know about her?"

"I knew her in uni, but I haven't seen her in more than a decade. I would never have believed she'd turn criminal. But her story doesn't add up."

Jacques nodded. "Yes. And something about the way she phrased her questions makes me think she came here to...encourage me to keep quiet."

A tense silence settled over the room. Harriet's mind raced. She couldn't ignore the way Alex continued to pop up, each appearance perfectly timed to seem innocent. And that cryptic warning outside the police station about never knowing what a criminal might do to avoid being caught? There was definitely something off about the woman.

Jacques's eyes slid closed.

"We'll let you rest," Will told him. "We wanted you to know we're here for you if you need anything. I left my number when they brought you in, so you can ask the nurse if you need to reach us. May we pray with you before we leave?"

A tear slipped down Jacques's cheek as he gave a single nod without opening his eyes.

Will rested his hand on Jacques's shoulder and bowed his head.

"Thank you," Jacques said after Will finished.

"You focus on getting well." Will's voice remained steady. "We'll look into this."

Outside, the day had grown as stormy as Harriet's insides. "Do you think Alex is somehow connected to this money-laundering business?" she asked Will as they drove home.

"The Alex I knew, never."

"But today's Alex?" Harriet said softly, recognizing that Will wouldn't want to believe his old friend could have changed so much.

Will heaved a sigh. "I don't know, Harriet. I realize you refrained from saying anything the other night, but even I clued in that she didn't seem to know much about the nesting habits of the birds she was supposed to be here to research."

"Couldn't you simply ask her what she's really doing here?"

"I doubt she'd confide in me." Will twisted his hands on the steering wheel. "And given what happened to Jacques, if she's in cahoots with criminals, I'd rather she not know we're onto her."

CHAPTER TWENTY-ONE

The next morning, Harriet made a hearty breakfast of bacon and eggs and crumpets and jam, hoping to shift the cloud of disillusionment that had hung over them since they'd returned home from the hospital. They'd spent hours the night before searching the internet for anything that would disprove their suspicions of Alex. Although they'd hit on a handful of mentions of her involvement in previous research projects, as well as one reference to the scope of her current one, the sparsity of information seemed suspicious.

Harriet brought the plates to the table as Will came into the kitchen. "Do you want tea or coffee with this?" She'd opted to brew herself a cup of coffee, deciding she needed the extra jolt of caffeine after the restless night they'd had.

Will motioned to a chair. "You sit. I'll get myself a cup of tea. Everything looks and smells fantastic." He added a tea bag and hot water to the teapot then joined her at the table with a kiss to her cheek. "I'm sorry. I guess my tossing and turning kept you awake too."

She smiled. "A little. Have you decided whether you'll talk to Van about Alex?"

"Yes, I plan to visit him first thing for a chat. I want to know why Jacques has been handcuffed to his bed for starters. I'll decide what, if anything, to say about Alex, depending on how forthcoming Van is with me. I don't want to throw her under the bus only to find out her visit was entirely innocent."

"Fair enough," Harriet agreed, wishing she could accompany him. But her schedule had her in surgeries all morning.

"You don't have to check on Edwina's horse today, do you?" Concern colored Will's voice, a reminder of how much he'd taken to heart Van's warning of the danger surrounding their investigation.

"Not unless they call with a concern."

Will clasped her hand. "That's good." He bowed his head and prayed a blessing on their meal. "If something comes up that requires you at the Castlegates', stick to the barn. No one who might be watching should get the wrong idea from that."

Harriet gave Will's hand a reassuring squeeze. The threatening note left on their windshield outside the church hadn't been far from either of their thoughts for the last few days. But, in retrospect, it was probably a good thing she hadn't acted on her suspicions and confronted Clifford about his bullying as she'd wanted to. Especially since it now seemed she'd been wrong about the note being his doing. Unless… The sight of Alex pulling out of the Castlegates' driveway last week came to mind. Maybe she was in cahoots with them somehow. But to what end?

A comfortable silence fell over Harriet and Will as they ate their breakfasts, each mentally preparing for the day ahead.

At the sound of Polly's arrival, Harriet hurriedly washed her dishes then kissed Will goodbye. "I need to go. Surgery this morning. Let me know how your chat with Van goes."

"Will do." Will gave her a warm hug. "Have a good day."

By the time Harriet joined Polly in the clinic, her able assistant had already begun prepping the surgery room.

"I've been thinking more about our Edwina-framing-Pierre theory," Polly said the instant Harriet joined her.

"Oh?" Harriet reminded herself that they were talking about the missing elephant statue, which Pierre insisted had nothing to do with the suspicious bag and its alleged connection to money-laundering criminals.

"Yes, because we don't know what brought Pierre to the Castlegates' estate in the first place, do we?"

"He told their maid he wanted to speak to Clifford," Harriet reminded Polly. Then she frowned. "Not Edwina."

"That's exactly what Edwina would've told him to do, because it would give her the perfect excuse to storm in and allege that Pierre was there to confront Clifford—a meeting that everyone would believe—mistakenly—she didn't want to happen."

Harriet must have looked as confused as she felt, because Polly rushed on.

"I think Edwina arranged for Pierre to come to the house and asked him to bring a bag or two to show her brother as a sample of his work. She knew his being seen leaving with a bag would incriminate him."

Pierre's declaration when she and Maisie had visited him in jail echoed through Harriet's mind. He'd made it clear that he didn't expect the police to believe him over the Castlegates. Was that why he hadn't bothered trying to tell the police that Edwina had invited him to the estate?

"But why bring that bag when it's not one of his designs?" A new unease rippled through Harriet. "At least he gave me that impression." What if he was innocent of the theft but not of being part of a money-laundering operation?

Before they could hash out their suspicions any further, Chimney arrived for his operation. Polly assisted, and they were too busy during the procedure to discuss the theft.

"I have two more surgeries this morning before I'll have time to examine the biopsied tissue under the microscope," Harriet said to Mr. Foster after Chimney was once again on his feet. "I'll let you know if I find anything of concern, but I doubt I will."

Mr. Foster thanked them profusely. By the time he'd seen to his bill with Polly, Harriet had the room prepped for their next patient, a twelve-month-old golden retriever named Finnegan.

As they started the operation, Harriet mused, "I always thought Finnegan was a boy's name."

Polly laughed. "Me too. I even researched it online after Mrs. O'Connell brought Finnie for her first checkup. The name means 'fair,' which suits this golden beauty. Their last dog was Winnie, so maybe they wanted a similar-sounding name. I hear them call her Finnie more often than Finnegan."

Finnie's procedure was simpler, so they continued discussing Polly's theory that Lady Edwina had hidden the elephant statue so her brother would think Pierre stole it and then hopefully see the man's downfall as a reason to stay in White Church Bay and try to win over Maisie.

"Did you discuss your theory with Van?" Harriet asked Polly.

"Yeah, actually. Did you see Pierre arrive with the bag?"

"No, I didn't see him arrive, only leave."

"Maybe that's why Van has been so cagey about discussing my theory."

"What do you mean?" Harriet asked.

"If Pierre didn't arrive with the bag, then Edwina must've given it to him, or he stole it too. Only the Castlegates didn't report that theft."

"If either of them used the bag to secretly move cash past authorities, they wouldn't report it stolen, would they?" Harriet's thoughts rioted.

"That's why Van keeps telling me Pierre isn't doing himself any favors by not telling them how he came in possession of the bag." Polly gasped. "Maybe Edwina caught Pierre checking out the bag and got scared he'd report it to the police, so she decided to beat him to the punch by framing him for the theft."

"That's a serious accusation," Harriet said.

"Moonlighting as a money mule would explain how Edwina affords all the designer clothes and high-end spas on her fixed allowance too."

Harriet fitted her stethoscope to her ears and listened to the dog's lungs before responding. "I don't think it quite fits though," she said. "Edwina went into the house to speak to Pierre. If she saw him leave with her duffel bag, surely she would've stopped him, especially if he threatened to tell the authorities about its secret compartment."

Polly frowned, her attention focused on Finnie. "Okay, then Pierre must've brought the bag with him, like we first said."

"But why would he? Unless it belonged to them. That's what we keep coming back to."

Polly's gaze snapped to Harriet's. "Do you think it's Clifford's? That's who Pierre asked to see, right? And since Clifford hasn't lived at home for over a decade, Edwina wouldn't necessarily know his luggage from anyone else's. So she wouldn't think anything of Pierre leaving with a bag. She must've assumed he'd brought it with him."

"Then we're back to why would Clifford frame Pierre if he wasn't interested in rekindling a relationship with Maisie?"

"You heard Isla's mum," Polly said. "Clifford talked to her about listing the estate before he clapped eyes on Maisie again. He could've changed his mind after the reunion."

"No, Lillian said she asked him after the reunion if he'd changed his mind about selling, and he was adamant that he still wanted to sell."

"Maybe when Clifford went inside, he realized Pierre had taken his bag and got scared he'd find the secret compartment, so he decided to set Pierre up before Pierre could incriminate him. It would explain why he was the one who 'discovered' the theft."

"Risky to incriminate the guy who holds incriminating evidence against you."

"No one's going to believe a tradesman over a titled gentleman, and he'd have been confident he could steer the police investigation whichever way he wanted to." Polly snorted. "Van's been acting like he's tiptoeing through a minefield ever since this case started."

"How closely did the police search the bag? Did Van say?"

"No, why?"

"I always leave receipts and other little things I pick up in my bags from trip to trip," Harriet said. "Chances are Clifford does too, and one of those things, if examined from the right perspective, might incriminate him big time."

"Like a credit card receipt?"

"Exactly."

"After we finish this morning's surgeries, we have two hours before your next appointment," Polly said. "We should go to the police station and share our theory with Van. I know he won't tell us what else, if anything, they found in the bag, but our theory might prompt him to examine the evidence from another angle." Polly affixed a cone to Finnie's head, then together, they gently lifted her into a large crate to recover.

"Given his concern over the danger surrounding this case, I doubt he'll want to see us anywhere near the station."

Polly waved dismissively, one hand already on the doorknob. "Leave that to me."

Later that morning, Polly dragged Harriet to the police station.

The weather had changed once more, today blessing them with sunshine and big fluffy clouds dotting the pure blue sky. A light breeze off the North Sea carried the slightest whiff of fish and brine. Despite the pleasant weather, an icy chill shivered through Harriet at the thought of her note writer watching their comings and goings.

But instead of going through the front door of the station, Polly had arranged for Van to let them slip in a rear entrance usually reserved for officers. He led them to an interrogation room, told them he'd be back in a minute, then shut them inside.

"I'm surprised Van didn't suggest coming to the clinic to speak to us," Harriet said. "I don't think he would be as nervous about someone seeing him come here as I am."

"He did. But I told him I needed to stop by the market anyway. I figured if we discussed the theory here, he'd be more likely to get straight onto reexamining any contents they'd removed from the bag."

Harriet scanned the dank room in which he'd deposited them. A metal table, scratched and dull from years of wear, stood in the center. She stared at her reflection in the large mirror covering the wall behind her—a one-way, she assumed—and felt a prickle of vulnerability under its anonymous gaze. A small recording device was in the corner, an unspoken reminder that every word they said might be recorded and dissected. She swallowed hard at the thought.

The doorknob rattled, making her jump, and Van strode in carrying a notepad and pen. He motioned for them to take a seat at the table. "What was so important that it couldn't wait until I got home?"

Polly launched into an explanation of their newest theory. "Think about it," she concluded. "If you could tell Pierre you know Clifford owns the bag, Pierre will be more likely to explain how it came into his possession."

"I appreciate you sharing your theory with me rather than attempting to test it yourselves by some other means. But the bag was empty." He glanced at the camera mounted in the corner and lowered his voice. "Besides the hidden compartment you're not supposed to know about, the only unusual thing about the bag was the odor."

"What kind of odor?"

"Some kind of perfume."

"Like a man's cologne?" Polly prodded.

"No, more like something a woman might wear, or maybe one of those overly scented laundry detergents. A couple of the female constables sniffed it and tried to place it, but the smell of the leather made it tough to match. The smell seemed to emanate from a small stain in the bottom of the bag. We figured that a bottle of perfume had spilled inside and soaked into the leather."

Thinking of the strongly scented leather glove they'd found in the Beast, Harriet said, "Could I smell it?"

Van shook his head. "Not a chance. The DI is convinced we've got the right guy locked up."

"What if we find something that has the same scent? Will you at least humor us by comparing the scent on the object we bring you to the one in the bag?"

Van's eyes widened. "You're not going to nick something from Castlegates' house to prove your point, are you?"

"No," Harriet assured him. "If the scent was one that lingered in the manor house, I'm sure you would've already picked up the connection."

"Actually," Polly interjected, "Van's been nursing a sinus cold for the past week. He can scarcely smell anything."

"Seriously?" Harriet blurted. "Have any other officers been to the manor house who have smelled the bag's interior?"

Van's cheeks flushed. "No. We never seriously considered that it belonged to either Edwina or Clifford."

"Could you pay them another visit with someone who has a good sense of smell?"

"I'll speak to the DI about it."

Harriet cringed. Given his boss's lack of openness to considering other suspects, she feared such a conversation might not be in Pierre's best interest. "Maybe wait on that until we get back to you." She'd now been in the Castlegates' home on three separate occasions, and she couldn't say that she'd noticed any particularly strong or distinctive scent while there.

"Where is this object you plan to bring me?" Van said.

Harriet turned to Polly. "What did you do with that glove we found in my vehicle?"

"I gave it to Lee, who tossed it into a pile of odds and ends. I'm sure we'll be able to find it again." Polly smiled at her husband. "For the church jumble sale."

"Do you know who donated it?" Van asked.

"No, but if it proves to be a match, hopefully we can find out." Harriet zipped her coat, preparing to leave. "Will and I collected boxes from only a half dozen houses or so before I was called to an emergency. So it must have come from one of them."

"The Castlegates being one of the donors, I presume?" Van asked.

"Actually, no."

"Yes, they were," Polly reminded her. "You went back there after the emergency call, and Rita gave you a box Edwina left for pickup, remember?"

"That's right." Harriet nudged Polly. "We've got to get to the church."

Polly stood up and planted a kiss on Van's cheek. "We'll let you know how we make out."

"No, give me five minutes to clear it with the DI, and I'll come with you."

Waiting by the back door of the police station for Van to join them, Harriet fidgeted, anxious to get moving. She hoped they were avoiding detection by the wrong people—whoever they might be.

An officer Harriet didn't recognize asked Polly if she was Van's wife. When she said yes, he told her that Van asked him to let her know to go ahead without him and he'd catch up in a few minutes.

"Great." Polly pushed open the door and held it for Harriet.

"I would've thought you'd know all the officers in a town this size," Harriet said.

"Most of them. He must be new. Or on loan because of this special investigation."

At the sound of a door clanking shut, Harriet glanced over her shoulder and noticed the same officer now approaching a cruiser, his cell phone pressed to his ear. She tugged Polly's arm. "Let's cut through the park."

Call her paranoid, but what if the officer had lied to them? The cruiser headed up the street. Relieved to see it turn away from the church at the next intersection, Harriet slowed her pace.

"What's wrong?" Polly asked.

"Doesn't it seem strange to you that Van didn't come and tell us himself? Or ask us to wait a few minutes longer?"

Polly winced. "I hope he hasn't raised the DI's ire by entertaining our theory."

Harriet's heart sank. The last thing she wanted to do was hurt Van's chances at promotion by steering him wrong. Hopefully they'd soon be able to give him the name of the bag's owner to smooth things over.

Reaching the church, Harriet unlocked the door of the parish hall and snapped on the lights.

Polly pointed to tables and racks on the far side of the room. "Lee was working at the tables over there on Saturday, but I don't see the pile of odds and ends anymore. Maybe she found the glove's match."

They wound their way around tables overflowing with donated items and past more boxes yet to be sorted.

"You start sniffing from that end, and I'll start from this end," Polly said when they reached the back of the room. "The scent on the glove was so potent, I imagine other items from the same box would smell too."

Harriet scanned a table displaying mittens and gloves, but the fine leather one they'd retrieved from the Beast wasn't among them. She leaned over tables, sniffing the air and randomly bringing items to her nose, but the scent they were after remained annoyingly elusive. She met Polly at a table halfway up the row, and they peeled off to repeat the same thing along the racks of hanging coats and dresses.

"Hello, anyone here?" asked a deep male voice that didn't belong to Van.

Not recognizing the voice, Harriet ducked behind a rack of clothes. Down the aisle, Polly did the same. "Who is it?" Harriet mouthed.

Polly peeked between two coats that otherwise shielded her from the man's view. "I can't see him," she whispered.

Harriet tried, but she couldn't spot him from her vantage point either. Were they being silly not to show themselves? Her pulse racing, she swiped her thumb across her phone screen to text Will to ask him to come to the parish hall if he was around.

"This is cute," a woman said. The voice was familiar, but Harriet struggled to place it. It didn't sound like any of the volunteers who'd been there Saturday afternoon.

"Psst." Polly beckoned to Harriet.

Staying low to remain hidden behind the racks of clothes, Harriet hurried to join her.

Polly's phone chose that moment to ring, and she scrambled to silence its dainty chime.

Thankfully, their company didn't appear to have heard it.

Harriet checked her watch. Polly had forwarded the clinic's calls to her phone while they took this extended lunch break, but their window of opportunity was quickly closing. She hoped whoever Polly had cut off hadn't been someone who'd driven to the clinic expecting to find it open.

Polly pointed toward a sliver of light seeping between the racks. "Do you recognize them? It's a man and a woman. But I can't tell who."

The pair had their backs to Harriet and Polly, making it impossible to identify them from their generic coats and dark hair. But they definitely weren't Edwina and Clifford, both blonds who typically wore designer outfits.

Harriet felt like a peeping Tom watching the couple from behind the clothes. "They must've volunteered to finish sorting the remaining donations," Harriet whispered at the sight of the pair pulling items from a box.

"I don't think so," Polly whispered back. "They're rummaging through the boxes, not setting the items out on the tables."

The same chill she'd felt at the police station shivered down Harriet's neck. Had someone been listening in on what they'd discussed about the scent in the duffel and come to see that they didn't find it?

The man moved to a table filled with an array of knickknacks, but all they could see of him was his back. "Look at this," he called to the woman, who immediately gasped in response.

"I can't see what he's found, can you?" Polly whispered to Harriet.

"No." She shifted for a better view and sent a hanger clattering to the floor.

The woman shrieked in alarm. The man spun on his heel and demanded, "Who's there? Show yourself."

Harriet met Polly's gaze. *What do we do?* If the officer at the station was telling the truth, Van should show up any second. And if they yelled loud enough, Will and the church secretary might hear them from the other end of the building—if they hadn't gone out.

The next instant, the lights snapped off, plunging the room into darkness.

CHAPTER TWENTY-TWO

The parish hall lights snapped back on. "Sorry, is someone in here?" Will's voice echoed through the room.

Harriet burst out from behind the clothing rack. "Will, am I ever glad to see you!"

The woman she'd been spying on, who turned out to be Rita, planted her hands on her hips. "What were you doing sneaking around over there?"

"Rita and Ryker delivered a couple more boxes of donations," Will said. He added to Rita, "Sorry I switched the lights off on you. I didn't realize you two were still here."

"They were looking through the donations," Polly said, sounding a bit like the pot calling the kettle black, considering that she and Harriet were doing the same thing. Harriet couldn't believe neither of them had recognized Ryker's voice, considering he'd recently been to the clinic.

"Come see what we found," Ryker said, seeming to take no offense. He held up a tarnished statue from the knickknack table—a tarnished *silver elephant* statue. "Do you think it's the one stolen from the Castlegates?"

"It couldn't be, could it?" Harriet fixed her gaze on Rita, the only one among them who'd have an intimate acquaintance with the statue.

Rita cocked her head, studying it. "It could be. I rarely leave the kitchen when I'm working at the Castlegates', so I've only seen it a few times."

A knock sounded on the parish hall's side door.

Polly ran to it and yanked it open. "Van, Ryker's found the missing statue!"

Drawing a pair of surgical-type gloves from his pocket, Van strode to where the rest of them huddled around the table. "Has anyone else handled it?"

Ryker thrust it into Van's gloved hands like a hot potato then pointed to an empty spot on the table. "It was standing right there."

"If the Castlegates positively identify it as theirs, I'll have to dust it for fingerprints. And I'll need to take yours to eliminate."

"How do we know—"

Harriet elbowed Polly's side before she could voice the same thought she'd had. But now was not the time for sharing. They could advise Van in private that Ryker came in with a couple of boxes, one of which might have contained the statue, which he could have then planted on the table to create the illusion that the thief had offloaded it there.

"How on earth did the volunteers setting out donations on Saturday not realize it might be the Castlegates' stolen statue?" Rita asked. "It seems everyone's been talking about nothing else for the past week."

Will motioned to three other elephant figures on nearby tables, one brass and two pewters. "Elephant ornaments are a somewhat common donation to our jumble sales."

"And this may not be the Castlegates' either, but I'll take it to the station until we can make that confirmation." Van lifted an empty box from under the table. "Okay if I use this, Will?"

Will nodded.

Ryker clasped Rita's hand. "If it's all the same to you, Detective Constable, we'll come with you now so you can take my prints."

Rita shuddered. "I'm glad I didn't touch it after all the rumors that went around about me helping you nick the thing to ruin Pierre."

Polly's gaze met Harriet's, mirroring her own skepticism. Were the pair playing up their innocence for Van's benefit? Or did they honestly have no clue how suspicious it was that they'd found the statue?

If they were guilty and Will hadn't caught them in here, would they have left the statue for someone else to find? Recalling Ryker's excited "Look at this" exclamation moments before Will shut off the lights, Harriet questioned her suspicions. Maybe they were entirely innocent, and the discovery had happened exactly as they'd said. If only Ryker hadn't picked up the statue, his claim would be much easier to believe. As it was, they couldn't be sure whether or not he'd deliberately handled the thing within their sight to give a valid reason why his fingerprints would be on it.

Had he heard Polly's phone ring then pretended not to and put on a show of finding the statue they'd in fact planted? Harriet hated to doubt them, but the discovery felt way too convenient not to question it.

Van headed for the door with the boxed statue, followed by Ryker and Rita.

"I guess this means you'll be able to release Pierre?" Will called after Van.

Van paused at the door. "Let's not get ahead of ourselves. We haven't confirmed this is the Castlegates' statue yet."

Polly grabbed her phone from her pocket and looked at the screen. "Oh no. I have four missed calls. We better get to the clinic." Heading for the door, she connected to the current caller and cheerily announced, "Cobble Hill Farm Veterinary Clinic, how may I help you?"

Harriet gave Will a quick kiss on the cheek. "I guess I'll see you later."

"Wait a minute. What are you doing here? Did you follow Ryker and Rita?"

Harriet laughed. "No, nothing like that."

"We need to hurry," Polly called from the open door.

Harriet tossed Will an apologetic shrug. "I'll explain later." Despite not being able to find the elusive glove or catch so much as a whiff of a similar scent among the donated jumble sale clothes, at least their excursion hadn't been a total bust.

If they'd truly found the Castlegates' elephant, then the police would have to believe that Pierre didn't steal it. There was no way he could have planted it in the jumble sale donations, since they'd locked him up before donation collections began.

Halfway home Harriet realized she'd forgotten to ask Will about his chat with Van regarding Jacques and Alex. She supposed they'd both have to wait until suppertime for answers.

Back at the clinic, Harriet checked on her two overnight patients then had a steady stream of clients until they closed at four. She closed the window blinds to help keep out the cold as Polly shut down the computer.

"Any update from Van about the statue?" Harriet asked.

"No confirmation that it's the Castlegates' yet. But apparently Maisie found out about the discovery and insisted they release Pierre. She was very nice about it too, suggesting the Castlegates must've inadvertently donated it."

"Something tells me Lady Edwina would still take offense," Harriet groused. "Did you tell him the Castlegates donated a box of items to the jumble sale?" Harriet thought of what the volunteer from the halfway house had said he'd have done if he were the thief—hide it in a car to retrieve later when the car was off-site. "If the box was already sitting around the day of the theft, the thief could've hidden the statue inside, intending to retrieve it later from the church."

"Maybe Clifford or Edwina put it in to make it look that way." Polly shrugged. "Or they'll accuse Maisie or some other accomplice of slipping the statue into the jumble sale to try to get Pierre off, once they realized he wouldn't get away with the theft."

"This is so frustrating," Harriet said, handing Polly's jacket to her.

"It gets worse," Polly said.

Harriet groaned. "How much worse?"

"Van lifted Pierre's prints from the statue."

"No way!" Harriet's heart ricocheted off her ribs. Had she been wrong to believe in Pierre?

Will came into the clinic from the kitchen. "No way what?"

"Van told Polly he lifted Pierre's prints off the statue."

"That's not as bad as it sounds," Will reassured them. "Pierre already admitted during his initial interrogation that he inspected the statue out of curiosity while waiting for Clifford."

Harriet pressed a hand to her chest. "That's a relief. But I'm still afraid this means they won't drop the charges, even with the statue being recovered." She ran her fingers through her hair. "Unless Clifford can convince his sister to have mercy on the poor couple now that the whole insurance argument doesn't matter."

Will winced. "I'm not sure it'll be that easy to get him released. They found the duffel bag during a lawful search, and it incriminates him in another crime. I think the theft has been a convenient excuse to hold him while they ferret out his connection to the money-laundering case."

Harriet stared at him, dumbfounded. "How do you know all that?"

"Van was a little more forthcoming during our chat this morning, since I already knew about the other case."

"Did he tell you why Jacques is handcuffed to his hospital bed?"

Polly's eyes widened at that news. "You didn't tell me that."

"Sorry," Harriet said. "We've been busy with so many other things today, it never came up."

Will hesitated. "We might be partly to blame for the cuffs."

Harriet stared at him in shock. "Us? How?"

"Our explanation of why Jacques wanted to talk to Pierre and how he thought he could help him—it sounded as if he might be prepared to blow the whistle on the criminal organization connected to the duffel bag. And our suggestion that the hit-and-run was no accident made them decide that if we were right and the organization was trying to silence him or intimidate him into staying quiet, then they'd better limit who had access to him."

"That explains the police officer at his hospital door, but not the handcuffs."

"If the hit-and-run was deliberate, then the situation has escalated, possibly beyond what Jacques had bargained for. He might change his mind about talking to the police and attempt to flee before giving them some answers."

Harriet frowned. "But they can't handcuff him unless he's under arrest or a danger to himself or others."

"I guess they must have something on him. He admitted he knows the criminals. And you know what they say—it takes one to know one."

Harriet cringed to think they'd left Maisie alone with him. "What about—" She hesitated before asking about Alex, because if Will hadn't mentioned his concerns about her to Van, he might not want Polly hearing about them.

"Alex?" Will finished the question for her.

"Your mate from uni?" Polly said. "What does she have to do with any of this?"

Harriet pressed her lips together, leaving it up to Will how much to reveal.

"We saw her visit Jacques's hospital room yesterday afternoon," Will explained.

"Wait, what?" Polly's brow furrowed. "She knows him?"

"Yes," Harriet chimed in. "Remember when I told you about Maxwell tipping over Alex's purse?"

"Yes."

"We got to talking about Lady Miltshire and then Van's file before I mentioned what tumbled out of the purse."

Polly sucked in a breath. "What?"

"A business card that might belong to Jacques. She apparently had a purse strap repaired at his shop during a recent trip to Paris."

Polly shook her head. "That's hardly enough of an acquaintance to prompt her to visit him in the hospital."

Will waved his hands. "I can explain. When she heard about the hit-and-run and realized she knew the victim, she alerted the police and asked if she could be of any help. Apparently, she's collaborated with the police before in an investigation involving illegal poaching of rare bird species and their eggs."

"Van told you that?" Harriet asked.

"More or less. I could tell he was straining to tactfully allay our concerns while saying as little as possible. I did some research and found a news article on the poaching that connected to one of the research stints she'd mentioned and filled in the blanks."

"That's a relief," Polly said. "I'd hate to have to add your old mate to our suspect list."

CHAPTER TWENTY-THREE

After Polly left for the day, Harriet filled Will in on their new lead concerning the duffel bag's owner. "Thanks to Ryker and Rita's arrival, however, we never found the glove or any other item that carried the same scent."

"Could you identify what kind of fragrance it was?"

"Van, who apparently couldn't smell it because of a sinus condition, implied the consensus among the police is that it's female. For me, the overwhelming impression I had from the scent on the glove was that it was too strong. It gave me an instant headache, so I'm certain I'd recognize it if I smelled it again. But we don't even know if it's the same as what's on the duffel, because Van won't let us near it."

"Well, we could revisit the homes where we picked up donations. See if you recognize the scent from the glove in any of them."

Harriet wavered at how awkward that would be. What excuse would they give for showing up uninvited?

"I can't say I've ever noticed a memorable fragrance on any of the halfway house residents at our weekly Bible studies," Will went on. "The place smells a bit like a gym locker."

Although heartened that, despite Will's earlier defense of the men, he hadn't completely written off the possibility that the bag could belong to one of them, Harriet said, "I know we could be way off the mark thinking the scent on the glove will match the one in the leather bag, but how about we go back to the parish hall? Polly and I didn't get around to all the tables."

"I'm game. Sure."

By the time they reached the church, dusk had settled over the town. Mist drifting in from the sea deepened the shadowy effect.

"I've got to say," Harriet mused, "night falls way too soon at this time of year."

"Think of it as a good excuse to stay in and cozy up to the fire with your hubby." Will winked.

Laughing, Harriet clasped his hand as they walked into the church. "If only my clients would confine their emergencies to daylight hours,"

They wandered up and down the rows of tables and clothes racks and even around the furniture. Finding the LPs they'd collected from Edwina's nearest neighbor, Harriet brought a few to her nose and inhaled.

"Any luck?" Will asked.

"Nothing," Harriet admitted. "Given the way the scent lingered in the duffel bag, I was so certain we'd still smell it somewhere in here."

Will enfolded her in his arms. "I wish we'd found it too. I hate to see what Pierre's arrest is doing to Maisie as much as you do." He dropped his hold and stepped back. "But I can't help being a little angry with him. Here you are, trying so hard to help him, and he's hurting his own case by refusing to tell the police who owns the bag."

Shuddering at a sudden chill, Harriet tightened her arms around Will. "You saw what happened to Jacques. It seems Pierre has good reason to fear retribution."

"But rotting in jail is no way to live. The police could protect him if he worked with them."

Harriet wasn't so sure. She'd watched enough television shows to know the police weren't as capable of keeping witnesses safe as they liked people to believe. "Do you mind if we stop by the police station before we go home? I'm afraid finding the statue might've made Pierre's situation worse."

Will grimaced. "I was already thinking that you going there this afternoon wasn't a good idea."

"Maybe not, but we can hardly be angry with Pierre for holding out if we're not willing to take a stand. Our God is bigger than the bully who left the threatening note on the windshield."

"Yes, but that doesn't mean He doesn't expect us to exercise caution."

"Like the caution that you're angry with Pierre for exercising?"

Will lifted his hands in surrender. "Touché."

They walked the short distance to the police station and found Van buying a can of soda from the vending machine in an alcove off the lobby.

"Lady Edwina still hasn't come to identify the statue," Van told them. "I have half a mind to head home for my tea and let her see how it feels to be kept waiting."

Harriet concealed a smile, knowing his higher-ups wouldn't look kindly on him snubbing one of the town's elites, however undeserved the title might be. "Will finding Pierre's prints on the statue be a problem?"

"I suspect Lady Edwina will want to make it one. But his weren't the only prints on it." Van slanted an apologetic look to Will. "That bloke from the halfway house—his were on it too."

"Brent's?" Harriet clarified.

"Yeah. The match came up because we have his prints on file. There were a couple of other distinctive prints that could be one of the Castlegates' or their maid's or whoever set out the elephant at the church."

"That must be how Brent's prints got on it," Will said. "All the halfway house residents were helping at the church Saturday, including Brent."

"But they were arranging the furniture donations," Harriet reminded him.

"When you were there. Earlier in the day they were emptying boxes onto the tables. I don't think identifying fingerprints on the statue will prove anything."

"I have to admit that the fact Ryker made a point of picking up the elephant this afternoon, giving him a ready excuse for his prints being on it, struck me as way too convenient," Harriet said.

"Maybe so, but we know the *only* place Pierre could've handled it was in the Castlegates' home," Van said.

"And Pierre admitted to that a week ago." Will's tone grated with obvious exasperation.

"Yeah, I'm just saying that if Lady Edwina wants to make a stink about it, she'll have grounds." Van jutted his chin toward the door. "There she is now. Excuse me, will you?" He left them standing in the shadows of the alcove and went to greet Lady Edwina at the lobby door.

After the two of them disappeared down the hall, Will asked Harriet if she was ready to leave.

Harriet wanted to hear what Edwina had to say, but they'd already been there longer than Will was comfortable with. She agreed.

The instant they exited the alcove to walk through the lobby, the distinctive fragrance she'd smelled on the wayward glove teased her senses. "Wait. Do you smell that?"

Will snorted. "Hard to miss. I assume Edwina plans to go out for the evening after this."

"No, you don't understand." Harriet pinched the skin above the bridge of her nose to stave off the pain already escalating in her head. "Oh, wow, Polly won't believe this. Except she will, because she predicted it."

Understanding dawned on Will's face. "That's the smell on the glove?"

The pieces tumbled into place in her mind. "It all makes sense now. Edwina frequently travels for horse shows and shopping trips and weekend getaways, giving her the perfect cover for her travels. No customs agent would give her luggage more than a cursory glance once they heard her title, would they?"

"I don't know about that. Possibly not," Will conceded.

"A little sideline operation neatly explains how she has so much disposable income, despite her apparently miserly allowance."

"But what was Pierre doing with her bag?"

"She must've taken it to him for repair. Oh." Harriet shook her head in self-recrimination. "I can't believe Polly and I didn't remember this before. Ryker told us he saw Edwina leaving Pierre's shop. That must have been when she took the bag to him."

"Do you think she would've risked that? I mean, she had to know Pierre would discover the secret compartment."

"Sure. That must be why she didn't take it to Ryker, their usual tradesman. She likely figured she could explain it away to Pierre if he was bold enough to question her about it. She might've assumed he wouldn't want to jeopardize potential future business with her family and their friends by calling her out on the discovery."

"But you said Pierre asked to see Clifford when he arrived at the Castlegates'."

"Which must be what got Edwina so freaked. I suppose she could've genuinely assumed he was there because of her brother's scene with Maisie." Harriet took a breath. "Then she must've noticed he had her bag with him and assumed the worst. Maybe she thought he planned to blackmail them and hatched her plan to smear his name before he could smear theirs. But to make her plan work, she had to deny ever seeing the bag."

Will shook his head. "But why would she let him leave with the bag?"

Harriet frowned. Why would she let him hang on to the very thing he'd threatened to use against them? Would Pierre even do something like that? If Harriet didn't think him capable of theft, how could she think him capable of blackmail? "Okay, I don't think Pierre would've threatened her. She must have assumed he was there to confront her brother about the scene at the school reunion. And she was so worked up that maybe she didn't notice that he had the bag with him."

"But then why would she frame him for stealing the elephant statue?"

"Maybe she watched him leave from the window, and seeing him with her bag, realized she might've misread his intentions. Then her guilty conscience kicked in, making her think he'd asked for Clifford with the intention of blackmailing them."

"Why would Pierre blackmail Clifford if Edwina brought him the bag?"

"Everyone knows Clifford holds the purse strings. What lord would want the embarrassment of having his sister charged with acting as a money mule?"

Will drew in a deep breath then slowly released it. "That's true. But you can't think Pierre would entertain blackmailing them."

"No, I'm suggesting the whole scheme was in Edwina's head."

"But Pierre did leave with the bag you're saying belongs to her."

"Yes." Harriet rehashed her theory in her mind. Blackmailing the Castlegates certainly didn't fit Maisie's portrayal of her husband. Not to mention that he'd told Harriet he was trying to do the right thing. "Maybe Pierre planned to offer Clifford his silence in return for Clifford promising to stay away from Maisie. But then Edwina thwarted him before he got the chance." Harriet frowned at the realization that didn't quite fit either, since Pierre claimed he didn't know about Clifford and Maisie until after he'd already asked to see Clifford rather than Maisie.

But before Harriet could solve that puzzle, Van and Edwina appeared in the hallway.

Harriet started toward them.

Will tugged her back. "Wait. I'd prefer Edwina didn't see you here." He squinted at the lobby door. "She might've brought along a 'colleague' or two to watch out for her."

Harriet's spine prickled. *Watching for me is what Will really means.* Or maybe for Pierre or Maisie. Or anyone else who'd figured out her secret.

The moment the door closed behind Edwina, Van strode over. "I didn't expect you two to wait around. You're not going to believe this."

"Oh, I think I'd believe almost anything at this point," Will said.

"Edwina says it's not her statue."

"What?" Harriet exclaimed. "Did you tell her you found Pierre's prints on it?"

"Yeah. I even suggested if she'd had donations boxed up and sitting within view ready to be delivered to the church, he might've seen it as the perfect way to sneak the statue out of the house while keeping his hands clean. He could have planned to be first in line at the jumble sale to buy it."

Harriet bristled at the unsavory suggestion. She'd thought Van believed in Pierre's innocence at least a little.

"But she didn't take the bait?" Will asked.

Van shook his head.

"So, to be clear," Harriet said, "you don't actually think that's what Pierre did?"

"No, but I'm sure that's what the prosecution would've argued if it had turned out to be the right statue. The fact she didn't bite has me wondering if the thing isn't as valuable as they've claimed, and she stands to gain more from an insurance payout than from its return."

"Or she could've thought she was throwing Pierre a bone," Will theorized.

Bafflement contorted Van's features. "Why would she do that?"

"Because Pierre hasn't betrayed her secret," Harriet interjected. "Didn't you recognize the scent she was drenched in?"

Van scrunched his nose. "Should I have?" Understanding slowly dawned on his face. "You think the duffel bag is Edwina's?"

CHAPTER TWENTY-FOUR

Harriet mentally catalogued the faces of the loiterers watching them as Van hustled her and Will from the police station's lobby into a conference room.

Van motioned them to the seats circling a large table then abruptly excused himself. After what felt like eons later, he returned looking more agitated than when he'd left. "Two other officers confirmed the scent on the bag matches the fragrance Edwina is wearing." Van paced the room. "But that doesn't prove the bag is hers. I need a lot more than the fact Edwina wears the same fragrance before I can go to my higher-ups with allegations against His Lordship's sister. Dozens of women in White Church Bay must wear the same fragrance."

Crossing his arms over his chest, Will shook his head. "Dozens? I doubt that. Edwina has never struck me as the type who'd go in for anything common."

"Exactly," Harriet said. "I can't believe we didn't see this sooner. It explains everything—how she can afford to travel all the time and live so extravagantly, despite her 'inadequate' allowance. She must be spending the cash she makes moving money for the bad guys."

"Wait." Van halted in front of her. "If the duffel bag is Edwina's, explain to me why she let Pierre leave her house with it."

Harriet straightened in her chair. "Will and I were discussing a couple of possibilities, although she isn't likely to admit to either of them if she knows the police are onto her sideline gig as a money mule. Why don't you ask Pierre? With any luck, once he learns that we know who owns the bag, he'll tell you why he took it from the Castlegates' home."

An officer knocked on the door, making Van jump. He stormed across the room, not like himself at all, and yanked the door open. "What is it?"

"Maisie Aubert is here to see you."

"Terrific," he muttered under his breath. Then he seemed to gather himself and told the officer to send her in.

Her fists clenched, Maisie walked in and scarcely acknowledged Harriet's and Will's presence before starting in on Van. "Why haven't you released Pierre yet?"

"The elephant statue in question is not the victim's," Van explained. "And there's still the question of what the duffel bag was doing in his possession."

"I've suggested Van ask him," Harriet said. "Since we've deduced who it belongs to, Pierre might be less squeamish about sharing what else he knows."

"You know whose it is?" Maisie exclaimed. "Who?"

Van glared at Harriet.

Harriet glared right back. "Seriously? Did you think you could keep her in the dark when her husband's refusal to give Edwina up was what skyrocketed your interest in him in the first place?"

"Lady Edwina?" Maisie's mouth fell open.

"Yes," Harriet said. "Was it any wonder Pierre didn't think the police would believe him after she'd accused him of stealing their silver elephant?" Harriet's gaze shifted to Van, who was wearing a groove in the carpet with his incessant pacing.

"How'd Pierre get his hands on the bag in the first place?" he countered.

"Ryker saw Edwina leaving Pierre's shop earlier in the week. My theory is she took the bag in for repair." To Maisie, Harriet added, "She'd normally take her business to Ryker, which is why he was offended to see her leaving his competition's store. I suspect she didn't want her brother to know about the secret compartment and couldn't be certain Ryker wouldn't mention it to him, given his long relationship with the family."

"Or"—Will straightened in his chair—"she could've taken the repair to him to figure out his reaction to her brother's scene at the school reunion and maybe in hopes of smoothing things over." Will traced a scar on the tabletop with his thumb. "Whatever the reason, I'm afraid it comes down to his word against hers. And she knows it."

"This is so unfair," Maisie lamented. "The magistrate won't believe Pierre over Lady Edwina. And you've seen what she, or whoever she works for, will stoop to in order to silence us."

Will pushed to his feet. "Which is why we should go. We don't want the wrong people getting the wrong idea about why we're here. The police have the information they need. It will be up to them to corroborate the evidence so Pierre is exonerated."

"As loath as I am to suggest it," Harriet said to Van, "you could offer Edwina a deal—keep her name out of the whole thing in exchange for her handler's name."

Van bristled. "That's above my pay grade. And the DI will want a lot more proof before she'd risk offending the Castlegates by making such allegations against Edwina."

Will groaned. "Edwina has more reason than Pierre to fear repercussion. She presumably knows who the real sharks are."

"Pierre's my husband," Maisie reminded Will. "I will not let these hoodlums scare me away from his side."

"Of course not. And hopefully they wouldn't question your being here. But you saw what happened to Jacques," Will said. "If that's the work of the note writer or the hit-and-run driver, it could be dangerous."

Maisie stiffened. "It's because of what happened to Jacques that I'm afraid Pierre will still hesitate to talk to the detective. But if Harriet and I tell him what she's figured out, maybe he'll tell us something more that will help the investigation move forward."

Harriet searched Will's gaze, acknowledging his extreme uneasiness with the idea. "We're already here. Would staying a few minutes longer to speak to Pierre do any more harm?"

Will heaved a sigh. "Give it a go then." He looked at Van. "If you think it's okay."

Van shrugged. "It's worth a shot." He opened the door and motioned them ahead of him.

A few minutes later, Van left them to wait in the same gloomy room in which they'd met Pierre the last time. A uniformed police officer returned with Pierre then stood sentry at the door.

Will and Harriet waited quietly while Maisie took advantage of the opportunity to give her husband a warm hug and kiss.

When the officer cleared his throat, Pierre obediently released his wife and focused on Will. "What's going on?"

Will motioned for Harriet to do the honors.

"We know the duffel bag belongs to Edwina."

Pierre's shoulders slumped. "How?" The single word sounded strangled.

"Her distinctive scent is embedded in its leather."

He closed his eyes.

"What we don't understand is why she let you leave the house with it."

Pierre opened his eyes and glanced at the officer at the door then at the video camera in the corner of the room, but no light flashed to suggest their conversation was being recorded. "Sit." He pulled out a chair for Maisie then sat next to her, opposite Will and Harriet at the table. Leaning across the table, he lowered his voice. "Lady Edwina brought me the duffel for repair a couple of days before the theft. When I discovered the secret compartment inside, I knew exactly what it was used for. Or at least what it was designed to be used for. I went to the Castlegate home to speak to her brother because I wanted to warn him that his sister might have fallen in with a bad sort."

"Only Edwina intercepted you," Harriet said.

Pierre nodded miserably. "I'm not sure what she thought I planned to do with the discovery. She was so hysterical about my needing to leave I didn't have a chance to say anything."

Will cocked his head. "Did she see you had the bag with you?"

"She must have. Why else would she get so riled up about my daring to come to the house?"

"She told Harriet she thought you came to confront her brother over his behavior at the school reunion."

Maisie ducked her head.

Pierre covered her hand with his. "Like I told the police, I didn't know about that or Maisie's prior relationship with Castlegate until the maid left me to wait in his office."

Harriet's thoughts whirred with possible scenarios. "But it's conceivable that Edwina worked herself into such a state trying to get you to leave that she didn't notice you had the bag with you, until maybe she looked out the window after you left and saw you with it."

Pierre shrugged. "I guess that's possible."

"Since running after you at that point would alert everyone to the bag's significance, she could've staged the theft so that no one would believe you if you went to the police."

"That is what I assumed."

The door burst open, and a second uniformed officer stepped into the room—the same officer who'd sent Harriet and Polly on ahead of Van earlier that day. "Time's up. The prisoner needs to return to his cell."

"Where's DC Worthington?" Will asked.

Harriet peered past the officers to the empty hall beyond, suddenly uncomfortable with how odd it was that Van was nowhere in sight.

"Seeing to other matters." The first officer shackled Pierre's hands and escorted him to the door as the second officer hitched his thumb in the direction of a handsome, dark-skinned officer standing in the hall. "Sergeant Oduba will see the rest of you out."

Harriet sighed with relief at Sergeant Adam Oduba's friendly smile. She'd met the young officer within the first month of moving to Yorkshire and knew they could trust him. "What's going on?" she asked him. "Where did Van get to?"

Sergeant Oduba shrugged. "He got called into a meeting."

Will must have sensed Harriet's concern, because he squeezed her hand, as if silently assuring her he was already praying Van's superiors would give their friend a fair hearing. Van had a big heart, and Harriet was certain he wanted to see justice served as much as she and Will did. But given the way he'd been pacing, he obviously knew the stakes would be higher if he pursued the evidence against Edwina.

After seeing Maisie safely to her car, they offered to follow her home.

"That's not necessary," Maisie said, although her voice cracked as she nervously glanced around.

"It would make me feel better," Will insisted.

A few minutes later, they pulled in behind her car in the darkened farmyard.

"That's strange," Harriet said. "Her yard light should've come on at dusk."

Will squinted through the windshield up at the lamppost. "Wait here. I'll see Maisie to her door and make sure no one's around."

Harriet unbuckled her seat belt. "I'll come with you."

Will reached over and gently grasped her arm. "No. Lock the doors as soon as I get out and keep watch. Make sure you have your phone ready to call the police if there's any trouble."

Harriet swallowed. "Okay."

Will reached into the glove box for the heavy-duty flashlight they kept there.

"Be careful," Harriet told him.

"I will." A few minutes later, with Maisie's house now bathed in light and Maisie safely inside, Will returned to their vehicle. "She said the yard light died a couple of days ago and she hasn't had someone change the bulb yet."

Blowing out a breath, Harriet put away the flashlight. "I guess we're getting paranoid."

"If it keeps you safe, paranoid is good." Will started the car.

"I texted Polly to ask her to have Van give you a call when he gets home," Harriet said.

"Good idea. He'll want to hear what Pierre had to say."

Harriet watched the countryside whisk by in the glow of the headlights. "I've been mulling over what Pierre said. Do you think Edwina has such an inflated opinion of her position that she honestly thinks a person like Pierre—one of the 'common folk'—won't report her?"

"Despite attending the local school, I suspect she's lived a somewhat insulated life," Will said. "Drawing attention to herself by staging the theft wasn't smart. But, like you said, she probably figured she had to act fast or she'd be in jail before she could save herself."

"Fortunately for Pierre, she never gave a thought to the possibility that her expensive taste in perfume could end up being her downfall."

"Of course, even if she acknowledges the leather bag is hers, she's bound to deny that she's used it for anything nefarious." Will slowed the car as their driveway came into view. "And any case the police might hope to make of the discovery will stall before it gets started."

"At this point, all I care about is seeing Pierre freed," Harriet said firmly. "Although Edwina should be made to pay for the damage to his reputation and business because of her false allegations against him."

Will parked outside their house and turned in the seat. "Except the elephant statue is apparently still missing."

"I don't believe it. I think she was too embarrassed to acknowledge the one we found was hers. How else do you explain Pierre's fingerprints on it?"

"I guess we'll have to wait and see what Clifford says about it," Will said grimly.

CHAPTER TWENTY-FIVE

Home at last, Harriet stepped from the vehicle and took a moment to gaze at the glorious night sky. "The stars are gorgeous tonight."

Will gently shut his car door, as if not wanting to disturb the peaceful quiet that had settled over the farm.

Harriet rounded the vehicle and slipped her hand into his. Without needing words, they wandered past Aunt Jinny's cottage to the field beyond that stretched to the cliffside path overlooking the North Sea. The crisp air carried a salty note that mingled with the earthy scents of damp grass and fading autumn leaves. They drew to a stop at the field's edge and soaked in the view. The sky seemed endless, dark as ink, save for thousands of pinpricks of light. Faint outlines of clouds drifted across the sliver of moon, giving the field a silvery glow.

From far below them, Harriet could hear the rhythmic lap of the waves, a constant presence against the hush of the night. She laid her head against Will's shoulder, letting the beauty of God's creation fill her.

Will pressed a warm kiss to the top of her head. "Would you like to stroll across the field?"

Relishing this quiet time, Harriet grinned. "Why not?"

But after only a few steps, Will slowed. At his gentle tug, she traced his gaze to a dark shape, still as stone, at the south edge of the field. Her heart gave a start. For a fleeting moment, she wondered if it could be Aunt Jinny walking home from a visit with the Danbys on the next farm. But something about the figure's shape seemed wrong—too tall, too solid, too hunched forward, as if walking into a stiff wind. But the figure wasn't moving.

"That's not your aunt, is it?" Will murmured, his voice carrying a note of unease.

Harriet squinted, and the figure turned in their direction as if sensing their scrutiny. When the silhouette of broad shoulders and a Scottish tam-like hat materialized against the pale smudge of the sea, Harriet's breath stalled in her chest. It was definitely a man.

Harriet's fingers tightened around Will's hand. "Maybe he's lost? Someone who wandered off the trail?" she suggested, her voice barely above a whisper. But the words felt thin, like an excuse she didn't quite believe.

The man advanced on them, his form becoming more distinct in the faint moonlight.

Will's hand tensed in hers. "We should go back to the house."

But as they retreated, Harriet looked over her shoulder and saw the man hurrying across the field, his figure gaining shape the nearer he drew.

Her pulse quickened.

Will looked back, and then he came to an abrupt stop and turned around, his eyes narrowing. "Dad?" His voice was a mix of surprise and relief. A slow smile spread across his face. "What are you doing here?"

Gordon closed the remaining distance between them, the moonlight revealing his familiar weathered face, underlined by a lopsided grin.

Harriet pressed her hand to her chest, feeling her heart pounding. "You scared me."

Will's father chuckled as he drew first one and then the other into a bear hug. "I was hoping to surprise you. I took the train in from Scotland, and a mate gave me a lift from Whitby. When I arrived here and found the place dark, I thought I'd ramble about while I waited. The moors are enchanting in the moonlight, aren't they?"

Will shook his head. "I can't believe you traveled all this way without letting us know you were coming. We could've met your train."

Gordon laughed again, a sound as deep and soothing as the waves lapping ashore far below. "It was a last-minute whim." He rubbed his hands together then blew on them.

Harriet hooked her arm through the crook of her father-in-law's elbow. "Let's get you inside and warmed up. Have you eaten supper?"

"I had a bowl of soup around four. But I wouldn't say no to a little something more."

"Well, we haven't eaten yet, so you're welcome to join us." Harriet was glad she'd put chicken masala in the slow cooker that morning. Will unlocked the front door, and she quickly shrugged out of her coat. "Give me a few minutes to check on my two overnight patients recovering from surgery. Then I'll get supper dished up."

"Don't rush for my benefit," her father-in-law said.

"I'll put the kettle on," Will volunteered. "And set the table."

Ten minutes later, as Harriet closed the door on the room where her patients were crated, movement outside the clinic window snagged her attention. Reassured to see the dead bolt engaged, she peered through the blinds. She could make out the shapes of the trees and shrubs in the moonlight, but nothing that shouldn't be there.

Telling herself she must have seen the lights of a passing car bouncing off the trees, or perhaps a barn owl swooping after its prey, she slipped into the kitchen to tend to supper. "I see Will has taken care of you three," she said to Maxwell, Charlie, and Ash, who were chomping away at the food in their bowls.

Harriet spooned the chicken into a serving dish and brought it to the table. "Nothing fancy, I'm afraid. The entire meal is in one pot tonight."

"It smells delicious," Will and his father said in unison then proceeded to prove their words.

After savoring his third forkful of chicken, Gordon added, "This is scrumptious. No wonder Will's put on a few pounds since the wedding." He winked at Harriet.

"Oh, trust me," she said. "Cooking around here is a team effort. I eat a lot better now than when I lived on my own."

After polishing off his food, Gordon pushed aside his plate and cleared his throat. "I didn't come all this way just for the good food," he said. He reached for his glass and paused to take a sip. "I've got news."

"What's that, Dad?" Will swiped the sauce from his plate with a piece of bread, not seeming to notice his dad's nervous energy.

"It's a bit of a story." His father took a long breath. "You remember that mate of mine I told you about that we found out was family—distantly, that is?"

Harriet nodded, remembering their recent telephone conversation about her father-in-law's visit to Sir Bruce's ancestral home on Fetlar Island.

Gordon circled his fingertip around the lip of his waterglass and rapidly blinked. "Sadly, he passed last week. The same night I talked to you, Harriet, as it turned out." His voice broke, betraying how moved he was by the loss.

"Dad, I'm so sorry." Will squeezed his father's shoulder as Harriet murmured her condolences.

Gordon's lips trembled into a semblance of a smile. "I'm going to miss the old codger. But at least he didn't suffer. Died in his sleep, they said."

"Still, I'm sure you would've liked the chance to say goodbye," Will said consolingly.

Gordon nodded. "That's only part of the story though. I think I told you he had no children." He cleared his throat then held Will's gaze. "Turns out he had no close kin to take on what he left behind either. And his lawyers have informed me that his title falls to me now."

"Are you serious?" Will exclaimed.

His father grinned. "I am. Sir Bruce was a baronet, and the title is passed down to the eldest son. But in Sir Bruce's case that wasn't possible, and his lawyers have determined I am the lawful heir. Then one day, the title will be yours."

Will let out a small laugh, clearly still trying to wrap his head around the news. "I never imagined that. So, you're Sir Gordon now? And someday I'll be Sir Fitzwilliam?"

"When the time comes." His father looked at Harriet, his smile widening. "And you'll be Lady Knight. It's a bit funny how the titles work. The baronet goes by his first name, while his wife's title is affixed to his surname."

Harriet managed a smile, but her stomach twisted. Warmth rose to her cheeks. *Lady Knight.* It sounded strange, foreign—like a name that belonged to someone else.

Clearly pleased, her father-in-law continued, "It's not every day a title falls into one's lap, and it's no small thing." He clapped Will on the shoulder, giving it a firm, affectionate shake. "How does it feel to be the son of a baronet?"

Will grinned, his surprise still evident, but he seemed at ease. "Guess I'll have to start acting more dignified."

Harriet chuckled, although it felt strange in her throat. The news sat like a heavy weight on her chest. The thought of Will with a title—and of herself someday as *Lady Knight*—stirred a deep discomfort she hadn't expected. It was all so far from the life she'd imagined, the kind of life she'd grown up in, rooted in simplicity, without any grand expectations of titles or formalities.

Warmth shone from Gordon's eyes. "It's a lot to take in, I know," he said gently, perhaps noticing her expression. "I don't imagine much will change. The lawyers said Sir Bruce's estate is not automatically entailed with the title. And it could still take some time until that's sorted. At any rate, it doesn't change who I really am. Who any of us really are."

"Of course not," Harriet said, but felt the words catch. He wouldn't change. He'd still be the same kindhearted man he'd always been. A man who put the needs of others above his own comfort. Yet hadn't everything already changed?

Titled people were treated differently, even if they didn't expect or demand it. She wondered if Will's father could sense her unease. She could barely imagine what being *Lady Knight* would entail. The title alone felt as if it carried a burden that had never sat on her shoulders before.

She slipped her hand into Will's, grateful for his comforting steadfastness.

He studied her, his expression softening. "You okay?"

She hesitated, but his gaze was full of the kindness she had always loved in him. "It's just that I don't know if I'm cut out to be *Lady* anything, honestly."

Will reached up and grazed his fingers across her cheek then tucked her hair behind her ear. "You don't have to change for anything." His voice was low and reassuring. "Not for me, not for a title. Whatever happens, we'll handle it together. It's just a name. It doesn't change us."

CHAPTER TWENTY-SIX

With her father-in-law's surprise visit and his even more surprising news, Harriet's concern about what had happened with Van completely slipped her mind until Will noticed the missed call on his cell phone the next morning. Unfortunately, when he tried returning Van's call, it went straight to voice mail.

"I'll ask Polly if there's any news when she comes in," Harriet said.

"Great. Let me know what you find out. I have meetings this morning, but Dad said he wants to visit his old mates while he's here, so I'll have him drop me off at the church and then he can use my car to get around."

"Will you both be home for lunch?"

"Don't worry about us. Chances are Dad will end up having lunch with his mates, and I can always pick something up in town."

After hugging both Will and her father-in-law goodbye, Harriet found Polly in the clinic checking on their overnight patients.

"Hey, did Van ever get ahold of Will?" Polly asked. "I gave him your message."

"He tried, but we got distracted with news you'd never even begin to guess."

Polly gave each patient one last pat then latched the crates and straightened. "Good news?"

"Some would think so. I haven't decided how I feel about it yet."

"Okay, now you've got me really curious."

Harriet led the way to the reception area. "Will's dad surprised us with a visit."

"That's lovely," Polly said. "Was that the news? But you said you weren't sure if it was good news. You didn't want him there?"

Harriet laughed at the sudden concern in her friend's tone. "Oh, his being here is great." Harriet loved the easy camaraderie she enjoyed with Polly. Surely she wouldn't lose that if she were to become Lady Knight one day. But it might make others act differently around her.

"What's wrong then?" Polly laid a hand on her arm. "You look as if Will's dad told you he's dying or something awful like that."

Harriet waved her hands. "Oh, no, nothing that dire. Actually, he's inherited a title."

"Are you serious? You mean he's now Lord Knight?"

"No, Sir Gordon. He's a baronet." Harriet nibbled her bottom lip. "And one day, Will is apparently going to inherit the title."

"And you'll be Lady Knight?" Polly laughed heartily.

"It's not funny," Harriet protested.

"Au contraire, my friend. It's hilarious. Here you spent all that time fretting about how to act around Lady Miltshire and her ilk, and you'll be joining their ranks."

Harriet covered her face with her hands. "Please don't remind me."

"I'm sorry. I shouldn't tease you." Polly's eyes sparkled with mirth. "Wouldn't want to get on a baronetess's wrong side."

Harriet swatted her arm. "You're incorrigible."

"Don't worry. Will's dad is only in his midsixties, right? You'll have years to brush up on your ladyship skills before you have to put them to work." Polly giggled.

"I can fire you, you know."

Polly laughed louder. "You'd be lost without me."

"That's true."

Before Harriet had a chance to shift the conversation to asking what had happened to Van the night before, the owners of their two surgical patients arrived to collect their dogs, followed by back-to-back appointments until nearly eleven.

Handing Polly the file of their last patient of the morning, Harriet said, "I'm ready for a tea break. How about you?"

"You read my mind."

They retreated to the kitchen, where they'd still be able to hear if someone came into the clinic. When Harriet sat at the table with her cup of tea and a couple of cookies, Charlie took it as an invitation to jump onto her lap and snuggle. Harriet stroked her patchy fur, and the cat purred contentedly.

Polly dunked a cookie in her tea. "So, what's all this I missed with you going to the police station last night?"

"Oh, big news. After I told Will about the scent the police noticed in the duffel bag and our idea that it might be the same one we smelled on that glove, we went to the church again to try to find it, or anything else with the same smell."

"And you found something?" Polly said excitedly.

"No, we didn't. But after we exhausted our search, I convinced Will we should stop by the police station to find out if the Castlegates had claimed the statue and to ask what the status was on Pierre."

"And?"

"Edwina hadn't been in yet."

Polly rolled her eyes. "Then what's the big news?"

Harriet took a long sip of her tea, enjoying a little payback for Polly's earlier teasing. "Edwina came in while we were there. Dressed to the nines for an evening out—and smelling distinctly of the same fragrance we smelled on the glove."

Polly's jaw dropped. "No way. Did Van say it smelled the same as the bag?"

"He did."

"I can't believe he didn't tell me. Lady Edwina really is our money mule?" Shaking her head, Polly pressed her fingertips to her lips. "That was one of our theories, remember? Like I said before, it explains where she gets all the cash she throws around despite her 'inadequate' allowance. And her frequent trips give her plenty of opportunities to move money from place to place."

"Pierre confirmed that she brought the bag to him for repair."

"So why were you asking after Van?"

"Because the idea of accusing Edwina put him all out of sorts. He allowed us to speak to Pierre to confirm our theory, but then another officer booted us out. We were worried Van might've been reprimanded for making allegations against Edwina, or maybe dissuaded from making them at all."

Polly frowned. "He was quiet when he got home last night. I assumed he was tired. I asked if they were any closer to releasing Pierre now that they had the elephant statue, and all he said was 'not yet' and that he'd rather not talk about work." Polly's lips tilted up once more. "We went for a moonlit walk and talked about other things instead."

"It was a lovely night for a walk."

Polly finished her cookie. "I get that Pierre's fingerprints on the statue make him look guilty. But since the Castlegates have the statue back, do you think Edwina will go ahead with the charges against Pierre?"

"She will. She said the statue Rita and Ryker found isn't hers."

"What? That's crazy."

"It's not as if the missing statue is the only elephant statue in existence," Harriet reminded her. "We saw others at the jumble sale."

"Sure. But none of those were silver. And who else's would it be, with Pierre's prints on it? You'd think Edwina would be jumping all over that fact as proof he took it."

Harriet shrugged. "The insurance payout could be worth more than the statue."

"Ooh," Polly said, her tone conspiratorial. "Do you think she's trying to bilk the insurance company as another way to line her pockets?"

"I'm not sure what to think. The entire case against Pierre seemed farfetched from the beginning. That she'd try to scam the insurance company makes as much sense as anything, I suppose."

The clinic phone rang, and Polly jumped up to answer it. When she returned a few minutes later, she was grinning from ear to ear. "I think God has opened a door."

"What do you mean?"

"That was the Castlegates' groom on the phone. He needs you ASAP. Thunder's leg is hot to the touch."

Harriet lifted Charlie from her lap and surged to her feet. "How long do I have before my next clinic appointment?"

"More than an hour, and I can push it back if you need more time."

"An hour should be enough." Harriet grabbed her coat, her mind already cataloging potential complications.

Polly trailed after her. "The groom said Edwina isn't home this morning, so if you see Clifford, maybe you could put in a good word for Pierre. You know, for Maisie's sake."

"I'll see. The horse is my priority." As Harriet drove to the Castlegate estate, she called Will. Getting his voice mail, she left a message letting him know Van hadn't said anything to Polly about what happened last night.

When she arrived at the farm a few minutes later, the groom waved to her from the stable door. As Polly had said, Edwina wasn't around. But Clifford's BMW was parked in the driveway.

Harriet followed the groom into the stable, where he once again had Thunder cross-tied in the aisle waiting for her. Harriet ran her hand along the horse's flank, past the injured joint, and finally down the affected leg. "I'm not feeling any hot spots. Where did you notice the warmth?" she asked the groom.

"The joint above the hoof." He pointed to an area she'd already assessed.

Harriet repeated her exploration then compared the warmth she felt, or rather the lack of it, to the same area on the other leg. "I'm not finding it. Could you feel the leg again?"

He blushed but did as she asked. A moment later, he looked at her with wide eyes. "You're right. I don't know what happened. I was sure it was hot before I called. I'm sorry to drag you out here for nothing."

"Better to be safe. It is peculiar that a hot spot would come and go so quickly." Harriet asked him to walk Thunder so she could check his mobility. Then she checked the horse's eyes, ears, and gums and took his temperature to ensure the groom hadn't picked up on some other ailment that had given rise to a temporary temperature spike. "I can't find anything of immediate concern. But you should check the area periodically. If you notice the heat return, don't hesitate to call."

The groom ducked his head. "I must've been distracted, thinking I felt something that wasn't there."

"Not necessarily. You're obviously more attuned to changes in the health of these animals than I can be, since you work with them every day. You may have picked up on an early, if somewhat fleeting, sign of something I can't yet detect."

Seeming somewhat heartened, he shook her hand and thanked her for her time.

Carrying her vet bag to her SUV, she checked her watch. Allowing for driving time, she could still fit in a ten-to-fifteen-minute chat with Clifford if he was free. Drawing a fortifying breath, she set her bag in the truck and traded her barn coat for her more respectable wool coat. Hitching her purse over her shoulder, she started toward the house. Its old arched windows sparkled in the midday sun, giving her an added boost of courage.

Until the groom drove off in a swirl of dust behind her.

Suddenly the ivy-clad stone walls of the sprawling estate didn't feel so inviting. The barn doors stood ajar but unmoving, as if holding their breath. The air felt heavy, too still. No sound of Brent hammering away on the new gazebo. No stable hand mucking out stalls. Not even the distant bark of a dog.

She searched the front windows of the manor house, but they stared back at her like unblinking eyes. A chill skittered down her spine. Her instincts told her to get in her car and leave. But the reaction seemed irrational.

God opened a window. Polly's words flitted through Harriet's mind, lending her courage. Ignoring the hammering in her chest, she gripped her bag tighter and took a slow, deliberate breath. It was time to get to the truth.

CHAPTER TWENTY-SEVEN

Harriet's heart thumped as she stood at the Castlegates' imposing front door and pressed the bell. If Clifford weren't Polly's age and only newly titled, she probably wouldn't dare speak to him again on the matter. She wasn't even sure what to say. She should have rehearsed something, but she didn't have time for that now. Should she express her concern for the danger his sister had unwittingly involved herself in with the duffel bag? Or merely talk about the statue found at the church as if it must be theirs and ask him again if he might urge his sister to drop the charges against Pierre for Maisie's sake?

Except that with the police so interested in the bag, the latter probably wouldn't be enough to secure his release. Sure, they wouldn't have the convenient charges to hold him anymore while they quietly investigated the money-laundering crime. But who knew what other charge they could trump up? Like how they'd come up with an excuse to handcuff Jacques to his hospital bed.

Any hope of mentally rehearsing her spiel died the instant the door opened, because Clifford himself stood on the threshold.

"Dr. Bailey, what an unexpected surprise." The man radiated an air of distinction in his finely tailored gray suit and pale blue silk tie.

He may be young for his title, but his bearing—shoulders squared, brow shadowed by something unreadable—made him appear older, more guarded. "I'm afraid my sister isn't here."

"I know." Harriet swiped her damp palms down the sides of her pants. "Her horse groom called with a concern about Thunder that turned out to be too elusive to diagnose, so I thought I'd take advantage of the opportunity to speak to you again."

"Of course. Won't you come in?" He waited for her to step inside then took the lead. "Excuse the disarray. I gave my staff a couple of days off while I sort through the house contents."

That explained why the place was so quiet save for the wind whispering through the eaves. "I heard you planned to sell." Although she imagined it would take much longer than a couple of days to sort through the contents of a house that had been in the family for generations.

"Yes, although Edwina is trying to convince me otherwise."

Harriet bet she was. As she followed Clifford down the corridor, she couldn't help but wonder how many secrets the walls had absorbed over the years. Clifford stopped two doors short of his office and showed her into what he called the parlor. "Would you like some tea?"

"No, thank you. I only have a few minutes."

He motioned her to a plush chair. Then he ambled to the sideboard, where he filled a tumbler with amber liquid. He turned to the fire and rested his hand on the mantel's edge. "Is this about Maisie again?"

"In part. Did your sister tell you we found an elephant statue in one of the boxes donated to the church's jumble sale?"

The hand holding his drink paused halfway to his mouth. "No, she didn't. So, Maisie has gotten her wish after all, without my intervention?"

"Not quite. There's a bit of a complication."

"How so?"

"Edwina doesn't believe the elephant we found is hers."

"Oh, bad luck. I imagine there are dozens of such souvenirs around these parts."

"I imagine, yes, but this one had Pierre's fingerprints on it."

Clifford cocked his head with an amused snort. "Well then, I guess it's a good thing Edwina couldn't identify the statue."

Harriet squirmed, sensing he wouldn't make this easy for her. "I apologize for coming unannounced," she said, her voice steadier than her heartbeat, "but this is a delicate matter."

Clifford crossed the room and sat in the chair across from her. "Go on."

Harriet let out a long, slow breath. "It's about your sister."

His gaze sharpened, but he said nothing, waiting.

"I'm afraid Edwina may be involved in something dangerous."

Clifford's eyes filled with mirth. "My sister? She's only dangerous to men."

"Hear me out, please."

He polished off his drink then set his glass on a side table. With a wave of his upturned palm, he signaled the floor was hers.

"When your sister went to the police station last night, she wore the same distinctive scent investigators had detected in the leather duffel bag they found in Pierre's car. Which suggests the bag belongs to your sister."

"You're saying Maisie's husband stole that too?"

"No. No. Not at all." Harriet closed her mouth. Discussing the duffel bag's secret compartment with Clifford would mean revealing information the police clearly wanted to keep quiet. Then again, he could be feigning ignorance, if the police had shared it with him in confidence. With how much deference the police were showing the Castlegates, how likely was it they'd kept details about the bag's secret compartment from them?

The mantel clock chimed the hour, reminding Harriet that she was running out of time. If anyone could convince Edwina to confess and accept the consequences, it was Clifford. But he couldn't do that if he didn't know what was at stake.

Stiffening her resolve, Harriet prayed Van would forgive her if she spoke out of turn, and plunged ahead. "A leather bag similar to the one found in Pierre's car was recently seized by police when it was used by a would-be tourist to transport money for a criminal organization."

Clifford's eyes narrowed. "What are you implying?"

"When your sister travels, she may be carrying more than her personal luggage."

Clifford's lips pressed into a thin, bloodless line, and he glanced briefly out the window before meeting Harriet's gaze again. "That is quite an accusation." His tone was measured but unmistakably cold. "Edwina can be reckless at times, yes, but this borders on the absurd."

Having expected his skepticism, Harriet nodded. "I don't make it lightly, Lord Castlegate. There have been signs. Her extravagant spending and frequent journeys are well known."

"Her dates are more than happy to indulge her expensive tastes," Clifford said, obviously not prepared to believe ill of his sister.

Harriet forged on anyway. "I suspect she feared Pierre had discovered her secret, so she framed him for the theft. That way anything he might tell the police wouldn't be believed."

Clifford's jaw clenched at the mention of Pierre's name, or maybe at the insinuation the statue was never actually stolen, and anger flickered in his eyes. His focus shifted to the fire for a moment, one hand curling into a fist on his knee. "Pierre claimed innocence from the start," he muttered, "but Edwina was so adamant."

"I know," Harriet said softly. "Rest assured Pierre has no intention of revealing what he knows, even if he could prove it. In fact, I believe he came here in the first place to alert you to his discovery so you could help your sister disentangle herself from these people before it's too late."

This time Clifford snorted derisively. "That's what you think, huh?"

"I believe it's the truth. Pierre simply wants the charges dropped so he can leave this in the past." Harriet fidgeted under Clifford's scrutiny, worried that telling him about Edwina's criminal connection had been a mistake. What did they say—possession is nine tenths of the law? And the bag had been found in Pierre's possession.

The fire crackled, sending up a warm waft of air. But the air between them was ice-cold. Clifford scrutinized her, and she braced for the likelihood he'd ask her to leave.

Then, with his voice barely above a whisper, in a tone more vulnerable than she'd expected, he said, "If you're wrong, my sister's reputation will never recover."

"And if I'm right?" she asked, in a tone equally as soft. She searched his face for a glimmer of understanding. "If I'm right, then she's already in a world of trouble she may not fully understand."

He closed his eyes briefly then nodded. "What do you want from me?"

She exhaled, feeling the smallest relief, although her heart still pummeled her ribs. "Convince her to drop the charges against Pierre. In return, Pierre will continue to stand by what he's said from the beginning, that the bag's owner has nothing to do with the missing statue."

Clifford's gaze shifted away again, as though he was already calculating the implications, weighing his loyalties against the risk. "You're asking me to accuse my sister of being a money mule, Dr. Bailey." His countenance darkened. "This isn't a simple misunderstanding over a misplaced statue."

Harriet tilted her head. "Is that what happened? Was the statue simply misplaced?" Remembering Polly's theory about Clifford hiding the statue in his safe, she wondered if his little slip meant he'd discovered that that was precisely what his sister had done. Only perhaps she'd convinced him that coming clean now would be too embarrassing.

"You know what I mean."

"I'm not sure I do," Harriet replied steadily. "We thought we'd found your elephant in the jumble sale donations. But your sister says otherwise. If Pierre didn't take it, and it didn't inadvertently end up in a donation box, it seems likely your sister hid it, don't you think?"

"No, I don't," he retorted, his tone sharp.

"Okay." Harriet gave him a moment to adjust to the idea. "Then it won't hurt to check. Perhaps there's a safe or a private chest where she could have hidden it." She paused again, watching his eyes flicker with indecision. "It's worth a look."

He held her gaze, his fingers tapping against his knee. Finally, he said, "Very well," although the reluctance in his expression was unmistakable. "Wait here, Dr. Bailey. I'll return shortly."

As Clifford's footsteps faded down the hall, Harriet settled back in her chair, allowing herself a breath of relief. The fire snapped quietly in the hearth, and the stillness of the room wrapped around her, settling her nerves. But then, a faint voice caught her attention—Clifford's voice, low and urgent, carrying from an adjoining room.

She rose from her chair, careful to keep her steps quiet as she approached a closed pocket door in the wall, her ears straining to make out the conversation.

"She knows too much," Clifford said, his voice sharp with frustration. "Harriet Bailey-Knight. She's far too clever for her own good, and if she connects the dots—if she realizes I'm the one behind all of this—"

Harriet's heart pounded painfully in her chest. Clifford was the real culprit? Not Edwina? She held her breath, pressing her ear to the door, listening. Was he talking on the phone? Or was someone else in there with him?

After a momentary silence, Clifford said, "Pierre is a minor inconvenience. It's Harriet who poses the true threat. I hoped she'd take my word and leave, but she's dangerously close to figuring it all out."

A cold wave of fear washed over her as she realized the extent of Clifford's treachery. She hurried to the hall door, but the knob rattled uselessly in her grip. He'd locked it behind him. She was trapped.

CHAPTER TWENTY-EIGHT

Panic clawing her chest, Harriet glanced desperately about the Castlegates' parlor for another exit. But the elegant walls of the grand room suddenly felt as inescapable as Pierre's cell.

A faint rustling at the window, followed by a quiet knock on the glass, caught her attention. She whipped around, her eyes widening at the sight of a familiar face peering in. *Alex.*

Harriet's already racing heart kicked up into a full-out gallop. Could the woman be trusted? She glanced back at the door Clifford might return through any second and decided she'd rather take her chances with Alex. She rushed to the narrow, lead-paned windows and unlatched one as quietly as she could manage.

Alex stood on tiptoes, her fingers curled around the window ledge. "You've got to get out of there. You're not safe."

"Yeah, I just figured that out." Harriet tossed her purse through the window then hauled a chair closer so she could reach to climb through after it. "What are you doing here?"

"I sensed something was wrong with Clifford, so I told him I was surveying for nesting sites to get a closer look at his estate."

Climbing onto the chair, Harriet gaped at her, relief and shock flooding her all at once.

Urgency lit Alex's eyes. "Are you going to be able to get out this way?"

"I'd better be able to, because he's locked me in here." Harriet swung one leg over the window ledge and slid through.

Alex grabbed Harriet's arm to steady her and guide her descent to the ground.

The welcome scent of damp earth filled Harriet's senses as she snatched up her purse. "You may have saved my life. Thank you."

"We're not out of the woods yet. Let's get you to your vehicle."

Harriet started across the grass, but Alex caught her arm in a firm grip. "Not that way. He'll see you from the windows." She tugged Harriet toward some bushes in the opposite direction.

"Clifford's behind the whole thing," Harriet said, racing to keep up with Alex. "He framed Pierre, and he's involved in something dangerous."

"I warned you to leave it alone."

Harriet stumbled. "What do you mean? Are you saying *you* left the note on my vehicle?"

"Yes. Now move." Alex tugged harder. "He's probably already discovered you've escaped."

Harriet dug in her heels and jerked her arm free from Alex's hold. "How are you involved in this? Why should I trust you?"

"Because I'm a cop. Undercover. Liaising with the Regional Organized Crime Unit."

"You're a cop?" Harriet narrowed her eyes. "How did Will not know that?" She shook her head. "I don't believe you."

Incoherent shouting came from the direction of the house.

"We don't have time to debate this. We need to get you out of here."

"No kidding." But Harriet was completely disoriented. She'd never been this far back on the property. Where was her Land Rover?

Alex whacked aside some shrubs and pointed. "The stables are there. The door at this end is open, so you can run through the barn to stay out of sight until you're close to your vehicle. Now go. I'll buy you as much time as I can."

Harriet raced for the stables. But her instincts revolted at the idea of going inside them for cover. What if it was another trap? With one last glance at the now visible manor, she dashed straight for the Beast—what she should have done in the first place. She rummaged through her pockets for her keys as she ran. She came up empty-handed. Reaching the Beast, she ducked inside. Lying low so no one could see her through the windows, she searched her purse. The keys weren't there either. She leaned her head against the cold steering wheel. This couldn't be happening. They must have fallen out when she threw her purse through the window, or from her pocket when she climbed out.

Unless Alex had pickpocketed them.

Had trusting her been a mistake? Harriet shook off the doubts. She didn't have time to second-guess what was done. She had a bigger problem here. No way could she risk returning to the house to search the grass under the window. So how was she going to get away? Still lying low on the seat, Harriet palmed her phone.

The Beast's door swung open.

Reflexively, Harriet drew her knees to her chest and kicked both legs with everything in her.

Caught in the gut, her attacker stumbled backward with a grunt. "What are you doing?"

"Alex?" Harriet sat up. "What are *you* doing?" She popped open the glove box and grabbed the heavy flashlight to use as a weapon. "Why did you follow me?"

"I have to make sure you get out of here." Still doubled over and rubbing her stomach, Alex grimaced. "Now go."

Harriet's jaw clenched. "I can't." She sat upright, one hand tightening around the flashlight, the other around her phone. "I lost my keys." She thumbed her password into her phone. "But I was about to call the police," she warned, her voice steely.

Alex's eyes flicked to Harriet's phone. "I already did. But we might be on our own a while yet. Clifford's got the kind of influence that stretches further than you'd think."

Harriet's heart stuttered. She tapped the call symbol beside Polly's name rather than dial emergency services. Polly knew she was at the Castlegate estate and would realize she was in danger faster than anyone. Hopefully she would use the clinic phone to call Van for help while keeping the line with Harriet open to hear her exchange with Alex. "Are you saying Clifford has police officers on his payroll, Alex?"

"Among other government officials, yes."

"But not *you*?" Harriet said suspiciously.

Alex pressed her lips in a firm line, her gaze flicking once more to Harriet's phone.

Harriet had turned the screen to her palm, but Alex no doubt suspected what she was trying to do.

A low rumble broke the silence—an engine starting up somewhere close. Harriet's gaze snapped toward the sound.

"That's Clifford's tractor," Alex murmured. "He doesn't like to get his hands dirty. But he'll have a plan. He'll delay you however he can until..." She trailed off, her attention shifting to the road. "Until someone else can make sure you don't have a chance to tell anyone what you know. Our best hope is to try to get to my car in the woods on the other side of that knoll." She pointed to the east.

Harriet's grip tightened on her phone, her pulse hammering. She wanted to run, to trust herself and her instincts. But Alex's expression, a mixture of warning and urgency, held her in place.

"If you don't trust me"—Alex's voice dropped to a whisper—"you're welcome to call and take your chances with the local police." Her gaze lifted to meet Harriet's, a flash of genuine worry flickering there. "But if you want to get out, you'll need to follow me. Now."

The rumble of the tractor grew closer, a reminder of the stakes closing in on them.

The look of worry in Alex's eyes shifted to real fear.

Harriet jumped from the vehicle. "Okay, let's go."

They made it as far as an old stone shelter on the far side of the pasture when the low thrum of approaching vehicles carried across the rolling hills from the gravel road beyond.

At the sight of a white car with the police force's traditional blue and yellow checkerboard on the side, Harriet's pulse skipped, her hopes flaring.

"Stay out of sight until we know whose side they're on." Alex pulled Harriet behind the stone building as the sound grew louder.

The tractor, which had already more than halved the distance between them, came to an abrupt halt. Through a gap in the stone wall, Harriet could see Clifford shoot an icy scowl in their direction before turning his tractor toward his driveway. Did he plan to intercept the police? Or elicit their help?

The rumbling engines of the police vehicles kept coming. But Harriet didn't know whether to be worried or reassured that their lights and sirens weren't on.

Two squad cars stopped in the driveway, their doors flying open as officers in uniforms emerged. A tall woman with russet hair and a focused expression emerged from a third unmarked vehicle. Harriet recognized her as Detective Inspector Kerry McCormick, who Polly's husband worked with on more involved cases.

The woman strode toward Clifford's now stopped tractor. "Clifford Castlegate," she called, eschewing his formal title, "we need to have a word with you."

Harriet couldn't see Clifford's reaction from her vantage point, so she maneuvered for a better view. Alex placed a steadying hand on her arm. Once again, Harriet's doubts about the woman flared. Was she keeping Harriet out of the picture for Clifford's sake? Or because she wasn't sure if they could trust these officers?

Harriet wavered. If only Van would show up, then she would know who to trust.

Clifford's voice drifted to them. "Officers," he said smoothly, raising his hands, "what's all this about?"

DI McCormick stood her ground. "We've had reports of suspicious activity on your property. Including an attempted restraint of one of our witnesses."

Harriet held her breath as McCormick's backup moved closer. Clifford's gaze flicked to Harriet and Alex, his jaw tight.

"You must be mistaken." His voice dripped with feigned politeness as his attention returned to the DI. "A simple misunderstanding, I'm sure."

"Save it," one of the other officers cut in, stepping up to flank him. "We have enough to bring you in for questioning. Get off the tractor."

To her surprise, Clifford complied. Harriet let out a long breath, relief flooding her system. Alex gave her a small, reassuring smile as the officers escorted Clifford to a police cruiser.

"You really did call them," Harriet whispered, a mixture of gratitude and disbelief in her voice.

"Sure. But I didn't know how long it would take them to neutralize any opposition that might arise." Alex tilted her head toward the throng of officers. "Let's go give them your statement and see if we can find those keys of yours."

DI McCormick nodded at Harriet in greeting. "Dr. Bailey," she said, her voice kind. "We'll take it from here. You're safe now."

Harriet looked between Alex and the officers, finally allowing herself to believe it. But as she watched Clifford being loaded into a police car, unease gnawed at her relief. His smile—a tight, twisted thing—hadn't faded even as they palmed the top of his head as he got into the cruiser. His gaze remained fixed on her, a wordless promise that this wasn't over.

Her stomach tightened. Suddenly realizing she still clutched her phone, Harriet raised it to her ear. "Polly, are you still there?"

"I'm here. Are you okay? Van and Will are on their way."

"I'm fine now. Thank you. The police arrested Clifford. You were right about him."

DI McCormick snagged Harriet's attention and held up her notebook. "We need to get your statement before you leave."

Harriet nodded. "Just one more minute, please," she pleaded. To Polly she said, "Listen Polly, I still need to answer some questions here before I can head back to the clinic. Can you reschedule this afternoon's appointments?"

"Already on it."

"Thanks for everything. I'll catch you up later."

DI McCormick, who told Harriet she had called Van away the night before and given the order that they be sent home from the police station, made short work of collecting Harriet's statement. She didn't seem surprised by Harriet's account of the conversation she'd overheard Clifford having, likely on the phone. "With a bit of luck, we'll be able to trace his call to someone higher up on the food chain in this network," she said.

Edwina's shiny BMW swerved into the driveway and screeched to a stop behind the police cruisers. She jumped from the car, her hair freshly coiffed and her gaze jerking from face to face. Not bothering to shut her car door, she rushed toward Harriet and the DI, her steps faltering when she saw Clifford sitting in the back of one of the cruisers. "What's going on?" She reached for the door handle, but an officer stayed her hand.

"Why is my brother in a police car?" she screamed, her eyes flaring.

With a brusque flick of her fingers, DI McCormick motioned Edwina over.

Edwina stormed to them. "What's going on here?"

Harriet caught a strong whiff of the same scent they'd connected to the duffel bag. Pressing the back of her fingers to her nose, she made eye contact with the inspector, who nodded affirmation that she had noticed as well.

"May I ask what perfume you're wearing?" she asked Edwina.

Clearly thrown by the seemingly unrelated question, Edwina scrunched her brows. "What do you mean?" She sniffed at her wrist. "I'm not wearing any perfume."

"I can smell that you're wearing something," DI McCormick said.

Edwina looked puzzled for another moment and then realization dawned. "You must mean my hand lotion. I just put more on before leaving the hairdresser. This cold weather is wreaking havoc on my skin." She frowned. "Now are you going to tell me what my brother is doing in that police car?"

"Your brother has been arrested." DI McCormick listed a litany of charges.

Edwina's jaw dropped in what appeared to be genuine shock.

The DI then cautioned Edwina as to her rights under questioning.

Edwina blinked hard and took a step back. "Am I under arrest too?"

"At this time we simply need you to clear up a couple of questions as best you can. You are welcome to call your solicitor, in which case we can wait and conduct this interview in town. But if you have nothing to hide, I don't see any need for that."

Edwina's expression hardened. "I don't know anything about what my brother's supposed to have done."

"The day of your alleged burglary, we found a weekend bag in the boot of Pierre Aubert's car. You're acquainted with this fact?"

"Alleged?" she repeated indignantly. "My grandfather's beloved elephant statue was taken from our home. I already told DC Worthington that the one he recovered from the church isn't it."

"Please just answer the question," DI McCormick replied serenely.

"Yes. I know about the bag." Edwina jutted her chin in Harriet's direction. "She told the DC she saw Aubert put it in his boot."

"When we recovered the bag in question, a strong smell was detected on it, identical to that of your hand lotion. Can you offer any insight into how that came to be?"

Edwina's expression morphed into a confused scowl. "Was it a brown leather holdall?"

"Yes."

"Then I guess it could've been the one I took to Aubert's shop for repair. I borrowed it from my brother for a weekend horse show. Then the lid popped off my hand lotion and spilled all over the inside. To make matters worse, its zipper also broke. So I took the bag to Aubert's shop, hoping for a quick fix before Clifford was any the wiser."

"Why did you take it to Aubert's shop when Ryker Williams has always handled the family's business?"

"Ryker isn't known for his speed." Her expression grew perplexed. "So you're saying Aubert had my brother's holdall with him when he paid us a call that day? And didn't return it to us?"

The DI asked a few more questions without answering any of Edwina's. After the inspector ignored yet another question, Edwina wrung her hands. "I think I'd like to consult a solicitor before answering anything more."

DI McCormick nodded and instructed a uniformed officer to escort Edwina to the police station once she'd made the necessary arrangements with her lawyer.

"Will she be arrested?" Harriet asked quietly after the officer led Edwina away.

"Yet to be determined. You're free to go."

"Thank you."

Alex strode up, brandishing Harriet's lost keys. "I found them in the grass under the window."

Harriet's face heated as Alex dropped them into her hand. "I'm sorry I doubted you."

Alex shrugged. "No worries. I can understand how hard it was for you to know who you could trust."

Another car Harriet recognized drove up the driveway, and her pulse quickened. Will opened the car door before Van brought his car to a full stop, and sprinted toward her, worry etched in every line of his face. Reaching her side, he clasped her hand to his chest and searched her face. "Harriet, are you okay? I got your voice mail, and then Polly called, and now this." He eyed the officers then Clifford, still restrained in the back of a police cruiser.

"I'm not hurt. Edwina's groom asked me to come see her horse. I thought I could have an amiable chat with Clifford about Edwina. I thought he'd be grateful." Harriet shook her head. "But there was nothing wrong with the horse. I'm not sure, but I think Clifford asked the groom to lie to get me here. Someone must've told him we'd been to the police station. Or my going into the house to talk to him alerted him that we'd figured out too much, even though I still didn't suspect him." Harriet shuddered. "He didn't intend to let me leave."

Will's face darkened, his grip on her hand tightening. "You're saying he lured you here? To trap you?"

"Maybe. I'm not sure. But the groom took off as soon as I told him the horse was fine." And the spot where his truck had been parked when she first arrived was still empty. Alex's warning about the length of Clifford's reach streaked through Harriet's mind, along with the memory of Jacques's horrible accident that wasn't an accident. Her gaze strayed to the police cruiser where Clifford sat, his shadowed figure radiating a nerve-rattling calm. When she refocused her attention on Will, her voice trembled. "I'm not sure we're truly safe even now."

Will's jaw clenched as he took in the implications.

DI McCormick, who stood nearby, grimaced. "Castlegate does have his fingers in too many places for our peace of mind. I don't doubt he'll attempt to use whatever influence he has left to try and keep you quiet." She glanced at Alex. "But we're hopeful we can outmaneuver him yet."

Will blinked with surprise, apparently noticing Alex for the first time. "What are you doing here?"

Alex smiled. "It's a long story. I'll let Harriet fill you in from the comfort of your own home."

"But given Castlegate's connections," DI McCormick cautioned, "it's important you stay vigilant."

Harriet swallowed, hearing the clear warning. Clifford's influence might stretch further than any of them knew. Even though he was in custody, the reach of his network remained uncertain.

Clifford caught her eye through the cruiser's window, his stare as sharp and venomous as ever, and she knew this was far from over.

Will wrapped his arm around her shoulders. "Perhaps now would be a good time to take that trip to the States while the police get this sorted."

"I don't think there's a need to rush into anything so extreme," DI McCormick countered. "But we'll set up a protective detail until the testimony is in place, in case his influence gets too close for comfort."

Harriet leaned into Will's side, letting his steady presence ground her. She'd walked into this blindly, but now, with the cold truth hanging over them, she understood. Clifford's reach was insidious, winding through the village, the local authorities, and likely much further.

CHAPTER TWENTY-NINE

Harriet sat across from Will in their quiet kitchen, the morning sun casting a warm glow through the farmhouse windows. She wrapped her hands around her mug of coffee, trying to shake off the lingering tension from the past few days. Will's father had headed home with a promise to return soon. Murphy's infected paw had completely healed, as had the horse who'd ingested sycamore seeds. The playful antics of Ash and Charlie batting about a toy mouse while Maxwell munched his kibble anchored her back to normality.

A knock at the door interrupted her thoughts. Will rose to answer it, meeting her gaze with a reassuring yet cautious look. Moments later, he returned with Alex, or Detective Sergeant Alex Lennox, to be precise.

Harriet sprang to her feet. "Has something happened?"

The DS motioned Harriet to sit. "No, it's all good. I'm heading home today and wanted to give you the good news myself before I left."

Will held up the teapot. "Want a cup?"

"That would be lovely, thanks." Alex settled herself at the table across from Harriet. "I think you'll find my news about the latest developments in Lord Castlegate's case relieving."

Harriet's pulse quickened.

Will set a cup of tea in front of Alex then sat next to Harriet and cradled her hand in his.

"As you know, Lord Castlegate attempted to use his influence to silence you," Alex said, "but thanks to your friend Polly making DC Worthington aware of how even as a youth Clifford manipulated situations to his own ends, we were prepared for his tactics. The officers he tried to inveigle to do his bidding worked under our supervision, gathering evidence against him and the larger organization."

Harriet let out a slow breath.

"So Harriet isn't in danger?" Will clarified.

"Not anymore. Quite the opposite, in fact." Alex's assuring tone was warm and steady. "Clifford made contact with his supposed 'allies' from inside the station, unaware they'd already turned on him. We recorded every piece of information he let slip, which has added to the case we've built against him. When faced with this, he realized there was no one left to shield him."

Harriet could hardly believe it. "So he made a deal?"

"Yes. To avoid a lengthy sentence, he agreed to disclose everything he knows about those involved in the money-laundering—men we are now quietly apprehending. His cooperation essentially neutralizes any threat to you. And effectively dismantles a small arm of an Eastern European crime family attempting to make larger inroads into the UK."

"How did Clifford get involved with the likes of them?"

"The same way many people get roped into bad company. Over an unpaid debt. Now our job is to gather evidence against the network that assisted him in bribing officials to look the other way."

Alex reached for her cup, her gaze kind. "But what's important where you're concerned is that the danger has passed. You're free to carry on as before."

Relief flooded through Harriet.

"Although," Alex added, "I'd advise you stick to veterinary investigations and leave criminal investigations to the police."

"I second that." Will raised his own mug in salute and sent Harriet a wink.

Harriet's face heated. Will had been so worried about her. This had to be a huge relief for him too.

"You're sure no one else will come after her?" he asked Alex. "Did you figure out who was sneaking around our place and setting the dog off the weekend after the theft? Because that would've been before Harriet was on Clifford's radar."

"Oh, I'm sorry." Harriet rested her hand on Will's arm. "I forgot to tell you. Polly found out that was Mike Dane dropping off lumber at the barn for one of the repairs."

Will relaxed at the explanation, much as Harriet herself had.

"We're confident that Harriet is now safe," Alex reassured them. "Clifford's cooperation took the teeth out of any remaining threats."

"That's good to hear." Happy she no longer needed to look over her shoulder everywhere she went, Harriet sipped her coffee, relishing the feel of its warmth seeping through her.

Alex drank the last of her tea and pushed back her chair. "I'd better be off."

"Wait." Harriet set down her mug. "Can you tell us what's happened to Pierre and his brother? The last time I spoke to Maisie, she didn't have a lot to tell us, and I wondered if she was afraid bad guys might be listening in on our calls."

Alex offered an empathetic nod. "Pierre was released this morning. We're satisfied that he had no direct involvement in any criminal activity."

Harriet's shoulders relaxed. "I'm so glad. I tried hard to believe in him, but I have to confess, his reluctance to cooperate with the police did leave me with a little doubt."

"His reluctance was out of loyalty to his brother. Jacques had crafted the duffel bag, and Pierre recognized his work. After Jacques woke up from the hit-and-run, he admitted to making the custom leather duffels for a client who used them for dubious purposes. The arrangement had been going on for some time, and it's why Pierre left Paris for White Church Bay. He didn't want to be entangled in such dealings."

Will leaned forward. "So Jacques has agreed to testify?"

"Yes. And due to his cooperation, his sentencing on the aiding and abetting charges will likely be lenient, if the charges aren't stayed altogether."

"Where does that leave Pierre?"

"Besides admitting to supplying the bags, Jacques assured us his brother was never part of it. His taking full responsibility allowed us to clear Pierre's name." Alex rose to leave. "He can return to his shop with no further repercussions."

"That's fabulous," Harriet exclaimed. "Maisie will be over the moon."

"Yes, we even nabbed the bloke who trashed their shop. A fix-it guy from London. He was the same one who ran down Pierre.

Unfortunately, he claims his orders came anonymously, so he can't identify who sent them. But we have enough corroborating evidence that we're confident we've got the man responsible."

"What about Lady Edwina?" Will asked. "How much did she know?"

Alex sank back into her seat with a wry smile. "Lady Edwina insists she knew nothing about her brother's activities." She turned to Harriet. "You heard her explanation about borrowing Clifford's bag."

"Yes, but how does she explain Pierre leaving with the bag, which he'd supposedly received from her earlier that week?"

"She claims that she was so certain he came there because of the scene her brother made over Pierre's wife that she didn't pay attention to what he was saying or to whether he had anything with him."

"And you believe her?"

"As you saw at the time of Clifford's arrest, she seemed genuinely shocked by the whole affair, and he also claims she knew nothing. So we're taking her statements at face value. For now, anyway."

"But where has she been getting all the money she spends?"

"Besides her very generous allowance, she has access to a trust fund established for her by her maternal grandmother. And her male companions are astonishingly lavish with their gifts, some of which she's apparently hocked for quick cash when needed."

"That's one way to do it," Will murmured.

"A woman does what she must to survive, I suppose," Alex said, her eyes twinkling. "As for Clifford, he isn't being entirely forthcoming. But from what we've managed to cobble together, when he returned to his office right after Pierre left and couldn't find his bag, the housekeeper told him Lady Edwina must not have been satisfied with the tradesman's repair. Louise told us Pierre brought the bag with him, but left with it again, just as he claimed."

Harriet smacked herself in the forehead. How had she never thought to ask Louise about the bag?

"Anyway, hearing that from Louise was enough to get Clifford good and worried about what Pierre intended to do with the bag. And he quickly decided to fit the man up for the bogus statue theft to ensure the police wouldn't believe a word Pierre said against them."

"Then Clifford hid the statue in their jumble sale donation box?" Will clarified.

"No. He hid the real statue in his safe to create the illusion of a theft, just as DC Worthington's wife suggested."

Harriet laughed. "Polly had Clifford pegged from day one. She had the motive all wrong, but she was onto him."

Alex chuckled. "Yes. DC Worthington shared his wife's theory with me. It's one of the reasons I kept an eye on the comings and goings at the estate."

"Wait a second," Will said. "You're saying the elephant Ryker and Rita found at the church really wasn't the Castlegates' missing statue? Edwina was telling the truth?"

"That's right. It was a similar pewter replica."

"But Pierre's fingerprints were on it."

Alex nodded. "He'd handled the statue at a mate's house some time ago. The resemblance of the Castlegates' statue to his mate's was what made Pierre curious enough to inspect theirs too." She shook her head. "Pierre could have helped himself from the very beginning by revealing the owner of the duffel bag found in his car."

Will poured himself another cup of tea. "You can't fault the man for being loyal to his family."

"That's true. As much as Pierre despised who his brother worked for, he didn't want to instigate his downfall." Alex rose from her chair again. "We have Harriet to thank for finally nabbing Clifford. Her confrontation with him ended up being the catalyst for his arrest."

Harriet's heart lightened. With the web of schemes and secrets finally unraveled, life at Cobble Hill Farm—her life with Will—could return to the hectic, unpredictable, and safe pace she loved.

Will rose too but shifted his weight from foot to foot as if he still had something on his mind.

Harriet slipped her hand into Will's. "Was there something else you wanted to ask Alex?"

"Um, yes," he started tentatively. Then he cleared his throat before continuing, his tone gaining strength. "Why didn't you tell me you were a police officer? A detective, no less?"

Alex folded her arms, offering a faint, apologetic smile. "From the very beginning, the force has used me in undercover operations. Some of them require me to pose as a research assistant, a conservationist, anything that allows me to work quietly in the background. Your mate DC Worthington wasn't lying when he said I've cooperated in investigations involving rare bird poaching. He just left out the part that I'm an officer myself and that most of what is written about me online is backstop to keep my cover from being blown."

Will raised his eyebrows, absorbing the revelation. "Van knew all along?"

"He did," Alex admitted, her voice contrite. "But please don't hold that against him. It was incredibly hard for him to shield the truth without outright lying to you—and to his wife. It's an ongoing issue I face, always having to balance what I can say and what I can't. That's why I've made it a rule not to tell anyone what I actually do, especially those I'm close to. That way they'll never have to lie or risk being pulled into something they didn't sign up for."

Will rubbed the back of his neck. "I guess I can understand that. It's a lot to take in though."

Alex's expression softened, and she placed a reassuring hand on his arm. "For what it's worth, I'm sorry for keeping you in the dark. But it's vital you don't mention my true occupation to anyone. Our uni mates, people in town—they have no idea, and it's best it stays that way."

Will managed a smirk. "So all those long afternoons in the field watching birds?"

"Legitimate fieldwork, mostly." Alex laughed. "And you'd be surprised how much information people will drop when they think you're the 'quiet bird lady.'" She gave him a gentle, almost pleading look. "It's the life I've chosen, Will, and I've made my peace with it. I need my mates to respect it too."

Will nodded, his expression a mixture of pride and lingering surprise. "Your secret is safe with me."

"Me too," Harriet said, squeezing Will's hand.

That evening, after the day's events had quieted, Harriet found herself drawn to the window. She stood there for a long time, gazing at the night sky. The house was peaceful, with the only sounds the soft creak of the settling wood and the occasional crackle from the fire in the hearth. But her mind remained in a tangle with thoughts about Clifford, about Will's father's title, and about what true nobility really meant.

Will joined her, his arm encircling her waist as he tracked her gaze out to the dark expanse. They stood there in companionable silence until Harriet voiced what was troubling her. "I keep thinking about Clifford and the way people held him in such high regard just because he was 'Lord Castlegate.'" She pressed her hand to her stomach. "People assumed he was trustworthy because of that title, but in reality, he wore it like a mask to cover up what he truly was."

Will's thumb traced gentle circles over her hand. "Titles like 'Lord,' or even 'Sir,' are merely words. It's what's beneath them, how one lives, that makes one truly noble—or not."

She hesitated until the question she hadn't been able to shake surfaced at last. "Doesn't it bother you? That one day you'll inherit your father's title, become 'Sir Fitzwilliam,' when we've seen firsthand that it doesn't mean what people think it means?"

Will smiled softly, seeming to understand her hesitation. "I've thought about it, sure. But to me, a title isn't a status. It's a responsibility. If it's anything worthwhile, it's the chance to serve, not to demand reverence. I would hope to use it in a way that lifts others—not myself."

His perspective soothed her troubled spirit. Clifford's title had shielded him, insulated him, and given him access to influence and connections. But in the end, his character had been devoid of substance, and his narrative nothing more than a house of cards easily toppled by the truth.

She lifted her gaze to his. "You're right. A title doesn't make a person noble. It's who they choose to be that matters, whether anyone notices or not."

Will's eyes held a gentleness that made her feel seen. "It reminds me of a verse I sometimes lean on from Proverbs: 'A good name is to be chosen rather than great riches, and favor is better than silver or gold.'" He stroked the back of his fingers across her cheek in a gentle caress. "It reminds me that integrity and humility are where true worth lies."

They gazed out the window in silence. Their life at Cobble Hill Farm might not be grand or gilded, but it was rich in the things that mattered most. Whatever the future held, Harriet knew she could meet it with courage and faith, knowing that true nobility came from within.

"Nobility," she said after a while, "comes from living by something greater than ourselves, whether we're given a title or not."

"Exactly," Will agreed, his voice low and warm. "You're already a princess in the truest sense—a daughter of the King of Kings. You couldn't ask for a higher title or a more noble calling."

Tears stung Harriet's eyes. She looked up at him, her heart swelling at the simple truth he'd voiced. In that moment, the last of her concerns over how they'd someday wear the mantles of "Sir" and "Lady" fell away. "Thank you," she whispered, a small smile tugging at her lips. "I needed that reminder."

Will brushed a thumb over her cheek once more. "It's easy to forget. We get so caught up in what people think of us, in the labels they give us. But none of that really matters—not when we're already loved and known by God."

Harriet rested her head against his chest, reflecting on the life they were building together—simple, giving, and full of love. It was the life she wanted. One grounded in faith, family, and the call to care for others. And whatever role or title might come, she knew they'd meet it together with humility, anchored by a purpose beyond themselves.

FROM THE AUTHOR

Dear Reader,

When I first began this story, I had no idea how deeply I would come to appreciate the journey on which it took Harriet. Her story was not merely about solving a mystery or untangling the web of intrigue surrounding one of White Church Bay's noble families. It was also about discovering what true nobility means.

As a veterinarian, Harriet is practical, grounded, and utterly uninterested in titles or social hierarchies. At the beginning of the story, she felt out of place among the noble class, unsure of how to navigate that elite world.

But as she interacted with lords and ladies, she began to see that nobility isn't just about birthright or wealth—it's about character, honor, and a willingness to serve others. She learned that her confidence didn't come from fitting in—it came from standing firm in her own sense of purpose and faith. I loved watching Harriet grow into the realization that her value isn't defined by societal standards or titles bestowed on us by other people, but by God's love and grace.

Her journey reminded me of how important it is to carry this perspective into our own lives. It's easy to feel insignificant in the face of power, wealth, or authority. But Harriet's bravery in staying true to herself—and standing up for justice and truth—is a reminder that real nobility isn't about who bows to you. It's about how you serve and love others.

I hope you enjoyed reading this story as much as I enjoyed writing it. And more than that, I hope it reminds you, as it reminded me, that each of us has a role to play in the grand story of the King of Kings. Step into it boldly, with the grace and confidence that only comes from knowing who you truly are.

Signed,
Sandra Orchard

ABOUT THE AUTHOR

Sandra Orchard writes fast-paced, keep-you-guessing stories with a generous dash of sweet romance. Touted by Midwest Book Reviews as "a true master of the [mystery] genre," Sandra is also a bestselling romantic suspense author. Her novels have garnered numerous Canadian Christian writing awards, as well as an RT Reviewers' Choice Award, a National Readers' Choice Award, a Holt Medallion, and a Daphne du Maurier Award of Excellence. When not plotting crimes, Sandra enjoys doing a variety of crafts, hiking with her hubby, working in their vegetable gardens, and playing make-believe with their dozen-plus young grandchildren. Sandra hails from Niagara, Canada, and loves to hear from readers.

TRUTH BEHIND THE FICTION

British peerage's complex history dates back to medieval times, when monarchs granted titles to reward loyalty, military service, or landownership. Over time, these titles became hereditary, creating an aristocratic class that held both political and social influence. Reforms in the twentieth century, however, and upcoming reforms promised by the UK's government, have limited the automatic right of hereditary peers to sit in the House of Lords, the UK's upper house of parliament.

In Will's native Scotland, titles and the peerage system have evolved with distinct features that reflect Scotland's unique cultural and political landscape. Most notably for the purposes of my story, in Scotland titles can be handed down along the mother's line to ensure the continuation of ancient titles and in some cases the estates associated with them. These days, however, many titles are passed on without any corresponding estates or wealth, although those inheriting such titles may still enjoy enhanced social prestige as a result.

As an interesting aside, the Shetland Islands of Scotland, where Will's father resides, were originally part of Denmark-Norway. They came under Scotland's domain in 1469 when King Christian I of Denmark-Norway couldn't raise his daughter's required dowry and pledged the islands as collateral to King James III of Scotland upon her marriage to James III. Although Norway later attempted to reclaim the islands, they were never successful.

I opted to have Will's father inherit a baronet title from his mother's line, because this was the most plausible option that explains why, up until this time, his family was oblivious to their connection to nobility.

Baronets were named by King James I of England in 1611 to raise capital and were never part of the political peerage system. They rank above knights, but lower than barons, and are addressed as "sir" (or "dame" in the case of women), rather than "lord"—the form of address bestowed on higher-ranked nobles.

By choosing a title that is inherited separate from land and peerage obligations, I could confer this on Will's father without creating a major upheaval where he lives and the way he lives. In fact, like junior members of peerage families, baronets are commoners, despite the status that might be afforded by their title.

YORKSHIRE YUMMIES

Chocolate-Orange Battenberg Cake

Battenberg cake is traditionally made with pink and yellow almond sponge cake, sliced and arranged in a checkerboard pattern held together with apricot jam. Then the entire cake is encased in marzipan. But taking my inspiration from Yorkshire's famous Terry's Chocolate Orange, I opted to add a chocolate-orange flavor twist.

Ingredients:

Be sure to read the important tips at the end!

For preflavored cake batter:*

175 grams** softened butter

175 grams brown sugar (demerara style is especially nice)

3 eggs

170 grams all-purpose flour mixed with 2¼ teaspoon baking powder and a pinch of salt (you may substitute 175 grams self-rising flour + ¼ teaspoon baking powder)

For the chocolate cake batter:

2 tablespoons cocoa powder (Dutch-processed is recommended for its more intense chocolate flavor)

½ teaspoon vanilla extract

For the orange batter:

2 drops food-grade orange essential oil or equivalent flavor extract

Zest of one orange

Chocolate filling:

Scant ½ cup heavy cream

¼ cup 50% dark-chocolate chocolate chips or grated chocolate

Marzipan:

1½ cups almond meal

1½ cups powdered sugar

1 egg white

Directions:

1. Prepare 8x8-inch cake pan by folding a sheet of foil to make a divider halfway across the pan, then separate the foil at the base to line the rest of the pan. Line each side with parchment paper to ensure batter doesn't leak through.
2. Preheat oven to 350 degrees.
3. To make cake batter, beat butter until light and fluffy. Add brown sugar and beat. Add eggs one at a time, beating well after each addition. Scrape down sides of bowl periodically. Add flour mixture and beat until thoroughly mixed.
4. Divide batter into two equal halves. To one half, add cocoa powder and vanilla extract and mix thoroughly. To second half, add orange flavoring and zest and mix thoroughly.
5. Carefully spoon orange batter into one side of prepared pan and smooth evenly into corners. Fill other side of pan with chocolate batter.

6. Bake in preheated oven for 30 to 35 minutes, or until a toothpick inserted in the center comes out clean.
7. Cool cakes for 10 minutes before turning onto wire rack.
8. Prepare chocolate filling by heating cream in small pan on medium-low until it starts to boil. Remove from heat and stir in chocolate until it melts and mixture is smooth. Pour mixture into a shallow glass dish. Once mixture cools, chill in fridge until spreadable.
9. For marzipan, mix almond meal and powdered sugar in food processor. Pulse in egg white until mixture forms a thick dough.
10. Transfer marzipan to work surface and knead. If dough is too sticky, add more almond flour. If dough is too firm, add a smidgen of water. Marzipan will become firmer once refrigerated. After kneading a few times, roll dough into a log then wrap in plastic and refrigerate.***
11. Before assembling Battenberg cake, make sure it's completely cooled. Using a long cake or bread knife, level off top of each cake and slice each in half, so you end up with 4 long rectangles measuring 2 inches by 8 inches. If necessary, trim sides so rectangles are the same size.
12. On a large sheet of parchment paper dusted with powdered sugar, roll marzipan into 8x12-inch rectangle. Place another sheet of parchment paper on top. Using a cookie sheet for extra support, carefully turn over rolled-out marzipan and peel off original parchment paper. Trim edges then spread chocolate filling thinly over marzipan.

13. Arrange one long cake rectangle of each flavor in center of marzipan, joining them with a thin layer of chocolate filling.
14. Spread chocolate filling over the pair of cake rectangles. Arrange last two rectangles on the opposite color in a checkerboard design, using a thin layer of chocolate filling to hold them together.
15. Carefully fold marzipan around the assembled cake. Turn cake over so seam is underneath. Trim ends of marzipan as needed.

Important Tips:

*Dividing the cake pan with foil can be fiddly. Save yourself the hassle by doubling the recipe and making one full cake pan of each flavor. Once cool, cut each cake into 4 long rectangles and build two Battenberg cakes. Or get creative by cutting them into 5 rectangles and making a 3-layer by 3-column checkerboard cake.

**Measuring your cake ingredients by weight ensures the best result. Please be aware that equivalent measurements by volume can vary widely depending on flour density and the way it's measured. For example, while developing this recipe, I found that 1 cup of my all-purpose flour weighed 150 g, whereas the estimate I found online for 1 cup of flour was 120 g, while another site said 1 cup weighed 170 g, which is why I opted not to provide an equivalent volume.

***Marzipan can be made in advance. It will keep for weeks in the fridge.

Mysteries of Cobble Hill Farm will return! In the meantime...

Read on for a sneak peek of the first book in an exciting new series from Guideposts Books—Mysteries of Blackberry Valley!

Where There's Smoke

By Laura Bradford

Earth to Hannah. Come in, Hannah."

Startled, Hannah Prentiss set down the cleaning cloth and raised her head to find her best friend, Lacy Minyard, watching her closely. "I'm sorry. Did I miss something?"

Lacy nodded to the long folding table erected in the middle of the yard. "Nope. Everything looks absolutely amazing. The sandwiches. The salad. Your special peach lemonade, and those *cookies*! Are you trying to fatten us all up?"

Hannah gestured toward the hustle and bustle that was their church group. "Everyone is working so hard to get this place cleaned up for Miriam that it only seemed right to give them a proper thank-you meal. It's easy enough when you own a restaurant."

Closing the gap between them with two long strides, Lacy commandeered the cloth from Hannah's hand. "Hold still. You've got a smudge of soot on your cheek." She gave it a quick rub. "And now you don't."

"Thanks."

"Of course. I suspect you'll do the same for me at some point before we call it quits for the day."

Hannah took the cloth from Lacy and tossed it into the bag at her feet. "Every time I walk through Miriam's front door, I praise God that she was at her son's place in Cave City when the fire broke out. If she hadn't been…" She stopped, drew in a breath, and held up her hands. "Miriam is fine. That's all that matters. And the house—well, we're making progress, right?"

"We are." Lacy hooked her thumb in the direction of the yard. "Are we ready to call everyone to the table?"

Hannah took a mental inventory of every place setting, every food platter, every waiting cup. When she was satisfied all was ready, she nodded to her friend.

Soon, after hands were washed and a blessing shared over the meal, a dozen members of their church women's group pulled folding chairs up to the table and began to eat, the exhaustion from the morning's work blanketing them in a rare silence. Occasionally, a pocket of conversation sprang up, but it didn't last long against the pull of the food as they worked to refuel their bodies.

"Hannah, this salad is amazing," said Connie Sanchez, the church secretary.

The round of nodding that accompanied Connie's words continued as Vera Bowman commented on the deliciousness of the sandwiches.

"If you haven't found your way to Hannah's restaurant yet, I can assure you that this"—Lacy motioned to the food around them—"is just a preview of what the Hot Spot has to offer."

More nods made their way around the table until Vera cleared her throat and took the conversational baton again. "I have to say, I was a little skeptical about a restaurant coming into the old firehouse, but you made it work, Hannah," she said. "My kids love your food, and I like knowing they're eating things that were grown and raised in and around Blackberry Valley."

"Thank you."

"I imagine you've had quite a lot of culture shock though," Connie said, eyeing Hannah across the top of her lemonade.

Hannah set her cup down. "You mean after working in Los Angeles?" At Connie's answering nod, she continued. "I mean, sure, LA and Blackberry Valley are very, *very* different. And the restaurants I worked in there were more high-end than the Hot Spot is, but high-end doesn't mean better, and I wanted to come home. To Blackberry Valley."

"And I'm so glad you did," Lacy said, resting her hand on Hannah's and giving it a squeeze. "Having you back in Kentucky these last few months has been such a blessing."

"For me too." Returning her friend's smile, Hannah pushed away from the table. "God led me home at exactly the right time."

The sound of tires against gravel drew her attention to the driveway and the navy blue sedan slowly making its way toward the one-story home. A glance into the passenger seat showed the reason they were all there.

"Miriam's here," Hannah said. She, Lacy, and a handful of others rose to their feet. "I was hoping we'd have everything done before she came."

"Miriam Spencer may be lovable, but she's also as stubborn as the day is long," Connie said. "She's no more capable of staying away than her son is of telling her no."

It was hard not to smile at the accuracy of Connie's words. It was even harder not to smile when Miriam opened the door and got out before her son could make his way around the car.

"Goodness, how long have you all been here?" Miriam asked, her sharp gaze darting from the women walking toward her, to the table, and then to her beloved home of nearly sixty years.

Connie stepped forward. "We got here shortly after sunrise."

"Sunrise?" Miriam shot an accusatory glare at her son, Tom. "Why didn't you wake me and bring me over sooner?"

"Because you need your sleep." Hannah sidled up beside the eighty-five-year-old and planted a kiss on her wrinkled cheek. "And we wanted to surprise you by getting everything cleaned up before you returned."

Leaning against the open car door, Miriam pointed the end of her cane first at the house and then the women. "It's *my* house that caught on fire."

"Yes, but Ecclesiastes chapter four, verse nine, says two are better than one because together they can work more effectively," Hannah reminded her. She gestured at the women assembled around them. "So we came, twelve strong. We plan to get right back to work after lunch."

Miriam lowered her chin and eyed Hannah over the top of her glasses. "And who's running your new restaurant while you're here?"

"I closed for the day."

"You closed a new restaurant for an entire day?" Miriam repeated, drawing back.

"Yes, but that's okay. Tuesdays tend to be slow anyway."

"And your staff is okay missing a day's pay?"

"I'm still paying them."

"You haven't been open long enough to be giving paid days off," Miriam scolded.

"It's one day, and I'll make it work. Being here, doing this, is more important. Truly."

Rolling her eyes, Miriam turned her attention to Connie. "And who's at the church office right now?"

Connie patted her pocket. "I've forwarded all calls to my cell."

"And you?" Miriam shifted her focus to Lacy. "Who's looking after those chickens of yours?"

Lacy swapped grins with Hannah. "My chickens are fine, Miriam."

"We *want* to be here," Vera said, and the others echoed agreement. "To help get you back into your house."

"Helping me is fine. Doing it without me isn't." Miriam planted the end of her cane on the ground and shoved her car door closed. "So let's get to it, shall we?"

The group made its way to the house, stopping en route to pick up the cleaning supplies and brooms they'd left beside the front door at lunchtime. Connie and her group of five broke right toward the kitchen, Vera and her helpers made a beeline for the primary bedroom, and Hannah and Lacy led Miriam and Tom into the living room.

"We've made a lot of headway on the smell in here, and we've pulled up the floorboards closest to the fireplace, as you can see." Hannah crossed the remaining scorched floorboards and retrieved the pry bar she'd left in the corner. "If we can get the rest of these up by the end of the day, the men can come and put in a new floor on Saturday."

Miriam gazed around the room, tsking softly beneath her breath.

"It's all fixable," Hannah said soothingly. "Even the guest room with all of its damage. Really. And you're safe and sound. That's all that matters."

"That's what I keep telling her," Tom chimed in.

"I don't know if I have the strength to pull up floorboards," Miriam murmured.

"You don't have to. Lacy and I have this covered. Right, Lacy?"

"Right." Lacy pointed at the stack of books they'd made that morning. "But if you could inspect those and rid them of any soot, Miriam, that would be helpful."

Miriam's gaze skirted to the books. "I can do that."

"Perfect."

When the elderly woman was settled in a folding chair on the other side of the room, Hannah, Lacy, and Tom got to the business of pulling up the rest of the floor. Board by board, they made their way from the fireplace to the center of the room, setting some aside and discarding others out in the yard.

It was slow, tedious work as they stood, crouched, and stood, again and again as the June sun made its way across the sky, trading the noon hour for the afternoon, and then the afternoon for the early evening.

Rolling her shoulders in an attempt to work out a growing kink, Hannah took a moment to survey what was left and weigh it against the chores she knew still faced Lacy at her farm. An hour's work, maybe, if they continued the course. Two hours if she took over from this point by herself.

"Lacy?"

Her friend wiped a bead of sweat from her face. "What's up?"

"Go home. I'll take it from here."

"I can't do that," Lacy protested.

"You still have farm chores to take care of. Go."

Lacy pulled her phone from her pocket and consulted the screen. "Are you sure? Because I could do those and come right back."

"I've got it. Really."

Lacy put her pry bar down and stood. "I'll clean up from lunch before I leave."

"Vera already took care of that," Tom said from the corner of the room where he was working.

"See?" Hannah waved toward the door. "All that's left are the horses."

"The horses and that corner of the room," Lacy said, pointing at the section behind Hannah.

"I've got it," Hannah repeated, smiling. "We can finish up."

In an effort to prove her words, Hannah crouched down, worked to hook the pry bar between the board she'd most recently dislodged and the loose one beside it, and pulled. Her gaze fell on a small wooden compartment cast in shadows. "Whoa. What's this?" she said as she leaned closer.

"What's what?" Lacy and Tom asked in unison.

She reached inside and ran her fingers along the intact wooden box. "It looks like a hiding place of some kind."

The thump of Miriam's cane was followed by her voice on the other side of Hannah. "A hiding place?"

"Yes, look." Pointing to the box, Hannah glanced at her elderly friend. "You don't know about this?"

"No. And I've lived here for nearly sixty years. Tom?"

"I had no idea."

Hannah handed him the pry bar and addressed Miriam again. "The lid isn't on right—it's crooked. Do you want me to look inside?"

"I think you'd better."

Hannah pushed aside the compartment's lid and reached inside the dusty box, her fingertips grazing paper before landing on something round and hard and—

She closed her hand around the object and drew it out. When the object was revealed, they all gasped.

"Whoa," Hannah murmured at the sight of an exquisite ruby brooch, its large gem sparkling in the early evening rays slanting in from the open window.

"It's magnificent," Miriam said in a raspy voice.

Tom squatted beside Hannah. "I don't understand. How could something like this be hidden under a floorboard in a house my mom has owned for longer than I've been alive—yet none of us knew it was here?"

Hannah heard the question, even registered it on some level, but her focus was on the brooch. A brooch that sparkled in the sun.

"I don't know how I *couldn't* know," Miriam said, shaking her head. "It's my house. Before now, I would have said I knew everything about this place."

"You never had a reason to pull up the floor, Mom," Tom pointed out.

Hannah looked from the polished jewel in her hand to the dusty box in which it had been hidden, her gaze landing on the other item she'd felt. Tom reached inside and pulled it out. "Is that a flyer of some kind?" she asked.

"I think so." Holding it to the side, he blew dust off the paper. "Put there as a cushion to protect the brooch, I'd guess."

Hannah watched Tom carefully smooth out the page to reveal an advertisement for what appeared to be classic cars and then returned her full attention to the ruby brooch as she rose to her feet. "I wonder how long this has been here."

"Based on the dust and the fact that Mom's lived here for almost sixty years, I'd say a long time." Tom balled up the flyer and tossed it in a nearby trash can. "A *very* long time."

"If you're right, and this was here before Miriam moved in, someone has come back to it since," Hannah said.

Miriam eyed Hannah. "How can you know that, dear?"

Hannah held out her hand and opened her fingers to reveal the brooch. "Look at it. Look at the way it shines."

Miriam gasped again. "You're right. It's been freshly polished!"

A NOTE FROM THE EDITORS

We hope you enjoyed another exciting volume in the Mysteries of Cobble Hill Farm series, published by Guideposts. For over seventy-five years, Guideposts, a nonprofit organization, has been driven by a vision of a world filled with hope. We aspire to be the voice of a trusted friend, a friend who makes you feel more hopeful and connected.

By making a purchase from Guideposts, you join our community in touching millions of lives, inspiring them to believe that all things are possible through faith, hope, and prayer. Your continued support allows us to provide uplifting resources to those in need. Whether through our communities, websites, apps, or publications, we inspire our audiences, bring them together, and comfort, uplift, entertain, and guide them. Visit us at guideposts.org to learn more.

We would love to hear from you. Write us at Guideposts, P.O. Box 5815, Harlan, Iowa 51593 or call us at (800) 932-2145. Did you love *The Elephant in the Room*? Leave a review for this product on guideposts.org/shop. Your feedback helps others in our community find relevant products.

Loved Mysteries of Cobble Hill Farm? Check out some other Guideposts mystery series! Visit https://www.shopguideposts.org/fiction-books/mystery-fiction.html for more information.

WHISTLE STOP CAFÉ MYSTERIES

Join best friends Debbie Albright and Janet Shaw as they step out in faith to open the Whistle Stop Café inside the historic train depot in Dennison, Ohio. During WWII, the depot's canteen workers offered doughnuts, sandwiches, and a heap of gratitude to thousands of soldiers on their way to war via troop-transport trains. Our sleuths soon find themselves on track to solve baffling mysteries—both past and present. Come along for the ride for stories of honor, duty to God and country, and of course fun, family, and friends!

Under the Apple Tree
As Time Goes By
We'll Meet Again
Till Then
I'll Be Seeing You
Fools Rush In
Let It Snow

Accentuate the Positive
For Sentimental Reasons
That's My Baby
A String of Pearls
Somewhere Over the Rainbow
Down Forget-Me-Not Lane
Set the World on Fire
When You Wish Upon a Star
Rumors Are Flying
Here We Go Again
Stairway to the Stars
Winter Weather
Wait Till the Sun Shines
Now You're in My Arms
Sooner or Later
Apple Blossom Time
My Dreams Are Getting Better

SECRETS FROM GRANDMA'S ATTIC

Life is recorded not only in decades or years, but in events and memories that form the fabric of our being. Follow Tracy Doyle, Amy Allen, and Robin Davisson, the granddaughters of the recently deceased centenarian, Pearl Allen, as they explore the treasures found in the attic of Grandma Pearl's Victorian home, nestled near the banks of the Mississippi in Canton, Missouri. Not only do Pearl's descendants uncover a long-buried mystery at every attic exploration, they also discover their grandmother's legacy of deep, abiding faith, which has shaped and guided their family through the years. These uncovered Secrets from Grandma's Attic reveal stories of faith, redemption, and second chances that capture your heart long after you turn the last page.

History Lost and Found
The Art of Deception
Testament to a Patriot
Buttoned Up
Pearl of Great Price
Hidden Riches
Movers and Shakers
The Eye of the Cat
Refined by Fire

The Prince and the Popper
Something Shady
Duel Threat
A Royal Tea
The Heart of a Hero
Fractured Beauty
A Shadowy Past
In Its Time
Nothing Gold Can Stay
The Cameo Clue
Veiled Intentions
Turn Back the Dial
A Marathon of Kindness
A Thief in the Night
Coming Home

SAVANNAH SECRETS

Welcome to Savannah, Georgia, a picture-perfect Southern city known for its manicured parks, moss-covered oaks, and antebellum architecture. Walk down one of the cobblestone streets, and you'll come upon Magnolia Investigations. It is here where two friends have joined forces to unravel some of Savannah's deepest secrets. Tag along as clues are exposed, red herrings discarded, and thrilling surprises revealed. Find inspiration in the special bond between Meredith Bellefontaine and Julia Foley. Cheer the friends on as they listen to their hearts and rely on their faith to solve each new case that comes their way.

The Hidden Gate
A Fallen Petal
Double Trouble
Whispering Bells
Where Time Stood Still
The Weight of Years
Willful Transgressions
Season's Meetings
Southern Fried Secrets
The Greatest of These
Patterns of Deception

The Waving Girl
Beneath a Dragon Moon
Garden Variety Crimes
Meant for Good
A Bone to Pick
Honeybees & Legacies
True Grits
Sapphire Secret
Jingle Bell Heist
Buried Secrets
A Puzzle of Pearls
Facing the Facts
Resurrecting Trouble
Forever and a Day

MYSTERIES OF MARTHA'S VINEYARD

Priscilla Latham Grant has inherited a lighthouse! So with not much more than a strong will and a sore heart, the recent widow says goodbye to her lifelong Kansas home and heads to the quaint and historic island of Martha's Vineyard, Massachusetts. There, she comes face-to-face with adventures, which include her trusty canine friend, Jake, three delightful cousins she didn't know she had, and Gerald O'Bannon, a handsome Coast Guard captain—plus head-scratching mysteries that crop up with surprising regularity.

A Light in the Darkness
Like a Fish Out of Water
Adrift
Maiden of the Mist
Making Waves
Don't Rock the Boat
A Port in the Storm
Thicker Than Water
Swept Away
Bridge Over Troubled Waters
Smoke on the Water
Shifting Sands
Shark Bait

Seascape in Shadows
Storm Tide
Water Flows Uphill
Catch of the Day
Beyond the Sea
Wider Than an Ocean
Sheeps Passing in the Night
Sail Away Home
Waves of Doubt
Lifeline
Flotsam & Jetsam
Just Over the Horizon

Printed in the United States
by Baker & Taylor Publisher Services